CHRISTMAS AT EMMERDALE

Christmas at Emmerdale is the first in a sweeping new saga, exploring the lives of *Emmerdale's* much-loved families during the run up to the Great War.

August 1914, and a terrible war begins, one that will affect the lives of everyone in the village of Beckindale. For Maggie Sugden, left to run Emmerdale Farm on her own while her husband, Joe, is at the front, it will bring grief and loss but also independence and the chance to find a place to belong – and perhaps even to love again.

CHRISTMAS AT EMMERDALE

CHRISTMAS AT EMMERDALE

by

Pamela Bell

Magna Large Print Books
Long Preston, North Yorkshire,
BD23 4ND, England.

British Library Cataloguing in Publication Data.

A catalogue record of this book is
available from the British Library

ISBN   978-0-7505-4745-1

First published in Great Britain in 2018 by Trapeze Books,
an imprint of The Orion Publishing Group Ltd.

Christmas at Emmerdale © 2018 ITV Studios Limited.
Emmerdale is a trade mark of ITV Studios Limited.
'Emmerdale' television series © 2018 ITV Studios Limited.

Cover illustration © Getty/Alamy/Shutterstock by arrangement with
Orion Publishing Group

Published in Large Print 2019 by arrangement with
The Orion Publishing Group Ltd.

Magna Large Print is an imprint of Library Magna Books Ltd.

Printed and bound in Great Britain by
T.J. (International) Ltd., Cornwall, PL28 8RW

1914

My thanks go to Linton Chiswick for the storylines and Ollie Tait, Alice Lee and Izzy Charman at Lambent Productions for their part in unearthing stories that inform the novel and the ITV factual series, *Emmerdale 1918*.

CHAPTER ONE

Maggie wedged the basket of eggs on her hip as she wrestled the barn door closed. Bustling past her, Toby gave a woof of pleasure as he spotted a familiar figure and she turned to see her father across the farmyard. His walking sticks rested against the dry-stone wall and he was hanging on to the rickety gate to keep himself upright as he gazed longingly across the valley.

Maggie's sigh blended exasperation with admiration. Albert Oldroyd could barely walk, barely speak, and still he insisted on dragging himself outside every day despite being told that he couldn't manage on his own.

And they called *her* stubborn and proud.

'You're a right chip off t'block,' Joe had commented once. It was one of the nicest things he had ever said to her.

It was a bright day but cool for early July and Maggie was glad of the shawl she had thrown around her shoulders earlier as she followed Toby across the farmyard. He was a bristly, long-legged terrier – not the prettiest of dogs – but with bright eyes, a cold black nose and a sweet nature that more than made up for his lack of looks.

A brisk wind was shoving great clouds across the Yorkshire sky, sending shadows sweeping over the fells on the far side of the valley and dazzling with sudden bursts of sunlight. It snatched at her

9

carelessly pinned-up hair and she swiped the strands away from her face with the back of her wrist.

Toby frisked around her father, nearly un-balancing him before Maggie called him sharply and he nosed instead under the gate onto the track. Hemmed in by two mossy stone walls and overhung in places by oaks, elderflower bushes and dog roses, the track led down to the lane into the village. A quagmire of mud in winter, it was lush now with feathery summer grass and Toby snuffled happily among the buttercups.

Maggie balanced the basket of eggs on the gatepost so that she could take her father's arm. 'You shouldn't be out here, Pa,' she said, know-ing that she was wasting her breath. 'You'll get cold.'

Albert's eyes were fixed on the fell opposite. She followed his gaze across Beckindale, a huddle of grey stone houses in the curve of the beck, to rest on the long, low farmhouse settled into the fold of the hillside beyond.

High Moor.

'Wish ... go ... home...' Albert's words were forced out with agonizing effort, and so slurred that only Maggie could understand him, and her heart clenched in sympathy.

'I know,' she said, her throat aching. 'I'd like to go home too, Pa, but we can't. The bank has sold High Moor to pay off our debts, remember?'

Now strangers owned the great iron key that sat, never used, in the front door of the farm-house that had been built by her grandfather's grandfather. Strangers would be learning the stair that creaked and the way the sunlight spilt onto the landing on summer mornings. They would stand at the parlour window and watch the rain racing across the fells, skimming over the long lines of the dry-stone walls and sweeping up and over the tops. They could step into the early morning dew and listen to the skylarks soaring over the heather and the distant bleating of the sheep dotting the hillsides, far from the squash and squabble of village life.

A tear squeezed out of the corner of her father's eye. 'Sorry,' he managed.

'It's all right, Pa,' said Maggie gently.

'Not ... right...' The gate to the farmyard hung drunkenly from the post. The wood was rotten, the iron hinges rusting, the broken sneck held in place with frayed binder twine.

When her father's grip on it shook in frustration, the whole gate lurched forwards and Maggie only just managed to haul him back before he fell.

'Pa, be careful! You know what this gate is like.'

She had tried asking Joe to fix the gate once, when she had been a new wife and had thought she could change things at Emmerdale Farm.

Joe had soon put her right about that.

Maggie sighed, remembering. She knew that the state of the farmyard must be distressing to her father, who had run a tight ship at High Moor until his collapse, but they had had nowhere else to go.

Emmerdale Farm had been their only option.

Without meaning to, she glanced down to the right, where Miffield Hall stood half hidden in

11

the trees. Once she had thought there might have been another choice, but she had soon been put right about that, too.

'Ralph is not for you, Margaret.' Lady Miffield could not have been clearer. She hadn't bothered to lower her voice as the congregation milled around outside the church, most listening avidly to Maggie's humiliation at the hands of Ralph's stepmother. 'The marriage wouldn't be successful. In the long run, you would be much happier with someone of your own class, and so would Ralph.'

'To hell with them.' White with fury, Ralph had come to find Maggie when he heard what his stepmother had done. 'They can't stop us getting married. We'll go away tonight.'

'And go where?' Maggie had asked dully.

'America! Australia! Anywhere!'

'And Pa? He's too ill to travel. I can't leave him, Ralph. Not now.'

Leaving High Moor was going to break her father's heart, Maggie knew. She couldn't take him away from Beckindale too, but where could they go? They had no money, no family, and isolated as they had been, few friends. Lord Miffield owned most of the land around the village and he was not inclined to rent so much as a cottage to a young woman who had, according to his wife at least, tried to seduce his eldest son and heir away from a sense of what was right and fitting.

And then there had been Joe Sugden, twisting his cap between his hands. His family had emigrated, leaving him Emmerdale Farm. He needed a wife, he said. He would give her father a home.

12

Ralph went out and got drunk when he heard. A week later, he left Miffield Hall.

There were those in Beckindale who felt Maggie had got above herself. They viewed her downfall with the satisfaction of those proved right in their predictions: Margaret Oldroyd would get what she deserved. They had been quick to pass on the rumours from Miffield Hall over the past year. Ralph was in New York, wooing an American heiress. Ralph was holidaying on a yacht in the Mediterranean. Ralph was shooting with the King at Sandringham.

Whatever he was doing, Ralph was a very, very long way from Beckindale. From Maggie.

She swallowed down the memory and made herself look away from Miffield Hall, only to find her father watching her and clearly able to read her unguarded expression.

'You...'

It was terrible watching his face contort with the effort of speaking.

'... here ... sorry...'

'Oh, Pa...' Maggie couldn't bear the anguished guilt in his eyes. He blamed himself for his seizure, for letting High Moor go, for her decision to marry Joe. She mustered a smile. 'It's not so bad, is it? We've got each other,' she reminded him. 'We've got Toby,' she added as a pheasant burst out of the long grass with a loud rattle, outraged at having been disturbed, and the dog recoiled in comical shock.

The corner of Albert's mouth twitched in an attempt at a smile. Encouraged, she tucked her hand into the crook of his arm. 'Remember what

13

you used to say to me and Andrew? That all we could do was to keep our promises and keep our heads up? Maybe Emmerdale Farm isn't what I dreamed of – what either of us dreamed of – but I'm not going to start weeping and wailing. I'm going to keep my head up, just like you taught me to.'

'My ... girl ... proud.'

Maggie wasn't sure if her father was telling her that he was proud of her, or if being proud was her problem. Perhaps it was. Ralph had used to tease her about being too proud. 'I love it when you look down your nose at me,' he had said. 'It makes me realise that the Verneys are Johnny-come-latelies to Miffield Hall, while the Old-royds have been at High Moor for ever.'

Disguising her sigh with a smile, Maggie kissed her father's cheek, hating how papery his skin felt. 'Come on, Pa. I don't want you catching a chill. Let's get you inside.'

Toby came bounding back at her whistle and wriggled under the gate to fawn adoringly at her skirt as she picked up the eggs and tucked one of her father's sticks under her arm so that she could help Albert back to the house. He was terrifyingly frail and light, and his hand trembled alarmingly on his stick. Very, very slowly they made their way across the farmyard, picking their way through the stale puddles that gleamed in the bright light.

Emmerdale farmhouse was a long, grey stone building, so old it seemed to sag into the ground. The dairy Maggie had made her own stood between the farmhouse and the cow byre where the cows were milked. A cartshed, a stable, an empty pigsty and a barn, all in various stages of dilapidation, formed the other sides of a rough square. A mess of rusting wire, broken wheels and pieces of wood cluttered the doorways and were guarded by a tangle of nettles and bindweed. In one corner of the yard, a muck heap sprawled, turning the cobbles slick and slimy with manure whenever it rained. Maggie wrinkled her nose at the stink of it. At least the wind was blowing the flies away today.

'I haven't got time to pretty up t'farmyard for you,' Joe had warned his new bride. 'You stick to the kitchen where you belong, and we'll get on.'

After the brightness outside, the kitchen seemed very dark and until Maggie's eyes adjusted all she could hear was the bad-tempered thump as Dot slammed the washing-dolly into the clothes, and the splash of water sloshing over the edge of the tub onto the flagstone floor.

Maggie knew she was lucky to have help in the house. There was no way she could do all the tasks that fell to a farmer's wife and care for her father at the same time. Besides, Dot was an excellent cook, while Maggie couldn't even manage the oatcakes that were staples in any Yorkshire farmhouse. Dot had stared at the burnt and crumbling mess on the iron griddle in disbelief.

'Ent nobody never taught you how to make havercake?'

'We had a cook at High Moor. I never learnt how to cook.'

Maggie imagined Dot regaling the gossips of Beckindale with mocking accounts of her inadequacies in the kitchen. She could almost see her lifting her nose with her finger and mimicking 'we had a cook'.

At least Dot went home in the evenings, unlike Joe's farm labourer, George Kirkby, and the farm lad, Frank Pickles, who had rooms above the stable. They might view her with a mixture of suspicion (George) and alarm (Frank) but at least they didn't treat her with the patronising contempt meted out by Dot. At seventeen, Dot was three years younger than Maggie, but that didn't stop her criticising or pointing out that growing up at High Moor had made Maggie a hopeless farmer's wife.

Maggie didn't need reminding. She had spent the year since her marriage to Joe Sugden learning how to do all those things she had taken for granted at High Moor, where her father had had a cook and maids and a shepherd and farmhands. Joe had George and Frank to help with heavy work on the farm, but Maggie had to cook and to bake and make butter and cheese. She had to feed the hens and salt the bacon. She had to wash and iron and mend. To clean out the range and get down on her hands and knees to polish the stone floor. To fetch water from the pump. To empty the slop bucket into the privy every morning.

And when Joe turned to her in bed and pushed up her nightgown, she had to lie there and let him grunt and thrust inside her. Because she had married him and that was what she had promised to do.

Keep your promises. Keep your head up.

Ignoring Dot's impatient tsks, Maggie helped her father into his chair by the range and tucked him in with a blanket. 'Comfortable?'

His face worked. 'Thank ... you.' It came out as *ank oo.*

Maggie set her jaw against the grief that barrelled through her whenever she remembered her father's intelligence and quick wit, the jokes and puns he and her brother had delighted in. He had been such a strong personality, with a vivid presence and a warm smile that had made High Moor a golden place.

Until Andrew came in from the fells that day, rubbing his neck. 'I've got a sore throat,' he said. Four days later, he was dead, and Albert Oldroyd had never been the same again.

'I'd better give Dot a hand with the washing.'

Monday was wash day. All the dirty clothes from the previous week had to be pounded in the tub, then rinsed and put through the mangle before being hung out to dry. It was a task that took the two of them all morning and Maggie was glad of the chance to escape the dark and dingy farmhouse when it came to hanging out the washing in the unkempt garden. Toby came with her to lie in the grass and sniff happily at the wind while the damp clothes snapped and billowed on the line.

Maggie was pegging out the last of Joe's shirts when she saw Toby's ears prick up and a few moments later she heard the cursing as Joe struggled to open the gate he could never be bothered to mend.

Her husband was back.

He had taken the carthorse, Blossom, into the smithy in Beckindale for a new shoe. Maggie suspected that he would have passed the time drinking in the Woolpack while Will Hutton, the taciturn farrier, dealt with Blossom. She braced herself for her husband to be in a surly mood when she went back into the kitchen, but for once he seemed almost genial as they sat down for dinner with George, Frank and Dot. Her father hated being fed like a baby so Maggie helped her father eat later when the others had gone.

'Any news in the village?' she asked Joe as she poured herself a cup of tea.

At twenty-five, Joe Sugden was a thick-set, sandy-haired man with ruddy cheeks. It could have been worse, Maggie often told herself. Her husband wasn't hideous, but his attitude veered between lust and a kind of resentful contempt that made him unpredictable and she had learned to treat him warily.

'Aye, some,' said Joe, shovelling potatoes into his mouth. 'The vicar talked my ear off about some foreigner, Archduke somebody or other, getting shot in a godforsaken foreign place I've never heard of. Vicar reckons it means war.'

'*War?*' Maggie looked up sharply as she helped herself from the plate of cold beef. 'Why?'

'Summat to do with Russia and Austria, Germany mebbe...' Joe wiped his mouth with the back of his hand. 'I stopped listening,' he admitted. 'Charles Haywood is an old windbag and probably wrong. It's nowt to do wi' us anyroads.' He removed a piece of gristle from his teeth. 'Vicar had other news, too.'

'Oh?'

'He'd just come from Miffield Hall.'

Maggie stiffened. She had made no secret of the fact that she had loved Ralph. Joe had known that when they married. He had said that he understood. But now when her eyes met his, it seemed to her that his smile was rife with malice.

'Aye,' he answered her unspoken question. 'Ralph Verney's back.'

CHAPTER TWO

Rose Haywood took a dainty sip of tea and surveyed the parlour at Emmerdale Farm with interest. It was not a welcoming room. It had dark, peeling wallpaper and the uncomfortable-looking chairs smelt musty, as if the parlour had been forgotten until it was needed to lay out Albert Oldroyd's body. Rose wrinkled her nose at the thought. His coffin wouldn't have been resting on a couple of stools for long. It was too hot to have bodies hanging around, and besides, it was haytime. Albert had died on the Thursday and been buried in the churchyard of St Mary's that afternoon.

The decencies were being preserved with a funeral tea, but the men would go back to the fields afterwards. No one wanted to waste the good weather, death or no death. As it was, Rose was surprised at how many people had crowded into the parlour. Mr Oldroyd had been much

19

respected, of course, but he had barely been seen since the seizure that had robbed him of speech and left him paralysed on one side. Rose suspected that people were more interested in getting a look at Emmerdale Farm.

That was why she had come after all, Rose owned to herself. As vicar, her father had taught his three children to be aware of their own faults, and Rose knew that curiosity was her besetting sin. But Emmerdale Farm had always seemed a kind of Bluebeard's chamber to her, at once alarming and intriguing. As children, Rose and her brothers had dared each other to go into the farmyard, but more often they had ended up running past the gate. There was something about the overgrown farmyard that appealed to Rose's romantic nature and she was intensely curious about what lay behind the firmly closed front door of the house.

And clearly she was not alone. Someone had managed to push open one of the windows, but the press of bodies was stifling and Rose could feel sweat trickling inside her corset. The cold meats laid on the table were curling in the oppressive heat. The last week had been one of the hottest she could remember. Every day, the sun had glared down, turning the limestone tops of the fells an eerie white and the normally muddy tracks to dust, and curdling tempers. Even her affable papa had snapped at their maid, Mildred, the day before.

'It's all this talk of war,' her mother, Edith, had sighed when Rose told her how she kept glancing over her shoulder, expecting every time to see an almighty storm building on the horizon. 'It feels as if we're just waiting and waiting for something terrible to happen and we can't do anything to stop it.'

'Perhaps it won't happen,' Rose had said hopefully. 'But I wouldn't mind a storm. Thunder, lightning and a downpour ... at least it would be cooler then and we could all sleep.'

But the sky behind the hills was still hazy in the heat; it would be August the next day and there was no sign of a storm any time soon.

'Not much of a show, is it?' Near Rose, Ava Bainbridge was making no effort to lower her voice as she surveyed the display of ham and cakes with Joan Carr, Betty Porter and Mary Ann Teale. 'When you think of Oldroyds of High Moor ... well, it just goes to show you can come down in the world, doesn't it? Poor Maggie. It must be hard for her.'

She clicked her tongue and shook her head in what Rose imagined was supposed to be sympathy, although Rose didn't know why she bothered to pretend. It was common knowledge that Ava was a cat and that she loathed Maggie Oldroyd, although whether that was for some long-forgotten reason or because Maggie looked at Ava as if she were no more bothersome than a summer midge, easily slapped aside and forgotten, Rose had never known.

'She doesn't look too upset about losing her pa,' Joan commented, and Rose followed their glances to where Maggie stood, stone-faced, at the far end of the table, dispensing tea from a battered iron pot.

'Dot says she never cried a drop,' Betty confided. She lived next door to Dot's mother and had heard all about it. 'Not. A. Drop. Just found him dead in his bed one morning and Dot didn't even realise until she saw Maggie was standing there staring at the wall. "He's dead," that was all she said. Course, Dot offered to get Joe Sugden, but Maggie wouldn't have it. He needs to get t'harvest in, was all she'd say. And then Dot said she'd go and get Eliza Booth to help with the laying out, but madam wasn't having any of that either. Insisted on doing it all herself!' Betty finished triumphantly.

'She was always supposed to be such a devoted daughter too,' agreed Ava. 'You'd think she could bother to look a little sad.'

Rose glanced at them in disbelief. She had always found Maggie cold and more than a little intimidating, if the truth were told, but it seemed obvious to her that Maggie's jaw was clenched with the effort of not weeping and that the strikingly pale grey eyes were full of pain. And when Rose thought of how she would feel if she lost her beloved papa, she knew she wouldn't want to stand in a stifling room pouring tea for a lot of nosy neighbours who had never done anything but gossip about her.

'That's typical of Maggie,' Ava went on with a sniff. 'She always has to be different. Although she's not as different as she thinks she is, as Lady Miffield pointed out.' She snickered at the memory of Maggie's very public humiliation.

Mary Ann leant closer. 'Do you think she knows Ralph is back?'

Rose didn't want to think about Ralph, and she moved away, murmuring an excuse here and there as she threaded through the crowd. The news that Lord Miffield's heir had returned had sped around the village and she had been thrilled to be invited to tea at Miffield Hall with her mother a few days after his arrival. Rose couldn't remember a time when she hadn't been in love with Ralph. Who could not be? He was charming, kind and ridiculously handsome and she had been bitterly disappointed when she had learnt that he was in love with Maggie Oldroyd of all people.

Rose couldn't understand it. Maggie wasn't even pretty! She was aloof and fierce-looking with intelligent, eerily pale eyes. Wolf eyes, Rose's brother, John, had described them once and even though Rose had never seen a wolf, she somehow knew what he had meant. But Ralph wasn't a wolf. He was a golden figure, a hero, like a knight from a story book and his inexplicable preference for Maggie had cut Rose to the quick.

When Ralph had gone away, life in Beckindale had been horribly dull. It wasn't that she had seen *that* much of him before, Rose could admit to herself, but just the chance that she might encounter him unexpectedly or be invited to Miffield Hall when he was there had been enough to brighten her days.

And if Ralph was back, it must surely be that his strange infatuation with Maggie was out of his system. He would be ready to settle down, Rose told herself, and why shouldn't it be with her? She knew without vanity that she was very pretty. And she wasn't a horrible person, whatever her younger brother, Arthur, might say. The Haywoods might not have a title but they were a good family, so it wasn't as if she were completely ineligible, like Maggie.

Rose had dressed carefully for the tea, in a pleated skirt and high-necked blouse with long sleeves and a lacy panel down the front. It was terribly hot, of course, but it made her look like a young lady instead of the schoolgirl she had been before Ralph went away. She had only been sixteen then. She wanted Ralph to see that she had grown up.

But though Ralph had been charming and chatty, not even Rose could convince herself that he had looked deep into her eyes or pressed her fingers meaningfully. He had treated her just the way he had always used to, like a fond older brother.

It had been awfully disappointing.

Carrying her cup and saucer, Rose headed towards her mother who was trying to engage Maggie Sugden in conversation. She would say everything that was proper to Maggie and then perhaps they could leave.

She moved through the press of people with difficulty, catching snatches of conversation as she went. Farmers with broad, weather-beaten faces, uncomfortable in their stiff dark suits, fidgeted, anxious to get back to haymaking. Their wives gossiped about their children and their neighbours and wondered if Ralph Verney had come home to announce his engagement, as rumour had it, and if so, how Maggie Sugden would react.

Why was Ralph's name always linked with Maggie's, Rose wondered disconsolately.

Her father was nose to nose with Mr Bates, discussing the latest news that had been displayed in the newsagent's window that morning.

'The government are taking things seriously at last, Mr Haywood. My boy came back from Bradford and said all the excursion trains for the Bank Holiday had been cancelled.'

'Not before time,' Charles Haywood said, fingering his pocket watch. 'With Germany under martial law and Russia mobilising, I fear war can no longer be avoided.'

'But will England join in?'

'We must, sir, we must!' Charles exclaimed. 'It is a question of honour!'

Rose was as tired of hearing about the prospect of war as she was about Ralph and Maggie. She had no idea why England should get involved in a dispute over Serbia and she had stopped asking, or her father would explain in tedious detail. All she knew was that until Germany and Russia had settled their differences, she was stuck in Beckindale and short of Ralph Verney falling miraculously in love with her, nothing was going to change.

'Ah, there you are, Rose,' Edith Haywood said with a trace of relief as she reached them. Evidently the conversation with Maggie had been a laboured one. 'I was just saying how tired we are of this heat.'

'And tired of talking about it,' said Rose crossly and was surprised and even a little gratified to see a fleeting smile cross Maggie's strange grey eyes.

What was it about Maggie that Ralph found so fascinating? Rose wondered anew. She *wasn't* beautiful, or even pretty. Her nose was big, her mouth too wide. Her jaw was too angular, her brows too bold, her expression cool. She held herself very erect, with her chin tilted at a defiant angle that seemed to put the rest of the world at a distance.

What was it like for such a woman to be married to Joe Sugden? Rose could see him across the room, his beefy face a dull red, sweating profusely in his black suit and waistcoat. He was drinking beer in a surly fashion. The other farmers might be heading back to the fields where their farm-hands would be making the hay they all depended on in winter, but it was clear that Joe would be going nowhere. If he felt the disapproving glances, he gave no sign of it, unless to drink more heavily.

'Would you like some more tea, Rose?' Maggie asked, and Rose flushed, sure that Maggie had been able to tell exactly what she was thinking.

'Thank you,' she said, handing Maggie her cup and saucer. 'That would be...' She broke off as she saw Maggie freeze, her eyes widening, and turned to follow her gaze.

As if pulled by an invisible string, all the other heads in the room turned too. The babble of conversation petered into a hush as they realised who was standing in the doorway: Ralph Verney, impeccably dressed in a tailored black suit and black tie, his hat in his hand. He held himself with an aristocrat's unconscious assurance and looked ridiculously out of place in the dingy parlour.

Rose's heart gave a little somersault at the sight of him, so tall, so glamorous, and her mouth curved into a smile before she realised that he wasn't looking at her at all. His eyes were fixed on Maggie and hers on his. There might have been just the two of them in the room. The air between them pulsed and crackled in the heat and Rose caught her breath. It was as if something dangerous had entered the room, zipping precariously through the hot air.

This wasn't the sweet, romantic love Rose had dreamed of. It was raw and powerful, and her mouth tightened at the painful pinch of envy.

The silence jangled. Rose could see people looking at each other, wondering if someone should say something, but then it was too late.

Joe Sugden was pushing his way through the crowd, his tankard still clutched in his meaty fist. He was very drunk, and the funeral guests silently made way for him as he staggered towards the doorway where Ralph still stood.

'What are *you* doing here?' he demanded.

Apparently unmoved by Joe's aggression, Ralph regarded him with only the faintest expression of distaste. 'I have come to offer my condolences,' he said in his deceptively languid cut-glass tones.

Joe's head was lowered like a bull's, his eyes red and mean. 'You're not welcome here, Verney.'

'You might remember that you only hold the lease of Emmerdale Farm,' Ralph said very softly. 'This farm belongs to my family, and I can go where I please.'

The shock of seeing Ralph seemed to have frozen Maggie into place. Rose took the cup and saucer from her before she dropped it, but she doubted that Maggie noticed as she jerked into belated action.

As Maggie stepped forward and laid a hand on Joe's arm, Rose couldn't help thinking it must be like trying to control a vicious dog, straining at the leash and trembling with suppressed violence.

'It was kind of you to come, Mr Verney,' Maggie said in a surprisingly cool voice.

'I am very sorry about your father, Maggie,' said Ralph. 'He was a fine man.'

'Thank you.' She glanced at Joe. 'I hope you will forgive Joe his outburst. It has been a difficult time – with my father dying,' she added quickly as Joe stirred ominously.

'I quite understand.' Ralph inclined his head. 'I just wanted you to know that I have been thinking of you.' His gaze swept the room briefly. Rose felt it pass over her face like a searchlight and although she doubted he had even registered her presence, she wished fervently that she hadn't been there.

'I must go,' he said formally as his eyes returned to Maggie. 'My sincere condolences for your loss.'

And with that he turned and left.

The silence in the parlour was broken by the clang and clatter of Joe's tankard flung into the fireplace and his inarticulate cry of rage as he shook Maggie's hand off his arm.

'Leave me alone!' he snarled and headed out after Ralph.

CHAPTER THREE

Maggie hurried after her husband into the hall-way. 'Joe, don't!' she said in an urgent undertone.

'Don't what? Don't tear your nancy lover-boy apart with my bare hands? Don't shove his condolences down his bloody throat?'

'Don't lose the farm,' she said.

Joe stood for a moment, his hot eyes on her face, his head swinging slowly from side to side as her words sunk in. His face twisted and he wrenched at his collar. 'I'm going to take off this bloody suit,' he said.

Maggie stood in the dim hallway, her hands folded over her stomach, making herself breathe – in, out – very carefully. She could hear Joe stomping up the stairs, the violent rattle of the latch on the bedroom door, thuds as first one boot and then another were thrown across the room, and then at last the creak of bedsprings that told her he had flung himself onto the bed.

In the parlour, a low hum of whispered conversations had broken out. Well, that little scene had given the village plenty to gossip about, Maggie thought bitterly. A vicious headache was tightening around her skull. She wanted nothing more than to run away, up to the moor, to lie in the heather and look at the sky and beat down the grief and the pain and the humiliation that surged inside her.

But only cowards ran away.

Lifting her chin, Maggie went back into the parlour where the whispers abruptly ceased. She knew that she looked cold and proud but she couldn't relax her expression. If she let herself go, she would unravel into a hysterical mess of screaming and tears and there was no way her pride would let her do that. 'I must apologise,' she began stiffly, but the vicar had evidently decided to take charge of the situation.

'My dear Mrs Sugden, there is no need to apologise. It is, as you said, a most difficult time for you both. And now we must go too.' Charles Haywood swept the room with a smiling glance that nonetheless held all the authority of his calling. 'And, I am sure everyone here has work to do. You men will be anxious to be back at the harvest.'

There were murmurs of agreement and some relief.

'You go, too, Dot,' said Maggie. 'I'll clear up here.'

Dot needed no second telling and at last Maggie was left alone.

She let Toby out of the barn where he had been penned during the funeral and he frisked around her as she walked back across the dusty farmyard. A cloud of flies swarmed over the muck heap and in the field behind the byre, one of the milking cows let out a mournful bellow.

Tying her apron around her waist, Maggie began listlessly tidying the parlour. She put any leftover pieces of ham and cake in the cool larder and gathered up the discarded cups and saucers. She moved sluggishly, barely aware of what she was doing, until a faint pattering caught her attention. A butterfly that must have found its way into the room through the window was beating its wings frantically against the glass.

Maggie put down the plates she was holding. Gently she cupped her hands around the butterfly, admiring its elegantly patterned wings.

'Off you go,' she said to it as she shook it from her fingers outside the window and watched it flutter away.

Lucky butterfly.

By the time Joe woke up, Maggie had drawn water from the well, boiled it in a great pot on the range and washed and dried all the crockery.

'Christ, my head's splitting,' said Joe, stumbling down the last step into the kitchen as Maggie was putting away the last of the cups in the pine dresser that had belonged to Joe's grandmother. Maggie often wondered what kind of life she had led. Emmerdale Farm had been thriving in those days.

Joe didn't comment on the fact that Maggie had cleared everything away, but there was nothing surprising about that. Gertie, the cook at High Moor, would have known what to say. What d'you expect from a pig but a grunt?

'I'm going t'pub.'

Maggie said nothing. What was there to say, after all? She just nodded an acknowledgment as she untied her apron and hung it on the hook by the range.

'Come, Toby,' she said when Joe had disappeared unsteadily down the track. 'Let's go for a walk.'

Turning the opposite way to her husband, Maggie headed for the moorland behind the farm. It was a steady climb and she had to hoist up her skirts to jump over the tussocky grass in places while Toby snuffled into rabbit holes, startling grouse that burst out of the bracken with their clattering cry and the skylarks that darted over the heather. Somewhere she could hear the mewing call of a buzzard and when she looked up, she saw it circling lazily overhead.

The heat had faded from the sky, but it was still warm and Maggie was soon sweating in her funeral blouse and dark, heavy skirt. Driven upwards by a determination not to let her swirling emotions get the better of her, she refused to stop until she reached a boulder high above Beckindale. Worn smooth by aeons of wind and rain, the rock was still warm from the sun. Toby flopped panting into its shade. Maggie sat, with her knees drawn up, and let herself think and feel at last.

Three days ago, her father had been alive. He had been ill and unsteady, but he had been there, and then she went to wake him that morning, and he was gone. Maggie had known she would grieve, but not how his absence would clang in the silence, beating at her until she wanted to cover her ears.

She was glad that he was at peace, glad that he no longer had to force himself to the gate to see High Moor, to yearn for home and grope through the confusion to realise what she was telling him about where he was, and why, glad that he no longer had to remember the pain of Andrew's death afresh every time. But the loneliness was a fist around her heart, squeezing and squeezing until she could hardly breathe with the pain of it.

Untethered by grief, Maggie had retreated into a cocoon of numbness, only fuzzily connected to the world around her. She had been going unthinkingly through the motions: sending for the doctor, for the vicar. Laying out her father's body, caring for him one last time. Eyebrows had been raised when she insisted on attending the burial, of course. The women were supposed to leave that to their menfolk, but Maggie couldn't abandon her father to Joe. She had accompanied him right to the end, to bear witness and watch dry-eyed as his coffin was lowered into the ground.

And now that was done, and the funeral tea was done and there was no more she could do for her father. He was gone.

Maggie didn't remember her mother. She had died when Maggie was barely two, and her father had never remarried. Maggie had always imagined that he had loved his wife too deeply to bear the thought of putting another woman in her place, and although the village gossips had disapproved of the way he let Maggie and her brother run wild, the truth was that Maggie had never missed having a mother. Her beloved father and Andrew were enough for her.

But now they were both gone and she was alone.

Except ... Ralph had come back.

The sight of him in the doorway had jolted Maggie's feelings back to life, the rush of awareness so piercing that it blotted out everything except the unthinking joy of knowing that he was there.

Ralph still loved her. He hadn't needed to say anything, she knew just by looking at him. He had come back for her.

Too late, too late, too late. The bitter realisation drummed along Maggie's veins. She was married to Joe. She had wed him with her eyes open. She had needed a home and he had provided one. She had stood in front of the altar in St Mary's and promised to stay with Joe till death parted them, not until her father died or Ralph came home.

Ralph loved her and she loved Ralph, but love wasn't a good enough reason to break the vows she had made, Maggie realised. She had made her choice the year before. There was no point in grieving for what was lost. All she could do was what her father had always said, to keep her head up and keep her promises.

And that meant going back to Emmerdale Farm and making the best of it.

'Where are you going?' Joe demanded.

Maggie stood in front of the mildewed mirror and secured her hat onto her hair with a pin. 'Church,' she said. 'It's Sunday.' She looked at Joe's reflection. 'You should come.'

'I've got better things to do than listen to t'vicar droning on.'

'Like what?'

'Like keeping this bloody farm going.' Joe jerked his head in the direction the river. 'We've still got to get in hay from t'far fields.'

The fields should have been done the week

before but Maggie knew better than to say anything.

'You haven't forgotten that you promised Frank
he could go home today? He hasn't had a day off
for three weeks now and his mother will be
looking for his wages.'

'The lad's simple,' said Joe in disgust. 'His ma
should be paying me to feed him!'

Maggie said nothing. Frank was not the bright-
est of lads, but he had a way with animals and
cheerfully milked the cows twice a day. Joe
wouldn't want to take on that job again, she knew.

Joe stomped over to mantelpiece and took
down the tin where he kept his money. He flung
the coins at Maggie. 'Take it then,' he growled as
if she had been nagging him for hours.

'Thank you,' she said coolly. 'I'm sure you'll be
able to manage with George.'

'George won't work when he finds out Frank's
having a holiday.' Joe looked out of the window,
his expression morose. 'We may as well do the
fields tomorrow.'

He would waste the whole day, Maggie realised
with an inner sigh. She knew that he had begged
his father to leave him in charge of the farm but
no sooner had Orton Sugden set sail for Australia
than Joe had started to resent the responsibility.
He lived his life in a constant state of dissatisfaction, yearning for something only to turn
around once it was achieved and blame it for not
making him content.

He had been the same when it came to her. He
had wanted her only until he had her, and now it
seemed that she was to blame for everything that

went wrong.

At fourteen, Frank was already as big as many men, but his expression was childlike with a round face and round blue eyes. He looked alarmed when told he was to accompany Maggie to Beckindale, but he was used to doing what he was told, and seemed to be reassured by Toby, who greeted him joyfully and ran around in excited circles as they set off down the track.

Maggie tried to talk to him while they walked, but couldn't get anything beyond a nod or a shake of his head, so after a while she left him alone and they walked in companionable silence, down the track, along the lane and over the bridge into Beckindale. It was another oppressive day, the heat pressing down from a hazy, strangely colourless sky, smothering the countryside which had a raggedy, inert look.

Surely it would rain soon? Maggie scanned the hilltops with narrowed eyes but she could see no sign of clouds, just a faint purple smudge along the horizon. All along the lane, the grass had collapsed and was leaning forward as if anticipating a blow while the normally muddy ruts had hardened into ridges that made for hard walking.

Nancy Pickles lived on the far side of the village in a mean cottage that seemed to be full of children, but her face lit up when she saw Frank and she took the money Maggie gave her gratefully.

'Thank ee, Mrs Sugden,' she said, fingering the coins. 'Likely as not the great gowk would have lost it if left to himself,' she added with an affectionate look at her son. 'I'll make sure he's back in time for milking, never you mind.'

Maggie smiled. 'Enjoy your day, Frank,' she said, and he blushed fierily and ducked his head.

Maggie's smile faded as she approached the church. Most of Beckindale – those who weren't Chapel, anyway – would be inside. She hadn't seen anyone since the scene at the funeral tea, and she was not looking forward to the stares and the whispers. If it hadn't felt like cowardice, she would have made an excuse not to come. At least everyone was already inside in the cool, so she could slip into a pew at the back.

Toby went to lie in the shade of a yew, and she squared her shoulders before pushing open the church door. Its loud creak cut through the murmured conversations and half the congregation turned to see the late arrival. Ava Skilbeck – now Bainbridge, Maggie remembered – was there with her husband and three timid stepchildren. Maggie saw her lean forward and exchange a significant look with Betty Porter, who twisted round, her plump face bright with curiosity. Janet Airey raised her brows at Mary Ann Teale. What did they think? That she was here to seduce Ralph in front of them?

Maggie met their looks with a defiant lift of her chin, but beyond the nodding bonnets and speculative gazes she had glimpsed a familiar wheat-coloured head in the front pew and in spite of her resolve, her heart lurched into her throat and lodged there, hammering.

Ralph was sitting between his stepmother, the young Lady Miffield, and the slumped form of Lord Miffield who was famous for sleeping

37

through the service. As if sensing her gaze, Ralph turned to look over his shoulder, and Maggie slipped quickly into a pew right at the back where she could hide behind a pillar. Her knees were trembling and she bent her head to rest on her hands, fists clenched in a pretence of prayer, to give the heat in her face a chance to subside.

Keep your head up, keep your promises, she told herself.

A buzz of anticipation ran around the church as the Reverend Haywood climbed weightily into the pulpit.

'There is a grave and troublous time before us,' he said in his sonorous voice. 'We are now at a point of crisis. I must tell you that today Germany has declared war on Russia and has invaded Luxembourg. If they continue to Belgium our ally France will stand in dire need of our help, and Britain will always stand with its friends. War may be upon us if Germany does not retreat.'

The congregation stirred uneasily.

'Whatever lies before us, know that we will all do our duty,' Charles Haywood continued, gripping the pulpit in his fervour. 'Honour, freedom, civilisation itself are at stake. We pray today for those who hold the wellbeing of our country in trust, and for our forces that may be called upon to fight for King and country and for the principles of our Lord Jesus Christ.'

Maggie stared at the vicar. She had heard rumours of conflict in Europe ever since the Archduke was assassinated in Sarajevo, but she hadn't thought that it would come to *war*, to fighting and to dying.

'We may be but a small village in the Dales,' Charles Haywood went on, 'but we are England too. If the call comes to serve, as it may, we *will* answer it. We will serve in whatever way we can and fight to preserve our country and our empire.'

Swept along by his fervour, the congregation was nodding and murmuring support, and when he suggested that they sing the national anthem together, they rose as one to their feet while the organist pumped the pedals for the opening refrain.

God save our gracious King
Long live our noble King

They sang lustily in unison, and Maggie found herself singing too. For those few short minutes, she forgot her grief for her father. She forgot her loneliness and the bleakness of her marriage. She even forgot Ralph in the conviction that something momentous was unfolding, and that somehow she would be part of it.

CHAPTER FOUR

After the service, the congregation filed out of the church. It was a slow business, as everyone paused to exchange sombre words with the vicar in the porch. The Verney party in the front pew left first, as was customary. Naturally, they weren't expected to shuffle along and wait their turn with everyone else.

Maggie was ready, and as Lady Miffield's hat appeared around the edge of the pillar, she dropped her hymn book and bent down to pick it up so that Ralph wouldn't see her if he happened to glance to the side. Pretending to fumble with it, she stayed down as long as she could, and when she did straighten it was just in time to see Ralph's back disappearing into the porch.

Ignoring the curious glances slid her way, Maggie fixed her eyes on the stained-glass window that her grandfather had donated to St Mary's after the church was gutted by fire in the previous century. It showed Christ in a rich red robe, holding a fat lamb, with hills in the background. Maggie liked to imagine her grandfather choosing a familiar scene from the pattern book, eyeing up the lamb with a Dalesman's critical eye.

She had never known William Oldroyd, but by all accounts he had been a formidable figure and one of the wealthiest men in Beckindale. What would he think if he knew that his granddaughter had to empty the slop pail and get down on her knees to polish the kitchen floor? Would he despise her for accepting her lot, or be proud of her for doing what needed to be done?

Outside the church, the people of Beckindale would be exchanging greetings and discussing the sermon, jostling to get a closer look at Lady Miffield's hat or perhaps even have a word with Ralph Verney. And there would be some, Ava Bainbridge chief amongst them, who would be waiting avidly for Maggie to emerge, hoping for another scene that they could shake their heads over for weeks and months to come.

Maggie had no intention of giving them the satisfaction of even noting that she walked past Ralph without saying a word. She sat on, watching the way the sunlight through the stained-glass windows threw puddles of soft colour onto the pillars, and thinking about the possibility of war.

It had been an expectedly uplifting moment, listening to the Reverend Haywood, the entire congregation united as they sang the national anthem. For those few minutes, she had felt as if she was part of Beckindale, but those sidelong looks as everyone left had reminded her that she didn't belong here, any more than she belonged at Emmerdale Farm. She belonged up on the fells, at High Moor, which was hers no more.

Loneliness wrapped itself around Maggie, settling onto her shoulders like a heavy cloak and she allowed herself a sigh.

War. Could it really come to that? She would be hard pressed to put Germany and Russia on a map, let alone Luxembourg. The vicar had talked about freedom, about honour and civilisation, but what did those things have to do with them? Maggie couldn't imagine anything changing at Beckindale. War or no war, they would carry on ploughing and harvesting, shearing and lambing, milking and making cheese. She would carry on being married to Joe. She would carry on grieving for her father and her brother. Her heart would carry on breaking for Ralph.

Nothing would change.

The verger was collecting up the hymn books and eyeing Maggie askance. Reluctantly, she got up to go, and was relieved to see that the congregation had dispersed. The vicar had abandoned his post in the porch and was walking back to the vicarage with his daughter, pretty Rose Haywood with her sweet face and the big brown eyes that held unmistakable hostility when she looked at Maggie.

As Maggie watched, she saw Rose tuck her hand in Charles Haywood's arm and lean against his shoulder. It was a simple gesture of affection, and Maggie's heart twisted savagely as she remembered doing the same with her own beloved father.

Toby had bellied out from under the shade of the yew and was jumping around her, anxious for attention. Maggie forced a wobbly smile as she bent to pat him. 'Good dog,' she told him. 'You're right. I've still got you.'

The streets of Beckindale were quiet as Maggie walked back to the bridge across the beck, Toby at her heels. In spite of the heat, most people would be sitting down to roast beef. Dot didn't come on a Sunday, so Maggie had left a huge joint in the oven at Emmerdale. They would have it for dinner when she got back, and the leftovers would see them through the week.

It felt wrong to be thinking of dinner when the country teetered on the brink of war. There was an ominous purple smudge behind the hills, and disquiet stirred in Maggie's stomach as she paused on the bridge to look down at the beck. It ran broad and shallow here, barely rippling over the rocks and slipping into quiet pools under the trees.

'Maggie.'

Her heart stuttered at the quiet voice.

'Maggie,' it said again. 'Down here.'

She leant over the parapet and there was Ralph, waiting for her in the dappled shadows under the bridge, a patch of sunlight picking out the gold in his hair.

'Come down,' he said.

Maggie shook her head, not trusting herself to speak.

'We have to talk,' said Ralph and when she still said nothing, 'I'll come up there then.'

He turned as if to climb up the bank, and Maggie found her voice. 'No,' she said, glancing around her. The road was empty but there was no telling who might come along and see her with Ralph and the whole cycle of gossip would start again. 'No, I'll come down.'

With a quick glance over her shoulder to check that no one was watching, she ducked under the branches of an elderflower and slipped down the bank into the damp cool shade under the bridge, Toby eagerly leading the way.

Ralph offered her a hand to help her down the last bit onto the sandy bank. Maggie felt his fingers close around hers and she clung to them before she made herself pull out of his grasp.

Toby was fawning over Ralph, pawing him and rolling onto his back, stubby tail wagging frenziedly. Ralph laughed and bent to rub the dog's stomach. 'Good boy, Toby!'

'He remembers you,' said Maggie and Ralph straightened with a final pat.

'At least *he's* pleased to see me.'

Maggie clutched her hands together to stop them reaching for him. 'How did you know I'd be coming? I didn't think you'd seen me in church.'

'I knew you were there. I could *feel* you,' he said. 'When you're near, the air changes,' he tried to explain. 'Like it's brighter and sharper somehow, and everything feels more vivid – like it does now,' he added, reaching for her.

She stepped back. 'Don't,' she said.

'Maggie...'

'We can't do this, Ralph. I'm married.'

'To Joe Sugden! How could you do that, Maggie?'

'You know how. You know why.'

She couldn't tear her eyes from him. It was as if she was devouring every familiar detail, testing her memory of the way his hair grew, the line of his jaw, of his mouth. His *mouth*. She could step towards him, kiss him and she knew exactly how it would feel, how he would taste. She wanted to do that, more than anything, so she made herself take another step back, made herself take a steadying breath. 'How could *you* leave me?' she countered.

'I couldn't stay and watch. I couldn't stand it. My beautiful Maggie, shackled to a brute like Sugden!' Ralph's face twisted at the memory. 'Just thinking of him putting his hands on you made me sick!'

And what did he think it had been like for her? Maggie thought with a flash of resentment.

'It sounds as if you got over me fast enough,' she said sharply. 'There are no secrets in Beckindale, you should know that. New York, the

Riviera, London. Champagne and balls. Seems to me that you managed to enjoy yourself all right.'

'Enjoy myself? Ha!' Ralph gave a crack of mirthless laughter. 'If only you knew. Yes, I tried to forget you, Maggie. I really did. But I was just going through the motions. I'd be at a party, dancing and flirting, or at the theatre, or drinking champagne on a yacht, and I'd find this terrible loneliness creeping over me, and I'd realise that all I wanted was to be with you. So I came home. I thought it would be easier if I was near you, if I could breathe the same air as you, but it isn't easier, it's harder. It's harder knowing that you're just up there at Emmerdale Farm and I can't touch you, I can't talk to you, I can't even *see* you.'

He paused. 'The truth is, part of me was hoping that when I saw you again, the magic would have died. That I'd realise I didn't need you after all.' He looked down into Maggie's eyes, his fingers tightening around hers. 'But when I walked into the room and saw you ... you looked so tired and so alone, but you were just the same. And then Sugden was drunk and I didn't realise... I should have realised,' he said, 'but God, Maggie, *Sugden!* The thought of you and that brute... How do you bear it?'

'I bear it because I have to,' she said. 'You shouldn't have come, Ralph. You humiliated Joe, and you humiliated me.'

'I'm sorry, I'm sorry!' Ralph dragged a hand over his face. 'I heard about your father. I couldn't just ignore it. He was a good man and I wanted to pay my respects but you're right, I shouldn't have

45

come. But that's why I wanted to talk to you today,' he said, catching hold of Maggie's hands and refusing to let her tug them away. 'Let's go away. Today,' he said urgently. 'Your father's gone. There's nothing to keep you in Beckindale now.'

'Ralph, I can't.'

'You *can!* You love me, Maggie. I know you do.'

'Yes, I do,' she said slowly. 'But I'm married. It's too late.'

He gripped her fingers. 'Don't say that! We'll go to New Zealand. A friend of mine has gone out to run a sheep station. We could do that,' he said, and Maggie laughed shakily.

'You don't know anything about sheep, Ralph, and nor do I. We may have grown up in the Dales surrounded by sheep, but we've never actually had to *do* anything with them.'

'We could learn. Or we'll do something else,' he said 'I'll come into money when I'm twenty-five. That's only another year away. It'll be a fresh start for us both. No one will know or care if we're really married or not.'

'I will,' said Maggie, extricating her hands from his at last. 'I *promised*. I don't love Joe, but I made promises to him and that's all I have left.'

How could she make him understand? 'I've lost Andrew, I've lost my father, I've lost High Moor. The only thing I have now, the only thing that makes me still feel like Maggie Oldroyd, is the fact that I keep my promises. If I don't do that, if I tell Joe that my promise was only good as long as my father was alive, or until you came back, or until I wanted to do something else, then what good is my word?'

Ralph's shoulders slumped. 'So that's it? This is goodbye?'

'It has to be,' said Maggie with difficulty. 'We can't meet like this, Ralph. It hurts too much. And I don't think there's much point in pretending that we can be just friends, do you?' Joe would never allow it anyway.

'I'll always be a friend to you, Maggie,' he said. 'But you're right, we're so much more than friends. That's why this feels so *wrong*.' He paced in a circle, raking his hands through his hair in despair. 'It's so rare to find someone to love the way we love each other! Leaving you before was like tearing off a part of me. Don't ask me to do it again.'

'You must, Ralph. You need to find someone else to love, to marry.'

'No.' He shook his head without hesitation. 'That wouldn't be fair. There's only ever going to be you, Maggie.'

'I'm sorry.' Her voice cracked at last. 'Oh, Ralph, I'm sorry. I love you, I do, but we can't do this. It's wrong.'

'You won't change your mind?'

She shook her head, her throat too tight to speak.

There was a silence while Ralph examined her face for doubt or hesitation, until he let out a long sigh.

'Very well. We'll say goodbye.'

Later Maggie couldn't remember if she stepped towards him, or if he pulled her into his arms, but suddenly she was where she wanted to be, held against the lovely lean length of him, they kissed

47

desperately, hungrily, pressing closer and closer to store up memories for a lifetime of missing each other. The buttons on his waistcoat pressing through her cotton dress. His clean male scent. His hard body, his hands moving insistently over her, how the feel of them made her blood thump with desire.

For the first time since leaving High Moor, Maggie felt as if she had come home. *This* was where she belonged, in Ralph's arms. Abandoning herself to the swirling pleasure of his mouth on hers, Maggie wavered. Of course she did.

The longing to abandon herself to him beat at her, and her hands tightened on his shoulders before she forced her fingers to relax, to smooth down to his chest, savouring the texture of his waistcoat, feeling his heart thudding beneath her palm.

'I love you, Ralph,' she managed in a voice that wobbled treacherously. 'I'll always love you, but I have to go.' Somehow she made herself step out of his arms. 'Toby, come.'

She couldn't look at Ralph as he helped her back up the river bank and held the branches of the elderflower so that she could pass.

'Goodbye, my love,' he said quietly.

Maggie could only nod an abrupt farewell and march up the lane with Toby prancing beside her, her whole body screaming in protest at leaving Ralph. Her eyes were so blinded by the tears she despised that she didn't notice Ava Bainbridge who had stepped sharply behind a tree as the two figures emerged from the riverbank and who was now watching her go with a spiteful smile.

CHAPTER FIVE

'It's war then.' Charles Haywood laid down *The Times* and looked around the breakfast table at the vicarage with satisfaction. 'Thank God we can all now hold our heads up high.'

'I don't know why you're sounding so pleased, Papa.' Rose buttered her toast crossly. 'War is a bad thing, isn't it?'

'Senseless war, perhaps, but this is a question of honour, Rose, as I have tried to explain to you.' Her father regarded her with a mixture of doting fondness and exasperation. 'The Kaiser is intent on taking over Europe and if we do not stop him, who will? We English have always stood up to bullies and if we had not stood by France now, well, I for one would have been ashamed. Instead, we will be fighting for justice and freedom and honour, so yes, I am pleased that the right decision has been taken – and so should you be.'

Rose didn't think she had ever felt less pleased, but she couldn't really blame the war. The truth was that she had been feeling peevish ever since Mr Oldroyd's funeral. When her mother had asked why she was so irritable, she had said that it was because of the heat, but that wasn't true either. Besides, the hot, dry spell had broken at last and rain was pattering against the dining room windows.

No, the scratchy, edgy feeling dated back to the

moment Rose had seen Ralph look at Maggie Sugden. She had been standing right beside Maggie, but Ralph hadn't even seen her. She might as well have been a teapot! The heat in his eyes had made Rose feel silly for loving him. The way they had looked at each other, that surge in the air, had made Rose feel ... excluded, she decided at last.

She was jealous of Maggie, that was the truth of it. Maggie had lost her father, lost her brother, lost her home and was isolated at Emmerdale Farm and married to that awful Joe Sugden while she, Rose, had everything. Her existence was a pampered one, Rose was well aware. She had a wonderful father, a sensible mother and her brothers, John, who she adored, and Arthur. Arthur was irritating, of course, but still, he was family. She lived in this comfortable vicarage with a maid and a woman to do the rough work. Her family might not be grand, but they had connections.

Rose was ashamed of herself for feeling jealous of Maggie, but she couldn't deny it.

Ever since she had been a tiny girl, her father had boasted of her beauty and promised to find her a husband. Until the prospect of war had loomed, he had talked of sending her to London to stay with her aunt so that she could have a chance of meeting a suitable husband, and Rose had been thrilled at the idea of balls and concerts and dinners.

But then Ralph had come home and she had realised that her feelings for him were more than just a schoolgirl crush. This ache in the pit of her stomach, this certainty that she would never meet anyone she wanted the way she wanted Ralph, this must be real love. Why would she want to go to London to find a husband when the perfect husband was right here in Beckindale?

Rose had known of his passion for Maggie, of course, but she hadn't seen it for herself. She hadn't understood it, and now she did. Ralph was never going to love her like that. She was spoilt, Rose knew. Until now, she had never had to accept that she couldn't have what she wanted, and now she did. Was it any wonder that she was out of sorts?

She was not the only one on edge, though. Everyone had been keyed up since her father's sermon on Sunday. Papa was obsessed with the news at the moment and was constantly rushing to the newsagent's where notices of the main news were put up in the window, or up to Miffield Hall to see if Lord Miffield had had any telegrams.

So they had known about the ultimatum the government had issued to Germany. Withdraw troops from Belgium, or there will be war. Assurances that the Germans would leave had to reach the Prime Minister by eleven o'clock the previous night. Rose and her brothers had been playing cards while their father paced around the drawing room, constantly checking his pocket watch. Edith, her mother, had carried on sewing calmly, but once or twice Rose had seen her glance at her husband and the muscles in her jaw had twitched as if she were gritting her teeth.

John had been up at dawn to cycle into Ilkley to meet the early train, knowing that his father

51

would be on tenterhooks for news from London.

Gentle and sensitive, her favourite brother was the exact opposite of Papa, who had charisma, a word Rose had only recently learnt but which described her father perfectly. When Papa talked, people listened. When he walked into a room, everyone sat up. And his children were just as much under his spell as anyone else. Rose understood exactly why her brother was so desperate to please their father. He had never captained the rugby team or excelled at debating the way Papa had. Papa never *said* anything, but John must have known that he was disappointed.

So his face had been flushed with triumph when he strode into the vicarage dining room a few minutes earlier and presented his father with a selection of newspapers, all with the same momentous news. 'We are at war,' he said.

Her mother's exclamation of distress had been quite drowned out by Papa's shout.

John brought back news of crowds at the station, all waiting for the train with the papers from London. They had stood five deep around the newsagent's window, too, reading the notice about the declaration of war which had been signed by the King the previous night.

'Everyone was excited,' John had reported while Charles devoured the papers. 'Anxious too, of course, but it felt like we were part of something historic.'

'We?'

The faintest of flushes stained John's cheekbones. 'Robert Carr was there to pick up the newspapers for Mr Bates.'

'The newsagent's boy?' Rose's father asked absently, scouring the pages of the newspaper. 'Is that his name?'

John's mouth tightened. 'He's more than a boy. He's twenty, the same age as me.'

'It must have been exciting,' Rose put in and he smiled at her gratefully.

'It was. And then when we got back to Beckindale, you wouldn't think anything momentous had happened at all! Everything was just the same as ever.'

'That's because nothing ever happens in Beckindale,' Rose sighed extravagantly. 'The King and the Kaiser could have a duel to the death outside the Woolpack and everyone here would keep talking about hay-time and whose havercakes got burnt and why Ralph Verney has really come home. I can't imagine anything ever changing here!'

'I doubt very much that we'll be that lucky,' her mother said quietly. She had been pushing scrambled eggs around her plate and now she put down her fork. 'John dear, would you like me to get Mildred to make some fresh eggs? You must be hungry after that ride.'

'Toast is fine, thank you, Mother,' said John. 'I'd better get used to short rations,' he added quietly.

There was a pause. Edith's cup rattled in the saucer and she put it unsteadily down on the table. 'Oh John, you didn't...?'

John answered her unspoken question with a nod. 'I went to see the adjutant when I was in Ilkley and enlisted straight away.' He glanced shyly at

53

his father. 'I thought it was the right thing to do.'

'I expected no less.' Her father was beaming. He picked up the *Daily Express* to show them the headline again: *England expects that every man will do his duty.* 'And you *have* done your duty, John. Without hesitation. I am proud of you, my son. Very proud.'

John glowed at his praise. Rose wanted to be proud of him but she could see that her mother had gone white. She watched as Edith made to pick up her cup and saucer once more, but the china rattled as her hand trembled with the effort of speaking calmly.

'But what about university?' she said to John. 'You have only a year left and then you can go into the Church as you planned. Could you not do just as much good that way as by fighting?' she said, and Rose winced at the pleading note in her voice. 'We would we just as proud of you then, would we not, Charles? It has always been your dearest wish that John should follow you into the Church, hasn't it?'

'Well, yes, of course, my dear, but in the circumstances...' Rose's father was clearly disappointed at his wife's lack of enthusiasm. 'This is a just war,' he reminded her firmly. 'We will be fighting with God on our side for the future of civilisation and Christianity itself. What could be more important than that? John is an able-bodied young man. He will make a fine officer, and the Church will still be there when war is over, which pray God will be soon.'

'You mustn't worry, Mother,' said John. 'I'm looking forward to doing my duty.'

54

Rose put down her toast. Papa made war sound glorious, and Rose had been able to cheer when it was about faceless soldiers fighting far away. But now her gentle brother would be fighting. John had always been bullied at school. How would he get on in the army? Her mother's reaction suddenly made sense.

'Oh, John, you're not really going to join up, are you?' Her voice wobbled. 'I wish you wouldn't! What if something happened to you?'

'Well, you females certainly know how to spoil a fellow's moment of glory,' her father said, throwing down the paper once more in exasperation. 'You should be telling John how proud you are, not weeping and wailing.'

'Rose and I are not weeping or wailing,' her mother pointed out quietly. 'And of course we are proud of John's bravery in volunteering without question, but you must allow us some trepidation too. I cannot imagine any mother waving her son off to war without a qualm.'

'I wish *I* could join up,' Arthur sighed before Papa could respond to her mother's reproof.

Rose wondered if she would have felt so upset if Arthur had been the one to enlist. Her younger brother was much more like Papa, although without the charisma, and of course Papa wasn't annoying in the way Arthur was. At fourteen, he was a boisterous boy, tall and well-built and ruddy featured like their father. Home from school from the holidays, he had been making Rose's life a misery. She couldn't wait for the new term to begin.

Arthur would do fine as a soldier, Rose

decided. John, though... She understood why he had signed up, but she wished he hadn't.

'You are not to think of it,' said Edith sharply.

'Besides, you're only fourteen,' Rose added. 'You're just a boy.'

'Yes, you are too young,' her father said, but he was obviously pleased at his younger son's enthusiasm. 'You must continue at school for now.'

Arthur scowled. 'It's not fair that John should have all the fun! I should think it would be jolly exciting to fight the Germans. I'd rather do that than go back to school!'

Edith pushed back her chair abruptly, irritably waving to Charles, John and Arthur to keep their seats. 'Stay and finish your breakfast. I will ask Mildred to come and clear later but I must get on. War or no war, there are things to be done.'

Her voice was high and tight, and they all looked at each other in silence as she left the room.

Her father cleared his throat. 'Don't take any notice of your mother, John. She's upset, naturally, but you mustn't take it to heart. Females always imagine the worst that can happen.'

The worst that could happen was that John would die, Rose realised and her stomach churned sickeningly.

'Wouldn't it be better if we could *do* something, Papa, instead of just imagining the worst?' she asked, and her father looked taken aback before swiftly recovering his assurance.

'There will be plenty for you ladies to do, I am sure, Rose. We will *all* have to do our bit, but John will fight harder knowing that those he loves are safe at home.'

CHAPTER SIX

'Robert Carr's joined up,' Dot reported, setting down the can full of milk in the dairy. She flexed her fingers, glad to be relieved of the weight. 'And Billy Hutton. Dick Swales and Johnny Skilbeck. Bert Clark. They've all enlisted. Oh, and t'vicar's son,' she remembered. 'He's joined up and all.'

'Not John?' Maggie was dismayed. She had known John Haywood slightly before he had been sent away to school, and he had always seemed a gentle boy. She couldn't imagine him fixing a bayonet to his rifle, let alone pointing it at anyone. *Killing* anyone.

Grimacing at the weight of the tin can she poured the milk carefully into the churn. 'I wonder what Mrs Haywood thinks about that.'

'I don't know about her, but the vicar, he's all for it,' Dot maintained. 'Him and Lord Miffield had a meeting in t'hall, got everyone all reckled up and now half t'village has enlisted. They got some recruiting sergeant out and they been handing out t'King's Shilling left, right and centre,' she told Maggie, her desire to impart news stronger than her dislike of her employer.

'George told Joe last night that he was going to enlist too,' Maggie remembered. Joe hadn't been pleased.

Dot sighed. 'At this rate there won't be no men left in Beckindale at all. Who's going to do all the work if all the men are in the army? That's what my mam wants to know.'

Maggie shook the last few drops of milk into the churn and set down the can. 'I suppose we women will have to do it instead,' she said. 'It's not like we don't work now, is it?' She showed Dot her rough palms and broken fingernails. Once her elegant hands had been her great vanity. No longer. 'Don't tell me these aren't working hands.'

'Women's work,' Dot pointed out, unimpressed. 'You ent never ploughed a field or sheared a sheep, have you?'

'Maybe I could learn.'

'You one of them suffragettes?' Dot gave a crack of laughter. 'Best learn how to make a cake first!'

She would not let Dot rile her, Maggie swore to herself, snapping the lid of the churn into place and taking hold of the handle. This was her life now. She was glad that her days were so full there was little time to mourn her father, although every time she passed the gate, she remembered him standing there, looking yearningly across the valley to High Moor.

It was easier when there was no time to think about the choice she had made, no time to re-member Ralph and the desperation in his blue eyes.

She was up in the morning to clean out the range and light the fire. She emptied the cham-ber pot into the privy and drew water from the well. She helped Dot with the cooking. She fed the hens and collected the eggs. She dug pota-toes. She made butter, she made cheese.

And at night she let Joe clamber on top of her. She listened to the creak and squeak of the bed springs as he shoved into her, her head turned on the pillow and her eyes tightly closed to blot out the image of Ralph reaching for her, Ralph's hands cupping her face, Ralph's lips warm against hers. 'Let's go away,' he had said. 'Today.'

She had said no. She was Joe's wife and she would make the best of it.

Joe had been furious when George had told him that he was enlisting. 'How am I supposed to run t'farm with just a halfwit like Frank to help me?' he demanded that night.

'Can Elijah not help with the sheep?' Maggie had suggested while she washed the supper dishes.

Elijah had been Joe's father's shepherd, rewarded with a little cottage behind the farm when Orton Sugden had set off for Australia in 1908, and, it seemed, a thorn in Joe's side.

'That old wazzock! He's ninety if he's a day. Too decrepit to get off his arse.'

'He must know a lot about sheep.'

'I'm not worried about t'sheep,' Joe snapped at Maggie. 'I'm more concerned about t'weather.' The long hot spell had broken the day war was declared, and he still had hay lying in the fields.

Carefully, Maggie put the plates back on the dresser, while Joe glared out at the rain. He would have to turn the hay again and dry it before he could stack it, and there was nothing he could do about it until the rain stopped. Of course, he should have finished cutting long ago while the grass was bone dry, but Maggie knew better than to say so.

Joe turned from the window. 'I'm off out,' he said abruptly.

'In the rain?'

'A bit of wet won't hurt me, and there's nowt else to do.'

Maggie dried her hands on the tea towel and watched her husband jam his cap on his head, turn up his collar and trudge out to the gate, which was still not fixed. Frank had eaten his supper, ducked his head in thanks and gone back to the stable where he slept in his little room in the loft.

She was alone. The light was so gloomy that she lit a paraffin lamp and watched it hiss into life. Then for want of anything better to do, she sat in one of the chairs on either side of the fireplace and picked up one of Joe's shirts to mend. Toby settled on the rag rug and rested his head on her foot with a contented sigh.

Maggie moistened the end of the thread with her tongue and pushed it through the eye of the needle. She wished she could keep her mind as busy as her hands. Alone, it was too easy to think about Ralph, to wonder where he was, what he was doing.

Too easy to remember the despair in his voice. *Leaving you before was like tearing off a part of me. Don't ask me to do it again.*

Too easy to imagine where they might have been if she had said yes instead of no. If she had simply taken his hand and never come back to Emmerdale Farm. If she hadn't let pride in being someone who kept her promises stand in the way of happiness.

She could have been standing beside Ralph on a ship on their way to New Zealand instead of sitting in the dreary light sewing buttons on another man's shirts.

At her feet, Toby twitched and dreamed, the warmth of his head on her foot a comfort. She could have taken him too.

It was Toby who heard Joe return. He sat up, soft ears cocked, long before Maggie caught the tell-tale scrape of the gate.

At first Maggie had no sense that anything was wrong. When Joe appeared in the doorway, his cap and shoulders were spangled with rain, she got to her feet, putting her sewing aside and pressing her palms against her apron.

'You're wet,' she said.

Joe didn't move and she went towards him, intending to offer to take his coat and hang it up to dry, only to stop dead when she saw his ominously blank expression.

'You lying little bitch,' he said, quite quietly and her heart jolted in shock.

'What is it?' she stammered.

'Did you really think I wouldn't find out?'

Ice trickled down Maggie's spine. She moistened her lips while Toby, picking up on her fear, crept beside her.

'Find out what?'

'You and Little Lord Fauntleroy, at it under the bridge.'

Maggie stiffened. 'If you mean Ralph, we weren't "at it".'

'But you were there?' Joe was dangerously calm but a muscle was jerking under his eye.

There was no point in pretending now. 'Who told you?'

'Ava Bainbridge saw you.'

'How helpful of her,' said Maggie tonelessly. 'I bet she couldn't wait to tell you all about it.' Clenching her fists in her skirts, she took a steadying breath. 'We were saying goodbye, that's all.'

'In the bushes under the bridge?'

The muscle was twitching uncontrollably now. Maggie couldn't take her eyes off it.

'Yes. I... Ralph asked me to go away with him but I told him that I couldn't. That I was married to you. That it was the last time I would see him and that this would have to be goodbye.'

'It's a pity you didn't remember that you were married to me before you slipped into the bushes with him, isn't it?' The rage in Joe's voice was straining at the leash. 'Do you take me for a fool?' He stepped closer until he was nose to nose with Maggie, and the threatening pose made Toby growl low in his throat.

'Do you expect me to believe that you weren't at it like stoats under there?'

Keep your head up. Maggie forced herself not to step back but to look Joe calmly in the eye.

'We were saying goodbye, that's all,' she insisted.

'Liar!' Joe's fist shot out without warning and the blow sent Maggie reeling backwards as pain exploded in her head. As if from a great distance, she could hear Toby on the attack, snarling savagely as Joe cursed.

'Bloody dog! Get off me!'

Desperately Maggie groped for something to drag herself upright. She had to get Toby to safety, but she could barely see and before she could clear her head she heard a terrible yelp and Joe steadily cursing.

'I'm going to fix you once and for all.'

'No ... no,' Maggie gasped, flailing to stop Joe as he stepped over her towards the gun cupboard. 'Please, Joe, I'll do anything...'

His only response was a vicious back-hander that knocked her back onto the floor. Her head cracked against the flagstones and darkness blotted everything else out. When she came round, Toby was standing over her, vibrating with aggression. His hackles were up, his ears flat, his lips drawn back in a warning snarl.

And Joe had a shotgun in his hand.

'Toby, down boy,' Maggie tried to croak but no words came out, or if they did, Toby was too far gone to hear her or obey. He was poised to spring for Joe's throat.

'No,' Maggie tried again, sobbing with effort. '*No, Toby.*'

But it was too late. In ghastly slow motion, she saw Toby's back legs brace to lift him off the floor and the next instant there was a huge bang, a scream and a thud as Toby crumpled onto the floor and the air reverberated with blood and horror.

Crawling towards the dog, careless of the man standing over her with a gun, Maggie fumbled to feel Toby's heartbeat. Frantically, Maggie felt him all over, but there was no warm huffing breath from the black nose, no rise of his ribs, just a cold slackness to his limbs and, at last, a great sticky hole in his side where the bullet had hit him.

'Toby!' Maggie pressed her face into Toby's ruff to muffle her scream of despair. 'No, no, no!'

'Get up!' Joe shouted and she lifted her face to look at him, white with grief and disgust.

'You've killed him!'

'It bit me! It were savage!'

'You're the savage!' she said in a trembling voice.

'It had it coming,' said Joe unrepentant. 'Now, get up and get rid of it. I'm not sitting in here with that stinking carcass. Take it outside or I'll put it on t'muck heap myself.'

'Don't touch him!' Heaving in painful breaths, Maggie hauled herself to her knees and bent to gather Toby's body in her arms. The dog was heavier than she expected, but somehow she got to her feet and staggered out into the rain with her burden.

For long moments she stood there, her face turned up to the rain, her mind blank with the horror of what had just happened.

Then she found a shovel and buried Toby down by the beck where he had liked to paddle in the peaty water. She was crying great, wrenching sobs of guilt and grief, weeping as she had never allowed herself to do for Andrew, for her father, or for Ralph.

This was where keeping her promises had brought her. No more, Maggie vowed. She would never forgive Joe for this, never. Tomorrow she would go to Miffield Hall and ask for Ralph. She would walk right up to the front door and demand to see him. She would tell him that she had changed her mind, that she would go away with him, tomorrow if need be. Next week they could be on their way to New Zealand and leave this wretched village and this wretched war behind them.

The thought gave her the strength to carry the shovel back up to the barn. Her hands were sticky with mud and blood. She rinsed them under the pump and then collapsed onto the straw, curling up to hug her arms around her. She was wet, cold, heartsick and so tired she could barely move. The barn was ripe with the smell of cows but she didn't care. Anywhere was better than the house where Joe was.

When the door slammed open, she didn't even look up. Joe stood over her, his hair wild, his eyes implacable.

'So this is where you're hiding. Get up.'

Maggie just shook her head and turned her face into the straw. 'I can't.'

'You can and you will.' Grabbing one arm, Joe jerked her upright and her legs gave way so that she slumped against him. 'You're going to get up and walk into the kitchen. Look at what your bloody dog did to me!' He shoved his arm in front of her face. It was badly torn and bleeding.

'Good,' said Maggie.

'What did you say?'

'You killed Toby!' Incoherent with rage and distress, Maggie beat at him with her fists, but she was too weak to hurt him. Joe dragged her back across the farmyard and threw her in through the kitchen door.

'Now clean yourself up and get a bandage for my arm!'

'No.'

Joe stared at her. She could imagine how she must look, her face drawn and streaked with mud, blood and tears, her hair matted with rain, but she didn't care. She lifted her chin and the hatred and contempt in her face must have got through because he swung his fist at her again, grunting in satisfaction as she stumbled and fell over a stool.

'You do as I say!' he screamed at her.

Maggie shook her dazedly, but her eyes when she lifted them to his were full of loathing. 'No,' she managed, coughing and spitting blood.

'Do it!'

'No.'

Drawing back his foot, he aimed a vicious boot at her side that sent her crashing back onto the floor tiles. 'Do it, do it, do it!' he grunted, kicking and kicking and kicking while pain bloomed all over Maggie's body, in bursts of red and agonising white until finally, mercifully, blackness swooped down and blotted out her mind and she lay sprawled unconscious on the kitchen floor.

CHAPTER SEVEN

A pounding dragged Maggie out of a darkness so thick and viscous that it pressed against her chest and made every breath a struggle. Someone was banging on the door, but she couldn't open her eyes properly, couldn't seem to move at all. Dot would have to answer it. She lay very still, squinting through slitted eyes at a patch of rough whiteness.

The ceiling, Maggie realised at last. She was looking at the ceiling in the bedroom at Emmerdale Farm. Slowly she became aware that the pounding was inside her head and that pain was drumming through her, banging in her bones, knocking on her nerves, smouldering under her skin.

What had happened to her, she wondered in confusion. Feebly, she wriggled her fingers, felt the coarse cotton of a sheet. She was in bed, that seemed certain, but why couldn't she move? A sense of doom slithered at the back of her mind. Something was terribly wrong. She had to get up.

Very, very carefully, she tried to lift her head from the pillow but even the smallest movement was enough to blot out her vision in a white burst of pain and with a whimper she sank back down.

But the movement had been enough to bring her memory back. It sliced through her like a knife through butter in cruel, vivid flashes: Joe's fists, the gun. Toby's snarl. His limp body.

Maggie's throat closed with anguish. Toby was dead. Toby, who had been her constant companion through the griefs of the past. When Andrew died, when her father collapsed, when Ralph left ... day after day, when Maggie woke here at Emmerdale Farm with Joe snoring by her side, Toby had been there, a quiet, trusting presence. His bright eyes had always been able to make Maggie smile, and the warmth of his body as he leant against Maggie had been a constant, word-

67

less comfort.

And now he was lying in the wet earth.

Abruptly Maggie leant over the side of the bed and vomited with pain and memory.

When she heard Joe's heavy tread on the stairs, she turned her face to the wall. She wasn't afraid. Joe could do what he liked now. He couldn't hurt her any more than he already had.

'Ah, Christ!' Joe exclaimed in disgust at the splash of vomit on the floorboards and stepped gingerly around it. 'You awake then?'

Maggie didn't answer.

There was a pause. Joe sat down heavily on the edge of the bed, and in spite of herself, Maggie tensed. Her whole body was a throbbing mass of pain and there was a redness behind her eyes.

'Mebbe I went a bit far,' Joe said grudgingly after a moment. 'But what's a man supposed to do when he hears his wife's been seeing another man? Sit down at t'table and talk about it? I don't know nobody who wouldn't have taken the back of his hand to you in the same situation. You were asking for it.'

'Toby wasn't asking for it,' she said, her voice barely a thread. 'You killed him.'

'What did you expect me to do? That were a vicious dog! About tore my arm to shreds,' said Joe. 'You can't keep a dog like that on a farm. If it could do that to me, what would it do to a sheep?'

Maggie refused to look at him. She was afraid she would be sick again if she did. 'A sheep wouldn't have been attacking me.'

'The sooner you accept the way things are at Emmerdale Farm, the better it'll be for you. You look a mess, but a few bruises won't kill you.' Slapping his meaty hands on his thighs, he pushed himself to his feet. 'I know how to protect what's mine. Accept that, and we'll get along all right.'

He stepped over the vomit and lifted the latch. 'Dot can come and clear up that mess.'

Maggie squeezed her eyes shut, listening to the sound of his boots on the wooden stairs. The red mass of pain was resolving itself into individual hurts. With her tongue, she probed her jaw where the blow from Joe's fist seemed to have loosened a tooth. Breathing was agony and she suspected he had cracked a rib.

There was a dull, nagging ache low in her abdomen. It might have been from a kick – she had a vivid memory of a boot slamming into her as she lay on her face, lifting her up and over onto her back to leave her exposed before she could curl up small once more, so it might have been from that or from any of the other blows that had rained down on her. When she lifted her arm, she could make out ugly marks where his fingers had grabbed her and dragged her back to the farmhouse.

She hurt all over, but that burning sensation in her stomach, that wasn't pain. That was rage. That was loathing. That was a determination to leave this house and this farm and this man who had killed Toby.

No more keeping her promises, Maggie vowed to herself. Oh, she'd keep her head high all right. She'd walk right through Emmerdale with it up. She would not be ashamed of leaving a man who beat her the way Joe did. The moment she could walk, she was going to find Ralph. She was going to tell him that she had changed her mind and she was leaving Beckindale for good.

It was a day before Maggie could stand up, two more before she could make it as far as the broken-down gate. She was breathless with pain by the time she made it there, and she clung to the top bar, white-faced. This time she looked deliberately right, to the chimneys of Miffield Hall. Ralph was there. She just had to be strong enough to walk a mile.

Dot's eyes had slid away from her bruises but Maggie was sure that she had taken the news that Maggie Oldroyd had finally had her comeuppance down to the village. Ava Bainbridge would be lapping up *that* juicy piece of gossip! She would be delighted at the effect of her tittle-tattling to Joe. Maggie could just imagine Ava whispering behind her hand. *That Maggie Sugden, Maggie Oldroyd as was, remember how proud she was? She's not so proud now. Carrying on with Ralph Verney and her a married woman. Disgusting, I call it. Is it any wonder Joe Sugden's taken his fists to her?*

Maggie told herself that she didn't care. Ava could say what she liked. She was going to New Zealand and leaving the gossip and the stares behind.

But first she had to get to Miffield Hall. It was a week before she was in any state to leave the farm, and she could feel Joe watching her. He must know how badly he wanted to escape. So Maggie bided her time and pretended that she could still barely walk, though the moment he was out of sight she would stretch and force her aching muscles to move again.

At last her chance came. Dot brought news of a parade in Beckindale for the new recruits who would leaving for training or, in the case of those like John Haywood who had been part of an officer training corps at their public school, straight for the front. Dot begged for the day off so that she could watch the parade and support the troops.

'Why not?' said Joe in an unexpected burst of geniality. He had been in a good mood since that terrible night when he had killed Toby. When he had nearly killed her. Maggie could see it in his eyes. He had enjoyed having her helpless and sobbing at his feet. It made him feel like a man at last. He looked at her now with a kind of gloating triumph, a conviction that he had mastered her at last. He thought that he had beaten her into submission.

He was wrong.

'We'll all go,' he said to Dot. 'Give George a proper send off, eh? Not you,' he added to Maggie. 'You're staying here. I'm not having you sniffing around for Ralph Verney.'

Maggie lowered her eyes as Dot smothered a smile. She said nothing, but hatred of her husband settled hard and cold in her belly.

On the morning of the parade, she made sure to hobble as she went to open the gate. To Joe, climbing into the trap next to Frank, it must surely look as if she was incapable of going any-

71

where. Frank took up the reins, clicking his tongue to get Blossom going, and Maggie smiled up at him as the trap rolled past her.

'Enjoy the parade, Frank.'

Frank's expression when, battered and bruised, she first made it down the stairs to the kitchen for a meal had been one of horrified confusion. Nobody had bothered to explain the situation to him, and she imagined he thought of her as a wounded animal, which, after all, was how she had felt. He was the only one at Emmerdale Farm she cared to say goodbye to, and although he darted her a baffled look and a quick nod of response, she could tell that he didn't understand why she wasn't going with them.

She took the photo of her father and Andrew in its frame but otherwise only what she stood up in: her Sunday skirt, a jacket, a sensible hat and sturdy boots. There was nothing of hers at Emmerdale Farm she had realised when she looked around the kitchen for the last time. There had been her father and there had been Toby, and they were both gone. There was nothing to keep her here now.

She was still stiff and sore, but it felt good to be walking away. Her heart lightened with every step that took her from Emmerdale Farm and she rejoiced as she marked off each staging point. The last time she wrestled with the wretched gate. The last time she made her way round that muddy patch in the track. The last time she turned into the lane and passed the Warcups' cottage with its pretty garden.

Newly married Polly Warcup was sweeping the

door step. She looked up as Maggie paused, but her smile of greeting faded as she took in the ugly bruises, and she turned away and went inside.

The last time she would be slighted by a neighbour, Maggie told herself. She didn't care.

Soon she would be with Ralph. It didn't matter what Lady Miffield had to say. Ralph loved her. He had promised to take her away and she would go with her head up. She would not be ashamed of leaving a man like Joe.

Her steps didn't even falter when she turned up the avenue that led to Miffield Hall. Walking boldly up to the front entrance, she rang the bell. She could hear it clanging and echoing in the entrance hall and she put up her chin. When the butler opened the door, she refused to look embarrassed although she could read in his eyes his shock and disgust at the remnants of the bruises on her face.

'I'm here to see Mr Verney,' she said as coolly as she could.

'Mr Verney is no longer in residence,' said the butler, unable to conceal his satisfaction at disappointing her.

Not there? How could Ralph not be there? 'I don't believe you,' said Maggie without thinking and dislike flashed across his face.

'I can assure you, madam, that it is true,' he said, his voice dripping with contempt. 'Mr Verney has enlisted in the army and is part of the patriotic contingent leaving Beckindale today.'

Maggie stared at him, aghast. Ralph had *enlisted*? Dear God, what had she done? She had told him so firmly that she would not leave Joe.

He must have thought there was nothing else to do, but enlisting? He could be killed! Why, why, why hadn't he waited?

But how could he have known that she had changed her mind? She had been a virtual prisoner and there had been no way to get word to him. It was not Ralph's fault, Maggie realised as her thoughts chased each other in frantic circles. It was hers for believing that her promise to Joe was worth more than her happiness.

She had to talk to Ralph, to show him what a terrible mistake she had made and persuade him to change his mind.

Swallowing her pride, she made herself smile at the butler. 'Please ... I must see Ralph. If you could just tell him I'm here–'

'Mr Verney has already taken farewell of his family,' he interrupted her. 'I understand that he will not be returning until the war is over, so I am unable to take a message. Good day to you.'

And he shut the door in Maggie's face.

Overwhelmed with hopelessness, Maggie stared dully at the great brass knocker. She had left her escape too late.

This cursed war! She had forgotten about it while she lay muffled in a red mass of pain. It had never occurred to her that Ralph would sign up. He was too warm, too charming, too passionate to be a soldier.

And now he would have to fight and he might die, and it would be all her fault.

CHAPTER EIGHT

Rose had never seen Beckindale in such a festive mood. The shops along the main street were festooned with bunting, and a brass band playing in the little square added to the jollity of the scene. Reg Webster had acquired a box of paper Union Jacks on sticks for the village shop and those who had been lucky enough to buy one guarded it jealously and brandished it whenever anyone in uniform appeared.

The atmosphere since the declaration of war had been a strange mixture of tension and excitement. In a burst of patriotic fervour, much encouraged by her father's sermons and a stirring speech from Lord Miffield, no less than ten Beckindale men had signed up to fight with the recruiting sergeant who had come out to the village. Today they were on parade before departing for a training camp or straight to France where the first British Expeditionary Force was already fighting the Germans in Belgium.

Rose had allowed herself to be swept up in the feverish atmosphere and she was not the only one. It felt as if everyone in Beckindale and the surrounding area was crowded into the main street. Percy Bainbridge had opened the Woolpack early and was offering free drinks to anyone in uniform, while Ava had found herself a prime spot to view all the activity from the upstairs window of the pub. Her stepchildren were running up and down the street, wildly excited like all the other village children.

Brusque Janet Airey had her lips pressed firmly together and was scowling ferociously to stop herself crying as she said goodbye to her gangly son, Jim. Alfred Porter's mother, Betty, clung to his hand, and dabbed at her eyes with a handkerchief. George Kirkby was strutting up and down looking pleased with himself. Rose had seen him take a passionate farewell of at least three different girls none of whom, she suspected, would have looked twice at him when he was just a labourer at Emmerdale Farm.

There was young Bert Clark, the cheeky butcher's boy more usually seen whistling on his bicycle in his striped apron, grinning self-consciously in his new uniform. Big Billy Hutton, the farrier's son, stood beside him. His father, Will, had shaken his hand and turned away, his expression grim. Even Joe Sugden was there, looking oddly pleased with himself, with slow-witted Frank Pickles looming beside him.

Rose couldn't see any sign of Maggie.

But everyone else was there and between the shouting children and the oom-pah-pah of the band and the babble of conversation, Rose was struggling to hear what John was saying. Now that the time had come to say goodbye, there was a terrible tightness around her throat. Dear John, with his finely chiselled features and sensitive mouth. Only two weeks ago he had been a Classics student at Oxford. Now he was Lieutenant John Haywood, with stripes on his sleeve to prove it.

Beside Rose, her mother's face was fixed in a smiling mask, but Rose knew how desperately sad she felt. Only the day before, she had found her weeping.

'Mama! Whatever is the matter?'

Edith dabbed hastily at her eyes, embarrassed. 'It's nothing.'

'It must be something,' Rose protested. She had never seen her mother cry before. Edith Haywood was muted compared to her charismatic husband, but she was always so steady and sensible that seeing her break down made Rose feel as if a pillar of her world had crumbled without warning.

'Is it the war?'

'Of course it's the war,' sighed Edith. 'Everything is the war now! It is like a great bird, a kestrel or a buzzard, circling high above us. And it feels far away but then you look up and you know it's still there, waiting to strike. John will be there, right beneath it. I wish, oh, how I wish he hadn't enlisted!'

'But we're all so proud of him,' Rose protested. 'Papa says it's a matter of honour.'

'What does your papa know of war?' Edith said bitterly without thinking. 'It is all very well to talk of honour from the safety of the pulpit. It is not your father who will be fighting the Germans.' She brushed angrily at the traces of tears on her cheeks. 'What is honourable about men killing each other?'

Rose must have looked shocked because she broke off. 'Forgive me, my dear,' she said after a moment. 'I do not wish to criticise your papa. He is right of course. We must fight to protect the

77

Empire. I just wish that John didn't have to go,' she finished brokenly

'I'm sure he'll be safe, Mama.' Rose put an arm around her mother's shoulders. 'And he won't be on his own. He'll have Robert as his batman.'

Robert Carr, a clever boy who used to work with Mr Bates, the newsagent, had enlisted at the same time as John, and was now a private. Rose liked the idea that John would have someone nearby to remind him of home but her mother only gave her an odd took.

'I think it'll take more than Robert Carr to keep John safe,' she had said.

Rose wasn't sure what to think now. She had been moved by the outpouring of patriotism she read about in the newspapers, the proud certainty that the people of Britain would do their duty. Even in Beckindale there was a sense that they were all part of a great undertaking and when Rose thought about her brother enlisting without hesitation she thought her heart would burst with pride. It was impossible not to be stirred by her father's sermons too, the fervour in his face as he banged the pulpit and charged them all to do their duty and support the war effort.

But when she thought about saying goodbye to John, to Ralph, when she looked at all the young men on parade who were marching so bravely off to war and might not come back, Rose was conscious of a hard lump in her chest. Who could fail to be moved by their courage, or by the cheers and smiles of the crowd who had turned out to support them?

It was marvellous to see them now, standing

straight and proud in their uniforms, lining up under the critical eye of a fierce-looking sergeant-major. Bert Clark, George Kirkby, Billy Hutton ... so many boys suddenly transformed into young men.

And then there was Ralph.

Captain Verney now. Rose had said goodbye to him at Miffield Hall the day before. Her heart had tripped when she saw him, the way it always did, but that flutter of excitement had died, flattened by the knowledge that she could never compete with Maggie Sugden. Ralph had been charming as usual, and he had kissed her cheek when they said goodbye, but there had been a remoteness in his eyes, an unreachability that had told Rose to give up hope at last.

Watching him now, Rose touched her cheek where his lips had brushed her skin. There had been warmth in his kiss, even affection, but no passion. He had said his farewells privately and stood alone, his eyes scanning the crowd.

He was looking for Maggie.

How could Maggie not have come to say good-bye somehow? Rose wondered.

'I must go.' John drew her attention back by bumping a fist lightly against her shoulder. 'Goodbye, sis.'

'Oh, John...' Face crumpling, ashamed of herself for wasting time thinking about Ralph in these last few minutes with her brother, Rose threw herself into his arms, unable to stop the tears. 'Oh, John, I will miss you so! Please, please be careful.'

His arms closed around her in a brief, hard

79

hug. 'I'll miss you too. Look after Mother for me,' he murmured against her hair as he released her.

Rose nodded, knuckling the tears from under her eyes. 'I will,' she promised. 'I'm sorry for crying, too. I really meant not to!'

'It's hard saying goodbye, but it won't be for long,' John said with forced cheer. 'Everyone's saying the war will be over by Christmas, so I'll be home before you know it.'

Now Papa was wringing John's hand in farewell. Arthur punched him enviously on the arm. Edith stepped forward last and laid her cheek against her son's, her eyes squeezed shut as she held him tight one last time. 'Goodbye, my dear,' was all she said.

She watched dry-eyed as John marched over to join Ralph.

Someone started singing *God Save the King*. The anthem spread through the crowd and the flags fluttered in a blur of red, white and blue as the contingent set off proudly. Small boys ran shouting beside them. Some of the mothers were looking anxious and trying to smile through their tears, but the younger women were starry-eyed and Rose saw last-minute kisses being blown. She tucked her hand into her mother's arm, but Edith was standing rigidly, her face white and set, and she didn't seem to notice Rose's attempt to comfort her.

Her father was beaming and telling everyone what a good show it was. Rose saw her mother turn her head to look at him, and the look she gave him was so contemptuous that Rose drew back her hand, shocked by the unwitting glimpse into her parents' marriage. Edith didn't even notice.

'I'm going to cut through the back, see if I can catch them before they get to the bridge,' she said and before her father could stop her, she picked up her skirts and ran off.

She was breathless when she reached the bridge, where she soon realised that she was not the only one with the same idea. Some of the boys who were too young to join up were clustered on the little knoll by the bridge, together with a few girls anxious for a last glimpse of their sweetheart.

And Maggie Sugden.

She looked ghastly, was Rose's first thought. Her face was swollen and marked with yellowing bruises. She was holding herself stiffly, a hand pressed to her side as if it pained her, and her desperate expression relaxed only at the sound of marching feet. She hadn't noticed Rose. She was peering at the advancing troops and her face cleared magically as she spotted Ralph at the front. 'Ralph!' She waved frantically. 'Ralph!'

Everyone on the knoll was calling out, cheering, whistling and blowing kisses. Rose saw John glance sideways with a grin at all the commotion, and she waved at him, but she was watching Ralph beside him. She saw the moment he heard Maggie's voice and spotted her, saw the remoteness in his face wiped out by a blaze of expression that made her heart jerk with envy.

An answering smile bloomed on Maggie's face and she looked suddenly beautiful as she cupped her hands around her mouth. 'I love you,' she yelled, and he waved his cap at her to show that he had heard, but the troops were marching behind him and he had to keep moving.

For a few minutes the air was full of the tramp of boots, and then they were marching out of sight around the bend and the noise receded into silence. Some blackbirds were squabbling in a hawthorn and a sheep bleated forlornly from the fell, but otherwise there was silence.

The boys drifted off, and the girls trailed disconsolately after them, pressing handkerchiefs against their eyes. Maggie had stood watching the lane long after the last of the troops had disappeared but now she turned, the eagerness draining out of her, and saw Rose at last just as she caught her breath at a stab of pain, staggered and had to grab onto the wall.

Rose rushed forward to help her upright. 'Are you all right?'

'Yes, I ... it's just ... I had to hurry,' said Maggie, her voice tight with pain. 'I thought I was going to miss him.'

Rose didn't need to ask who 'he' was. 'Here, sit down.' She helped Maggie over to a boulder and sat down next to her.

'Thank you.' Maggie's hand was still pressed to her side and she winced.

'What happened?'

Maggie turned stiffly so that Rose could see the ugly bruises on her cheek, the scab on her forehead, the still swollen lip where a cut had just healed. 'What do you think happened?'

Rose flushed and looked away from the brutal evidence of a beating. 'I'm sorry,' she said.

'He killed my dog.'

'What?' Rose's hand crept to her mouth in horror. She remembered the bright-eyed little terrier that had accompanied Maggie everywhere.

'Joe,' Maggie said in a flat voice. 'He killed my dog before he nearly beat me to death. I was leaving him this morning,' she went on. 'I went to Miffield Hall to find Ralph. I was going to tell him that I would go away with him wherever he wanted but he'd gone. I only just made it here to see him, to say goodbye. And now I don't know what to do,' she said as if the words had been forced out of her against her will. 'I don't want to go back to Emmerdale Farm. I *can't*.'

Rose looked down at her hands. 'I used to envy you, you know,' she said abruptly, and Maggie was surprised into a laugh that turned into a grimace at the jab from her cracked ribs.

'*You* envied *me?*'

'I know. It's ridiculous, isn't it? But Ralph never once looked at me the way he looked at you.'

There was a pause. 'You're in love with Ralph?'

Rose sighed. 'I thought I was. I mean, how could I not love him? He's so ... so *Ralph*. You know.'

A slight smile softened Maggie's face. 'Yes, I know.'

'But I saw him look at you at when he came to Emmerdale Farm after your father's funeral and I realised that I don't really know what love is,' Rose went on. 'I love Ralph, I *do*, but I'm never going to have what you and he have. I know that.'

'And I threw it away,' said Maggie bitterly. 'I thought that staying with my husband would be doing the right thing. I thought I should keep my wedding vows.' Her face set. 'Not any more. I'm not staying with Joe now, not after he killed Toby, but where else can I go? What else can I do? If I were a man, I could just leave. I could get a job. As it is, I'm trapped. I have no family, no money, no skills.'

What a pampered existence she herself had, Rose realised. The unfairness of a woman's position had never ever struck her before. She had just taken it for granted that there would always be a man to look after her.

'My brother says the war will be over by Christmas,' she told Maggie. 'Can you bear to stay at Emmerdale Farm until then? It's less than four months.'

'But how will Ralph know that I'll be waiting for him?'

'You can write to him, tell him to come back for you.'

Maggie shook her head. 'I've already thought of that but how will I find out where to send a letter? And even if I write to him, Ralph can't write back. If Joe finds out that I've had a letter from Ralph, he really would kill me.'

'Give me your letters,' Rose heard herself say. 'I'll send it to Ralph. He can write back as if to me and I'll pass his letter on to you. No one else need know.'

Maggie stared at her. 'You'd do that for me?'

'And for Ralph. I want him to be happy.' And it was true, Rose realised.

'What about your parents? They wouldn't approve of you encouraging adultery. That's what it is,' Maggie said when Rose shifted uncomfortably.

'I'll tell them that Ralph and I are writing to each other as friends, which will be true.'

'Are you sure?' Maggie asked after a moment and Rose nodded.

'I'm sure. Think of it as my contribution to the war effort. Papa won't let me do anything else,' she added, resigned, and got to her feet, brushing off the back of her skirt. 'Bring a letter to church on Sunday. I'll make sure it gets to Ralph.'

CHAPTER NINE

Somewhere in France, 11 September 1914

My dearest and only love,
I am not allowed to tell you where we are, only that we are well back behind the firing lines and waiting for our turn for a scrap with the Germans. We can hear the big guns – that unmistakable crump, crump, crump – in the distance but are comfortable enough in our billet here. I expect we will be sent forward soon and the men are in fine spirits.

As for me, my spirits are as high as they have been for more than a year now. The last time we said good-bye, I was hopeless. What does it say that I am more joyful sitting here preparing to go into war than I was dancing and drinking champagne a year ago? This time my heart is full of hope. This time I know that you will be waiting for me when I come home.

I cannot tell you what it meant to me to see your smile as we marched out of Beckindale, although the

85

bruises on your beautiful face filled me with horror. That brute Sugden! I knew he must be responsible. How dared he lift a hand to you? If I could have broken rank there and then to deal with him as he deserves, I would have done but for now the war makes us all prisoners to a higher cause, and I had to march on and leave you there.

My darling, when I had your letter, it left me wild with joy and yet raging at your unhappiness. I know how much you grieve for Toby, and that your disgust of Sugden must be greater even than mine. Please, please hold on just a few months more. I am confident this whole show will be over by Christmas and then I will come for you. I will take you away and devote the rest of my life to making you forget that you have ever been anything but the happiest woman alive.

There are precious few hills here. I miss the fells. I miss you. Sometimes when I can't sleep I remember those days walking high on the moors with the wind blowing in our faces and the smell of the heather, lazy summer afternoons in the shade, dangling our feet in the beck, and always you, you with sunshine in your eyes, your hair falling around your face. I torture myself remembering the way you turn your head, the way you tilt your chin at me. I miss you, Maggie, I have been missing you for too long, but now I only have to miss you until Christmas.

Take care until then my dearest one. I love you always and forever. We were meant to be together, and we will be.

Your ever loving Ralph

Maggie straightened and pressed her hands to the small of her back. The previous day's rain had left the earth clogged and heavy. Digging potatoes was hard work but at least it got her out of the house and away from Dot's grumbling. She rested for a moment, enjoying the view as she leant on the fork. It was a mild autumn day, the air rinsed with a watery light, and so still that the smoke from the chimneys in Beckindale drifted straight upwards. Across the dale, the moors above High Moor were smudged with purple heather while the bracken-covered slopes below had turned a bright russet colour.

A red squirrel ran along the dry-stone wall and paused as if to study her, its head cocked and its eyes bead-bright as it clutched a nut between its paws. 'And good morning to you, too,' said Maggie. She missed having Toby to talk to, missed the comfort of his warm, sturdy body pressed against her leg, and the coldness of his nose nudging her for attention.

Every time Maggie thought of what Joe had done to her dog, hatred squeezed her heart.

The squirrel darted off with its prize. Sighing a little, Maggie put her foot on the fork and pushed it into the claggy ground. Perhaps she should be preparing for winter too. There were crab apples to be gathered and made into jelly, blackberries for jam. The blackthorns were heavy with sloes and she could coax Dot into showing her how to make the rosehip syrup that the cook at High Moor had claimed was a cure-all for every minor complaint.

But perhaps she wouldn't be here. Maggie picked out a potato and shook the worst of the earth from it before dropping it into the trug.

Perhaps she would be gone.

This whole show will be over by Christmas, Ralph had written in his first letter. *I will come for you.* The thought had kept her going for the past few weeks. It helped her sit opposite Joe at table, helped her bear his heavy tread on the stairs, the sound of his chewing. It helped her pretend that he had broken her.

She was quiet and submissive and careful not to provoke him, and when he heaved himself on top of her at night, she let him do what he wanted, which was not very much. He grunted and swore but more often than not would flop back onto his side with a curse, and Maggie would smile grimly into the dark. She could endure this now that she was leaving him. Joe would learn then that he had not broken her. He had made her stronger.

Ralph's latest letter crackled in her pocket. Thanks to Rose Haywood, she heard from him often and she pored over his letters before hiding them in the dairy where Joe never went.

But the news was not good. Soon after that first letter, Ralph and his company had been moved up to the front. He wrote of howitzer shells exploding around him, of a sea of mud criss-crossed by planks and trenches full of water and entanglements of barbed wire, and crawling into dugouts only big enough to sit up in. Of the incessant rat-tat-tat of machine-guns and the dull crump of heavy shells burrowing into the earth and the rising, tearing, shattering burst of shells exploding overhead. He told her of his fellow officers, shot through the lung or carried from the field having lost a leg or an arm, and his men, his brave-hearted men, who scrambled over the top of the trench and ran into the German guns.

The newspapers reported that the troops were fighting splendidly, but even they had had to acknowledge in the end that the British Expeditionary Force was in retreat as the Germans swept into France. Ralph always ended his letters the same way. He was safe, he loved her always and forever, they would be together soon. Maggie was to wait for him and he would be home soon.

She *was* waiting, Maggie thought, but there was no sign that the war would be over by Christmas as so many people had claimed. Perhaps all the new recruits would make a difference. Maggie hoped so. The Army had leased two of Joe's far fields to put up a training camp. The first batch of recruits from Bradford had just arrived and Maggie could hear shouted commands in the distance as they drilled. She wished they would hurry up and get to France to support Ralph.

Five more potatoes and Maggie reckoned she had enough for dinner and supper. She washed the worst of the earth off under the pump and took them into the kitchen where she warmed some water so that she could scrub away the earth packed under her fingernails. She had hoisted up her skirt as much as she could but the hem was still splattered with mud, and her boots were filthy too, in spite of having scraped off the worst of it at the door. If only she could wear trousers like Joe. They would be so much more practical.

She set the potatoes on to boil while Dot finished the ironing. Joe had gone to market to sell the few wether lambs they had, and Maggie hoped he wasn't spending all the profit on beer. She didn't expect him back until the evening, but when supper time came there was no sign of him. Dot had gone home to Beckindale, so Maggie fed Frank and sent him back to his room above the stable while she put Joe's supper of bacon cakes to keep warm between two plates.

It was nearly dark when Joe came back. Maggie had lit the fire against the damp evening chill and was knitting socks for the troops by the hissing light of a paraffin lamp.

Joe was swaying slightly. He had been drinking – the fool, Maggie thought contemptuously, but she said nothing. She just put aside her knitting to fetch his plate from the warming oven in the range.

'There's apple pie if you want it, too.'

Joe grunted as he sat down at the table. He ate fast, shovelling the food into his mouth, but he was watching her in a way that made her uneasy.

'Did you get a good price for the lambs?' she broke the silence at last.

'Enough.'

'You were gone a long time.'

'Why don't you come out with it and ask if I was in t'pub?'

'Were you?'

'Later,' he acknowledged. 'After I'd joined up.'

Maggie had picked up her knitting once more but at that she paused and stared at him. 'After you did *what?*'

'I joined up,' said Joe with a touch of defiance.

'But ... you're a farmer! Farmers aren't expected

to fight. It's a reserved profession, surely?'

'Maybe I want to fight,' he said belligerently. 'Maybe I'm sick of watching them volunteers training out there in t'fields and not being able to do my bit. Maybe I want to do my duty – or is it only your precious Ralph Verney who gets to fight for King and country? And maybe I'm sick of all this,' he said, gesturing around the kitchen. 'Maybe I'm sick of shovelling shit all day just to pay rent to those blasted Verneys. I never wanted this farm,' he said. 'I never had a chance to do owt else, but now I have, and I'm taking it.'

'You can't just walk away from a farm,' said Maggie, shocked out of her pretence of being submissive. 'What about the milking? What about the sheep? The crops?'

'You'll have to manage.'

'How? George has already gone. Elijah's too old. If you go too, there'll just be Frank, and he's only a boy.'

'He's strong enough,' said Joe indifferently. 'He can do t'milking and t'ploughing. Get some help in for rest of it if you must, or do it yourself.' His lip curled. 'Them suffragettes are allus on about you women being equal. Now's your chance to prove it.'

We women will have to do the work instead. Hadn't she said as much to Dot? But she had never imagined being left on her own to run a farm. There was more than milking and ploughing to think about, as Joe well knew. How could she possibly manage the sheep and the cattle on her own, quite apart from the crops and general maintenance? She had been busy enough with the dairy and the vegetables and the hens, with running the farmhouse, without having to think about the farm itself.

But Joe would be gone. The thought of it set a giddy relief uncoiling inside her. No Joe. How much more bearable would the next months be without him! A smile threatened to break out over her face and she bent her head quickly to school her expression to indifference. If Joe knew just how much she wanted him gone, he would stay just to spite her.

It would be worth the struggle with the farm.

The war would be over in a few months, Ralph still assured her. And when it was over, Joe would come back and she would be gone.

'I daresay Tom Skilbeck up at Barter Farm will take t'stock off your hands.' Joe interrupted her spinning thoughts. 'He might even give you summat to use t'fields if you can't manage.'

Maggie's head came up at that. Tom Skilbeck was Ava Bainbridge's father and as tight-fisted a farmer as you would find anywhere. 'We'd never get the fields back,' she pointed out.

'He'd let you stay here,' said Joe indifferently. 'If you've got any sense, you'll let him take over the whole farm. I might sell up anyway after t'war,' he said.

It was on the tip of Maggie's tongue to ask what he could possibly do instead, but then she reminded herself that it wouldn't matter to her. She would be on her way to New Zealand with Ralph.

'I'll think about it,' she said, mentally vowing not to let Tom Skilbeck anywhere near Emmerdale Farm. If she were to be left to manage on

92

her own, manage she would. Somehow.

'When are you leaving?' she asked Joe.

'Tomorrow morning. I've to report for training near Hull.' Joe pushed his plate away.

'Will you get a chance to come home before you go to France?'

'Mebbe. We should get embarkation leave at least. I might come back then. I'll see. Or mebbe I'll get other leave and come back and surprise you.' He made it sound like a threat, which Maggie supposed it was.

'Don't think you can do what you want while I'm gone,' he warned, pointing a stubby finger at her. 'I'll be keeping tabs on you. There's plenty of folk in Beckindale will know if you're messing me around while I'm doing my patriotic duty, and they'll let me know. You won't be able to keep any secrets from me.'

A thick mist enveloped the farmhouse the next morning and Maggie had to grope her way through the fog to the privy. It seemed appropriate somehow that the farm she was now responsible for should seem muffled and unfamiliar. She could hear the cows shifting and lowing in the barn but the hens were silent, bamboozled by the eerie light.

Over breakfast, Joe told Frank that he was going to war. 'You'll have to help t'mistress,' Joe said, jerking his head at Maggie.

'Don't worry, Frank,' Maggie told him kindly, seeing Frank's eyes grow round with alarm at what 'helping' might involve. 'Finish your porridge and get on with the milking.'

The milking. Frank could understand that.

When he had gone, Joe drained his tea and pushed back his chair. 'I'll be off then.'

'I've packed some bread and cheese for you to take with you,' said Maggie stiffly and handed him the packet wrapped in waxed paper.

Joe grunted and shoved it into his pocket as he went to the door. His gaze swept around the kitchen and rested at last on Maggie, who stood by the range with her hands folded over her apron at her waist, her expression rigid. She hoped he wasn't expecting any tender words before he went off to war. He had been rough with her the night before and only the thought that he was leaving had kept her from crying out.

But it seemed Joe wasn't thinking of tenderness either. 'I'll know what you're up to,' he said. 'Don't think I won't.' And with that, he turned and walked out to be swallowed in the mist.

CHAPTER TEN

A fine drizzle seeped through the khaki of Levi Dingle's uniform as he hung around outside the tent. He was waiting for his brothers. Nat was finishing a letter to his wife in Ireland and Mick was somewhere doing what Mick did best, working the system to their advantage. The other recruits that made up their company of the Bradford Pals were daunted by the army's rigid rules and regulations, but not Mick. It had taken him no time at all to find out how to secure the best bed in the tent and an extra blanket, how to avoid the worst of the fatigues – no emptying of the urinal tubs or peeling hundreds of potatoes for the Dingles – or how to get his buttons polished to a shine that would satisfy the eagle eye of the sergeant-major.

'He's like a cat, that one,' Mammy had used to say with a mixture of pride and disapproval. 'Throw him as far as you like, and he'll land on his feet.'

Nat was the eldest and steadiest of the family and Levi loved and admired him, but it was Mick he idolised. He longed to have Mick's daredevil charm and confidence, and envied his carefree approach to life.

Especially, he envied Mick's ability to talk to girls. Where Levi's tongue would tie itself in knots, Mick didn't need to try. A wink, a smile, and the girls would blush and giggle and let Mick tease and flatter them – and do a whole lot more, too. A whole lot of things that Levi could only fantasise about in the dark while his blood pumped with a hot mixture of confusion and longing.

He had never even had the courage to kiss a girl.

Mick was the reason Levi was standing here in this muddy field in the Yorkshire Dales. Behind him stood row upon row of tents that leaked like sieves in the incessant rain. 'Mother of God,' Mick exclaimed with a grin every night. 'It's like being back in Ballybeg. Tell me again why we left the bogs, Nat.'

In front of him was the parade ground, already

reduced to a quagmire of sticky mud a foot deep in places, where they drilled incessantly. Every muscle in Levi's body ached and his feet were permanently wet.

He hunched his shoulders and gazed morosely out over the valley. Grey, that was all he could think. Grey rain from grey clouds pressing down over grey hills divided by long grey stone walls. A grey village next to a grey river.

How he missed the green of Ireland!

At least Beckindale was better than Bradford. Levi hadn't liked that at all. Bradford was hot and dirty and noisy. The sky was grimy with factory smoke which clung to the inside of your nose and the back of your throat. The streets were full of rattling vans and even cars, with their arrogant, tooting horns, and the sky was full of belching smoke. The people were friendly enough, but they spoke in a harsh accent that Levi could barely understand.

He was horribly homesick for Ballybeg, but he couldn't admit it. When he'd heard that his two elder brothers were heading for England to find work, he had stowed away to join them. It was the bravest thing Levi had ever done, but they had been dismayed when he had appeared after the ship had docked at Liverpool. He'd been a sickly child and their mother had coddled him until her death earlier that year, so Nat and Mick still thought of him as a child. But he was seventeen now and he wanted to be treated like a man.

Levi had heard them talking about him in low voices.

'What are we going to do with him?'

'We can't send him back to Ballybeg, not now. At least now he's here we can keep an eye on him.'

'I don't need you to look after me,' he protested but they both shook their heads.

'But we do,' said Nat. 'We promised Mammy on her deathbed, didn't we, Mick?'

'We did. She made us swear we wouldn't let anything happen to you, and it's not easy, you have to admit, Levi. You're a dreamer. You'd walk into a wall if we didn't look out for you.'

Nat had wanted to find work in one of the Bradford mills, but it was a hard time. There were plenty of local men hanging around on the streets, drawing dole money for half the week, eking out their beer and cigarettes. The Dingle brothers had managed to get a few days of work here and there but Levi hadn't liked it. He hated the constant clatter of the machines, the grimy heat, the smell of people and wool, wool, wool. He missed working with the horses in the stables at the big house near Ballybeg, but having made such a fuss about getting to England, he couldn't say so.

They had arrived in Bradford just as the city was a-swirl with talk of war. Levi remembered the febrile atmosphere as they were caught up in a crowd around the newspaper office on 4th August. The British government had given Germany until eleven o'clock that night to withdraw from Belgium or it would declare war.

The Dingles were Irish through and through and no lovers of British rule, but in the middle of that solid, seething mass of people, even Levi was caught up in the excitement. As the clock struck eleven, he found that he was holding his breath while they waited for the telegram that would be sent to the newspaper office.

At last a great murmur rose from the front of the crowd and as the word spread back – *It's war! We are at war with Germany!* – an exultant swell of cheering broke out, and somehow Levi and his brothers were throwing their caps in the air too, although afterwards he couldn't have said exactly what he had been cheering for.

'There you are!' Mick clapped Levi on the shoulder and brought him back to the damp September afternoon. 'Ready for an afternoon off?' He put his head in the tent. 'Nat, get out here!' he shouted. 'I'm told there's a fine pub in Beckindale. I think we should go and introduce ourselves.'

Having rousted out Nat, Mick led his brothers down the track towards the village. They passed a ramshackle farm, two of whose fields had been requisitioned for the training camp, but on this murky afternoon there seemed to be no one about. Levi was just happy to get away from the camp for a while. There had been times during the endless drilling when he had wished that he had never enlisted. He had only done it because Mick had.

Nat had been furious when Mick confessed.

'Jesus, Mick, what were you thinking? We didn't come all this way to fight for the English! We might as well have stayed in the bogs.'

'Ah, come on, Nat,' Mick had coaxed. 'It'll be a lark, and you know I could never resist one of those!'

The Curve
William Street,
Slough, SL1 1XY
Renew books by phone 0303 1230035

Borrowed items 16/11/2019 12:31
XXXXXXXXXXX6007

Item Title	Due Date
* The factory girls [text(large print)]	07/12/2019

* borrowed today

Talking books are available to borrow free
from Slough libraries
Ask staff for details
Thank you for using Slough's Self Service Unit
www.slough.gov.uk/libraries
Follow us on Facebook and Twitter
Did you know? There are no overdue fines
for children aged 13 and under!

'What about that lass you've been seeing?'

Mick's face darkened at the memory. 'She was only after giving me a white feather yesterday! Said I was a coward and she didn't want to be seen with a man unless he was in khaki.'

'So that's it? You've joined up because of a silly girl?'

'It's not just that.' Restlessly, Mick lit a cigarette. 'You've seen all the posters. Your country needs *you*,' he mimicked, pointing a finger at Nat in imitation of Lord Kitchener. 'You must have heard about the German atrocities. When I think about what they did to those babies in Belgium, it turns my stomach! A man can't just stand by and do nothing when that kind of thing is going on.'

Levi had regarded his brother with admiration. 'What did you have to do to join up?'

'Ah, it was easy,' said Mick. 'A few questions, strip for a medical – there wasn't much to that, just open and close your hands a couple of times – then all I had to do was take an oath of allegiance in return for a shilling.'

He tossed the shilling in the air and Levi watched it glinting in the light as it fell back into his palm.

'Swearing allegiance to the English king stuck in my throat a bit, I'll admit that,' Mick said, 'but you know I'm not cut out for steady work, Nat. I'd rather fight than spend all day in the mill. Besides, when I was in the queue at the recruiting office, I heard they give you three meals a day in the army, and a full uniform. I don't mind doing a bit of fighting for that.'

Nat hadn't been convinced. His wife, Molly, was expecting a baby, and he had come to England precisely for some steady work. 'Well, there'll be no stopping you now,' he had sighed. 'With all these men joining up, Levi and I should be able to pick up some more work here.'

But Levi had no intention of staying safely in Bradford. If Mick was joining up, he would too. He knew better than to say anything to his brothers, though. They would only try to stop him.

The next day he joined the queue outside the recruiting office. 'Age?' the recruiting officer barked when Levi finally stood in front of the desk.

'Seventeen.'

There was a pause, then a regretful shake of the head. 'Too young. Next!'

'But–' Levi started to protest, only to be taken by the arm and propelled outside by a burly sergeant.

'Clear off, son,' he said sternly, but then he winked. 'Come back tomorrow and see if you're a couple of years older by then, eh?'

So Levi firmly announced that he was nineteen when he went back. His medical was more thorough than Mick's had sounded, but then it must have been obvious that Mick was fit and well. Standing naked in a line with other men, Levi was burningly conscious of his weedy physique, but he was passed and he beamed with relief as he swore the oath of allegiance and accepted his shilling in turn.

Mick was furious when he heard what Levi had done, but there was no going back. And then, of course, Nat had to enlist too. 'To keep an eye on you both,' he grumbled. 'I don't know what Molly is going to say when she hears I'm fighting for the English King!'

The Woolpack was a sturdy Yorkshire pub, all dark wood and the smell of spilled beer and cigarette smoke curling in the air.

'Ah, heaven!' said Mick, taking a deep breath with every appearance of delight. A group of older men with hard, weather-beaten faces and shrewd eyes stood at the end of the bar. Nodding at them, Mick stepped up with an easy smile and leant on the bar.

'Three pints of your best, please, landlord.'

The stout landlord grunted an acknowledgement and pulled the pints while eying the three of them distrustfully.

'You from the training camp?' came an abrupt question from the end of the bar.

'We are indeed. We're part of the proud contingent of Bradford Pals.'

'You don't sound like you're from Bradford,' growled one of the men, but Mick was unfazed.

'Now, that's very astute of you. We're from Ireland, from Ballybeg, to be precise.' He waved an arm at Nat and Levi who had taken a seat at a table in the corner. 'The Dingle brothers at your service: Nathaniel, Michael and Levi.'

'Bloody paddies,' someone muttered. 'That's all we bloody need. Them buggers from Bradford is bad enough.'

'Least they're doing their bit,' a milder voice put in.

'I've got no problem with them doing their bit

at t'training camp, but putting on a bit of khaki don't excuse thieving. I lost three hens last time them Pals had an afternoon off. Aye, and a spade. Tom's missus, she reckoned they pinched a cheese and one of her pies. Ent that right, Tom?'

There was a rumble of agreement.

'I'm sorry to hear that,' said Mick peaceably, 'but this is our first visit to Beckindale and we're just looking to enjoy a quiet pint here in your pub.' He handed over some coins and carried the glasses over to the table where Nat and Levi sat.

Levi saw one of the men standing at the bar turn to follow Mick with his eyes. 'We know the Irish,' he called after Mick. 'They used to come and help with harvest. Worked hard enough but they'd steal as soon as look at yer. You paddies are no better than gyppos.'

'Ignore them,' said Nat in a low voice as Mick stiffened.

Levi watched the men nervously at first, but Mick and Nat seemed to be able to shrug the hostility off. They were chatting easily about the family at home and the chances of specialist training, and as the strong beer hit him, Levi began to relax. He was feeling pleasantly fuzzy as he drained his glass.

'Another round?' he suggested.

Nat regarded him with affectionate amusement. 'I think you might have had enough, Levi. They make strong beer round here.'

'I'll have another.' Mick tipped back his own glass and set it down on the table. 'It's our afternoon off, isn't it? We've nothing to go back to but a tentful of smelly socks.' He dug in his pocket for some coins. 'You get them, Levi. I suspect I've worn out my welcome.'

Levi fumbled the coins that Mick tossed at him, and nearly tripped over a stool as he got up. Burningly aware of his brothers exchanging looks, he went to the bar and ordered three more beers loudly, hoping that a show of confidence would make up for his clumsiness. The landlord had disappeared and been replaced by a plump blonde with an officious manner and a pursed mouth. She made a point of biting the coins he gave her to check that they were good.

Levi's mouth tightened as he gathered up the three glasses and turned, only to bump into one of the men from the end of the bar who had crowded him deliberately and who now decided to take offence at the beer spilt over his shirt.

'Now look what you've done.' The man pushed at him and Levi fell back against the bar, slopping more beer around.

Over the man's shoulder, Levi could see Mick get to his feet with a sigh. 'Ah, Jesus...'

'Henry Porter, you take any trouble out of here,' snapped the landlady.

'I'm not the one causing trouble, Ava.' He shoved at Levi again, only to find himself spun round by Mick. When the good humour dropped from Mick's face he looked dangerous.

'That's my little brother you're pushing around there. If you want to fight, come outside and pick on someone your own size.'

Henry was only too glad to oblige. To the landlady's shrieks for her husband, they barrelled out into the street and started grappling, slipping and sliding on the damp cobbles. Nat and Levi tried to pull them apart but Henry's friends soon weighed in and it turned into a nasty scrap. A fist hit Levi in the eye and he went down, seeing stars, just as a booming voice ordered them all to stop *'at once!'*

From the ground, Levi blinked up to see a big man standing over them. The vicar, judging by his dog collar and the sheepish way the locals were dusting themselves down as he harangued them. 'This behaviour is unacceptable. We are at war,' he reminded them, 'and we must all pull together. Henry Porter, get back to your work. And all of you! What are you doing in the pub at this time of day anyway?'

But Levi had stopped listening. He had caught sight of a girl standing behind the vicar and for a moment he wondered if he had died and gone to heaven, because surely this was what an angel looked like. She was standing under an umbrella, the fingers of one hand pressed to her mouth in what might have been shock but could also have been an attempt to suppress a smile. She had golden hair, dewy skin and huge, mischievous brown eyes and Levi thought she was the most beautiful thing he had ever seen.

Levi saw Mick risk a wink at her while her father ordered the local men away with a sternly pointing finger. She coloured and looked away, but not before a smile had trembled on her perfect lips.

Mick rearranged his expression to look repentant just in time. 'And as for you men,' the vicar said, turning to the Dingle brothers with a scowl.

'You're a disgrace to your uniform! You are supposed to be training in discipline, not drunken
brawls.'

'But–'

He flung up a hand. 'I do not wish to hear any
excuses. I will not have my daughter exposed to
this kind of behaviour in the open street. I will
have a word with your commanding officer if
these incidents do not stop. We wish to do everything we can to support the troops, of course, but
we must preserve standards in Beckindale, too.
Now get on with you,' he said, dismissing them.
He offered an arm to the angel. 'Come along,
Rose. I'm very sorry you had to witness such a
disgusting scene.'

'Pompous old fart,' muttered Mick as Nat
helped Levi to his feet. 'He should try cleaning
out the latrines at the camp if he wants disgusting! But did you see his daughter now?' He kissed
his fingers. 'Pretty as a picture!'

'Rose,' said Levi, looking after her dreamily.
'Her name is Rose.'

CHAPTER ELEVEN

Dot heartily approved of Joe's decision to sign up
but was appalled to learn that Maggie intended
to run Emmerdale Farm by herself.

'You? Run t'farm? You'll never do it! You can't!'

'Why not?'

'You're a woman,' said Dot as if that was ex-

105

planation enough. 'It's not fitting. You're not strong enough, and you don't know anything about farming.'

Maggie put up her chin. 'I can learn,' she said, but Dot only shook her head.

'You should let a proper farmer take Emmerdale off your hands. Tom Skilbeck would be glad to help you out.'

'I dare say he would,' said Maggie, 'but I've no intention of handing this farm over to him.'

'You won't have any choice,' Dot predicted. 'It were hard enough running it when Mr Sugden had George, but now there's nobody. You're on your own.'

'I've got Frank.'

'Frank?' scoffed Dot. 'If you're relying on Frank, you're really in trouble!'

'We'll see, won't we?' said Maggie.

In spite of her show of confidence, she was overwhelmed by the enormity of the task she had taken on. She would never admit as much to Dot, but she had no idea how she would manage. That night she sat at the kitchen table with her head in her hands. There were fields to be ploughed, crops to be sown, walls to be repaired and fences mended. There were cattle to be fed, calves to be castrated, cows to be milked. The sheep would need to be brought down from the fells at some point, to be tupped and sheared and lambed.

Frank was only a boy, but he was strong. He had come in for supper, obviously puzzled by the changes that had been taking place. Maggie explained again, slowly and clearly.

106

'You remember George?'

He nodded.

'Where's he gone?'

'To war,' said Frank after a moment and Maggie felt like cheering. She thought they might have been the first words he'd ever said to her.

'That's right. George has gone to war. And now Joe – Mr Sugden – he's gone to war too.'

Frank didn't say anything but Maggie thought she saw a flicker of relief in his expression. For a gentle boy like Frank, Joe's surliness and outbursts of temper must have been frightening.

'And Toby?' he said after a moment.

'Toby?'

'Toby's gone too.'

She hadn't thought he'd noticed. 'Yes, Toby's gone too,' she said, her heart twisting as it always did when she remembered her faithful little dog. She drew a breath. 'So it's just you and me and Dot,' she went on. 'You're the man now, Frank. We're relying on you.'

Frank didn't say any more, but he puffed up a little, and the next day when she asked him to show her how to harness Blossom to the plough, he did it slowly but competently. Maggie walked beside him as he led the great horse out to the field where they grew winter oats.

'You and Blossom plough this field,' she told him when they got there. 'Can you do that?'

Frank nodded.

'Off you go then.'

Maggie stood and watched for a while as he took the long reins in his hands and guided Blossom up and down the field, the plough tearing up the earth behind her. Perhaps it wasn't as neatly ploughed as some fields, Maggie thought, but it would do the job.

Satisfied, she pulled the shawl closer around her shoulders. Frank was occupied and Dot had been left, grumbling, in charge of the farmhouse. The next step was to get some advice and Maggie knew where to get it.

Nobody knew how old Elijah Aske was now. He had been a shepherd since Joe's grandfather had first taken him on as a young lad and there was nothing he didn't know about sheep or the hills that rose behind Emmerdale Farm. Joe resented him for it and cursed whenever Elijah's name was mentioned, but Maggie admired the old man's dignity. He kept himself to himself and seemed content to live alone in an isolated cottage below the moor but he accepted the occasional boiled pudding or cheese that she took up to him.

Tucking a hunk of fruitcake and a jar of Dot's blackberry jam into her pocket, Maggie set off up the overgrown track, missing Toby as always. It wasn't the same without his bristly body bustling ahead or his pink tongue lolling as he galloped back towards her, dark eyes black and bright with pleasure.

Little more than a single room, Elijah's cottage was dark and pungent-smelling and a peat fire was burning. His seamed face showed no surprise when Maggie turned up at his door. He took the cake and the jam with a nod of gratitude and invited her to sit on the settle as courteously as if it were the drawing room at Miffield Hall.

He spat into the fire when he heard about Joe's

decision to join up. 'That lad were never a farmer,' he said. 'Doesn't have t'backbone for it. He were always a disappointment to his pa. Mind, Orton Sugden were a hard man,' he allowed. 'Joe were allus running after summat he thought he wanted, then throwing it away as soon as he got it.'

Like he had done with her, thought Maggie.

'Orton hoped leaving t'farm would be the making of him,' Elijah went on. 'He reckoned Joe would never amount to anything as long as he was around, so off he upped and went to Australia.' He spat again. 'Might as well have stayed here for all the good he did. Joe Sugden weren't never going to be t'man his father were.'

Elijah looked doubtful when Maggie told him that she was planning to run the farm herself in Joe's absence. 'It's a lot for a lass to take on.'

'I just need to know where to start with the sheep.'

'You can't do owt wi' sheep without a dog,' he told her. 'A proper dog,' he added, obviously remembering that Toby used to accompany Maggie everywhere. 'Not a house dog like that one you take around with you.'

'I don't have Toby any more,' said Maggie evenly. 'Joe killed him.'

Elijah regarded her for a moment before spitting into the fire once more. 'Joe's a bad 'un,' he said after a moment.

'What about Joe's dog?' asked Maggie, thinking of the collie Joe had never even bothered to name. He kept it in a bare kennel in the barn and fed it occasionally with scraps of meat. On the

109

few occasions Maggie had seen it, it had cowered away.

'Aye, she might do. She'll take some coaxing,' Elijah warned. 'Joe, he never knew how to treat a dog. A good dog will look to you, so if you're in bad temper, you'd best take it back to its kennel. And he were always in a bad temper.'

It was almost an hour later that Maggie made her way thoughtfully back to the farmhouse. Elijah had given her a lot to think about. But she had been encouraged to learn that the sheep would be fine on their heaf, the familiar patch of moor they rarely wandered from, so she could leave them up there while she trained the dog.

'You need to treat it right,' he had told her. 'Not too soft, mind. It needs to know who's boss.'

Ignoring Dot's protests, Maggie cut off some slices of roast beef and went out to the barn. Hens pecked around the door and as she pulled it open, one of the wild farm cats streaked past her. Inside, the barn smelt of straw and dung and old wood. A bare pen had been constructed in one corner, and when she unfastened the door, she saw the dog press back into the corner.

Her throat closed at the fear in its expression. 'It's all right,' she soothed, putting down a slice of the meat where the dog could see it. 'It's all right, he's gone. You're my dog now.'

She called the dog Fly. It took her much patient coaxing with scraps of meat, but eventually Fly would crawl out of her kennel on her belly when Maggie opened the door and take the food from her hand. Very gently, Maggie lifted a hand to stroke the soft ears, her heart cracking when the dog immediately shrank back.

'You're a good lass, I can tell,' she told Fly. 'Joe didn't deserve you.'

'Do you think I'll be able to work her?' she asked Elijah, when she walked Fly up the track to see him.

Elijah studied the dog who waited warily at Maggie's side. A black and white border collie, she had the nervous air of a dog who might break and run at any moment. 'Think you can get an understanding between you?' he asked.

Maggie crouched down and stroked Fly's head, pleased to see that this time she didn't flinch. 'I think so.'

'You make sure you're boss and you'll do all right,' said Elijah. 'She'll want to please you and it's bred in her to work. Wasn't her fault young Joe never had patience to train her up.'

Under Elijah's direction, Maggie taught Fly to lie down on command, and when that was mastered, to go left when she shouted, 'way here,' and right if called, 'come by'. They trained every day, and it warmed her heart to see how Fly's eyes brightened and how her coat was gradually losing its dullness. The dog loved to work and was in her element running up a hillside. She spent the day at Maggie's side. Whatever Maggie was doing, there was Fly. Maggie wanted to take her into the farmhouse at night, but Elijah told her firmly that she should leave her in the kennel.

'She's a working dog, not a pet,' he said. 'Don't spoil her. She'll be happy where she is.'

111

Maggie took his advice but when no one was looking, she snuck an old blanket for Fly to lie on in her kennel. 'Don't tell Elijah,' she told the dog.

'I reckon you can try her with some sheep now,' Elijah decided one day. He had been leaning on the wall while Maggie and Fly demonstrated what they could do.

'Really?' Maggie flushed with pleasure.

'And you'll need this.' Elijah held out his crook.

She took it, feeling the warmth of the wood worn smooth by years of use.

'Oh, I couldn't...'

'It's no use to me now,' he said gruffly. 'You've got the dog, but you can't deal with sheep without a crook, too.'

'Thank you.' Absurdly moved, Maggie held it between her hands and thought about how many times Elijah had climbed the fells with the crook in his hand. 'Thank you.'

There were encouraging moments over that autumn, but there were times when she had to admit defeat, too. Frank was happy to milk the dairy cows, but Maggie had swallowed her pride and sold the rest of the cattle to Ava Bainbridge's father, Tom Skilbeck, a flinty-eyed farmer who made no secret of his distaste at dealing with a woman, but who nonetheless drove a hard bargain.

'I'll take them fields off yer hands too,' he suggested once he had beaten her down on price. They were standing in the field with the grazing cattle and he jerked his head in the direction of the half-ploughed fields with their tumbledown

112

walls and raggedy edges adjoining his land.

'They're part of our tenancy.'

'Nowt to stop you sub-letting.' He cocked a grizzled brow at her. 'You'd be wise to let me have the ploughing of them. We all know Joe's left you with nowt but that lackwit Frank Pickles. You won't manage.'

Maggie drew a breath and folded her hands tightly together. She knew what he was thinking: there was no way a woman would be able to run a farm by herself, let alone one as hoity-toity as Maggie Oldroyd. She could practically hear him telling the other farmers in the pub that she didn't know the arse end of a sheep from another. She would come crawling back, she was sure Tom was calculating.

They would see about that.

'I don't want to sub-let,' she said.

'On yer own head be it,' he said sourly.

Maggie was sad to see the cattle being driven off by Tom Skilbeck's man, but she knew she had done the right thing. She was left with five milking cows, a small herd of a hundred or so sheep and yearling lambs, the hens, and Blossom the carthorse. Two of the fields had been requisitioned for the training camp, but that left her with two to grow oats, three hay meadows and the hillside pasture where, as Elijah had told her, the sheep rarely wandered far from their heaf.

Frank milked the cows twice a day and loaded the churns onto the trap to take them to the bottom of the lane. They were collected there and eventually made their way by train to Bradford. Maggie had no time now to make butter or cheese. Dot maintained she had enough else to do with the cooking, cleaning and laundry, which Maggie supposed was fair enough. She spent her days feeding the animals, cleaning out the barn and stables, and then walking her boundaries with Fly. Together they counted the flock, kept an eye out for any sheep in trouble and note any repairs that were needed. The list grew dismayingly long: tumbledown walls, broken gates, crumbling troughs.

She soon abandoned her skirts which dragged in the grass and got snared in brambles, and adapted a pair of Joe's trousers to wear, tightly belted at the waist. Dot's mouth tightened with disapproval when she saw them for the first time, and Maggie was sure the news that she was wearing scandalous trousers would be around Beckindale in no time. She didn't care. The trousers were comfortable and practical and that was all she cared about.

As it grew colder, she started carrying hay up to the sheep on their heaf high in the hills. The first time, she had to almost crawl under the weight of it, but she soon grew stronger.

I wish you could see me, she wrote to Ralph. *I must look like an old crone from a fairy tale, bent almost double under my load of hay, as I climb the hill with Fly trotting beside me. When I reach the top and drop the hay, the sheep converge as if by magic from all the ghylls and walls where they've been hiding, and Fly and I get out of the way sharpish or we'd be trampled underfoot. You don't want to get between a flock of sheep and its feed!*

114

It is so beautiful up there, Ralph. So quiet and cold. On frosty mornings the ground glitters and sometimes the light is so bright and clear that I feel as if I could reach out and touch High Moor across the dale. And then I think of you at the front, slipping and sliding through the mud, with shells exploding around you and gunfire and screams, and it is hard to believe we exist in the same world. Please stay safe, my dear and only love. I am waiting only for you to come home.

Sometimes Maggie felt as if she were living two separate lives. The Maggie who yearned for Ralph at night seemed to have little to do with the Maggie who spent her days tramping over the fields or pitchforking straw and manure out of the stable.

Rose Haywood had been as good as her word and forwarded the letters between Maggie and Ralph. Every Sunday Maggie walked down to the village with Frank. She sent him to see his mother while she went to church and waited for an opportunity to slip Rose a letter for Ralph and with any luck receive one in return. Sometimes there were none, but at others she would receive two or three at once.

She hoarded those letters and read them again and again on the long, lonely evenings as if to remind herself of who she really was, to remind herself of him: of the warmth of his skin, of the way the edge of his eyes creased when he smiled, of the thud of her own heart whenever he was near.

As the weeks wore on there was less mention of the war being over by Christmas, but in her head

Maggie had that fixed as the date when everything would change. She refused to think beyond it, to what would happen to Frank and the farm and the animals when she left with Ralph.

She thought only of Ralph and of being together at last.

Christmas, she reminded herself whenever her courage flagged or whenever she was so tired she could hardly crawl up the stairs to bed. All she had to do was to hold on until then.

CHAPTER TWELVE

Rose could never walk up to Miffield Hall without thinking of Ralph. As she and her mother turned into the long avenue, she couldn't help remembering how hopefully she had almost run up to the Hall when she heard that Ralph had returned in July, fizzing with excitement at the prospect of seeing him again. Was it only three months ago? So much had changed since then.

How carefully she had dressed! How pleased she had been with her new cartwheel hat! Rose cringed now at her own foolishness, at the silly dreams she had had, of herself as Lady Miffield one day, entertaining to tea in the drawing room, no longer a guest but at home. That had been before she had realised how hopeless her feelings for Ralph had been.

Acting as a go-between had brought her closer to Ralph. He wrote to her often, enclosing a letter

116

to Maggie but with news for Rose, too, and always telling her how grateful he was. Rose wasn't sure whether she missed Ralph himself or just the idea of him, but she always read his letters with a pang. Of course she was glad to hear from him, but the letters only underscored how brotherly he felt about her. They might have been written by John.

Naturally, her correspondence with Ralph hadn't gone unnoticed. Her father was delighted when he heard that Ralph had written to her.

'You don't mind if I write to him, do you?' Rose had said.

'No, no, not at all. He's just the kind of young man I hoped you would develop a fondness for.' Rose could practically see him planning the speech at her wedding, puffed up with pride at the idea of his daughter as the future Lady Miffield.

'It's nothing like that,' she said honestly, glad that Arthur had gone back to school. She would never have heard the end of this otherwise. 'He's writing as a friend.'

It was true, but her father would never believe it.

Rose let out a sigh thinking about it, and her mother eyed her in concern. 'You seem very low at the moment, dear. Is anything worrying you?'

How unlovable she was. How useless she was.

'No,' said Rose. 'It's just ... oh, everything! The war is so depressing.'

Edith acknowledged that. 'But you can't give in to despair. We are all in the same boat, after all.'

'I know. I'd feel better if I could *do* something.'

'You are doing something. That's why we're

going to Miffield Hall.'

Regular bandage rolling sessions had been instituted by Lady Miffield, who invited all the ladies in the area to tea and conversation, with an hour or so of rolling strips of gauze in the dining room to make them feel as if they were all doing their bit for the war effort. It wasn't that Rose didn't think the bandages would be used, but she couldn't help feeling there was more she could do.

'I mean something useful,' she told her mother. 'I've heard girls are going to work in munitions factories to release men for the army. Couldn't I do that?'

'Your father wouldn't hear of you doing anything like that, Rose,' said Edith. 'He'd say it wasn't suitable work for a young lady.'

Rose looked at her sideways. 'What would *you* say, Mother?'

There was the tiniest of pauses. 'I would agree with your father, of course,' Edith said, faint colour staining her cheekbones. 'I don't think you would cope at all well working in a factory.'

'I can't work in munitions because it's not suitable. I can't go to London because it's too dangerous...' Rose lifted and dropped her arms in frustration. 'What *can* I do?'

'Rolling bandages is useful,' said Edith firmly. 'So is knitting socks. So is keeping cheerful and writing to those we love who are fighting to protect us.' She paused. 'I know it is hard, Rose, and frustrating at times, but you must accept that there is a limit to what you can do, especially when we cannot easily leave the village.'

'I wish the army hadn't requisitioned Dora,' said Rose. The vicar had been furious when they had taken the pony that pulled their trap away. Rose hated to think what Dora might be doing now. She had been used to a pampered existence at the vicarage – just as she was, Rose acknowledged. At least Dora was part of the war effort. She sighed again.

'Please put on a cheerful face for Lady Miffield,' Edith said quietly as she rang the bell, and Rose fixed on a smile.

The butler led them across the tiled hall with its grand staircase and opened the door into the drawing room. 'Mrs Haywood and Miss Haywood,' he announced them.

Violet, Lady Miffield jumped up and came towards them with her hands outstretched. 'Oh, my dears, I am so grateful you could come! I have been going quite mad with only Gerald to talk to, and he has nothing to say except about recruitment for this wretched war!'

Four years earlier the village had been astounded to hear that the widowed Lord Miffield had been snared by a pretty young debutante some thirty years his junior. Very obviously delighting in her new title, Violet found herself with a handsome and charming stepson who was only a couple of years younger than herself. Rose had sometimes wondered if Violet's fury at Ralph's love for Maggie was partly jealousy that he hadn't fallen in love with his pretty new stepmother.

Still, Violet had duly presented Lord Miffield with a second son, George, who was occasionally brought down from the nursery to be admired.

119

Violet claimed to dote on the child, although as far as Rose could see, he spent most of his time with his nanny.

George was the only male they ever saw at Miffield Hall now, apart from the elderly butler. Lord Miffield was busy with the Territorial Force, Ralph at the front from where the news seemed to get worse daily. Most of the footmen and grooms and gardeners seemed to have enlisted too.

'Now, you'll remember Mrs Haddington? And Mrs Dauntry and Sylvia?'

How could they forget, thought Rose irritably. They had all been there the previous week. Mrs Haddington was a relentless social climber who lapped up Violet's stories of staying at Windsor Castle for Royal Ascot week, dinner with the Northumberlands or a ball at Blenheim Palace. From a neighbouring village came Mrs Dauntry and her daughter Sylvia, who had somehow managed to avoid having their pony requisitioned, much to the Haywoods' envy. Sylvia was always bright and cheerful in spite of being nearly thirty and unmarried and possessing a mouthful of unnaturally large teeth. Rose was terrified of turning into Sylvia, which she knew was unkind and unfair, but surely, *surely,* there had to be more to life than living with her parents for ever?

The ladies exchanged greetings and sat down while Violet rang for tea. It was a large room with long windows looking out over the terrace to the lawn and the ha-ha beyond. Wallpapered in rose pink and hung with paintings and portraits, the room was furnished in a grand but rather old-fashioned manner: elegant armchairs with padded backs, a slippery sofa with gilt arms and elaborately carved legs, a writing desk, occasional tables covered with framed photographs. There was a grand piano where Rose had once sung a duet with Ralph, and in the middle, a huge palm in a brass pot, reaching almost to the ceiling.

They had tea served in delicate porcelain cups with dainty scones and fish paste sandwiches. Rose told herself not to remember sitting next to Ralph, shimmering with happiness because he had told her how pretty she was looking.

Violet prattled on about her connections and events she had been to before the war. Rose had little to contribute, having never been a house guest at a castle or danced at a ball. She had never been to London, or drunk champagne on a yacht in Nice or ... or done *anything,* Rose thought, trying not to feel resentful. She was fairly sure Sylvia had done none of those things either, but Sylvia was smiling and prompting their hostess with questions and looking suitably impressed. Rose wanted to stand up and scream. How would Violet showing off help the war effort?

At last Violet put her teacup down and announced that they should all 'get to work'. This involved traipsing back into the hall and along to the dining room where they spent an hour cutting up gauze into strips, spreading them the length of the magnificent mahogany table and rolling each up tightly before securing the end in a neat knot.

Bored and frustrated, Rose let her mind wander. As in the drawing room, long windows opened onto the terrace, but from the dining room Rose could see the great cedar tree where they had picnicked in the shade earlier that summer when she had been so innocently happy just to have Ralph nearby.

Oh, she was being tiresome! Rose scolded herself angrily. It wasn't as if she had suffered any great tragedy since then. She had just had to accept that Ralph loved Maggie. She would survive – but what was going to do without Ralph to love?

'Rose,' Edith's voice held a warning note, and Rose jerked her attention back to the gauze strip creeping along the table towards her as she rolled it up. The roll was lumpy and bulged out to one side because she hadn't been concentrating on keeping the sides straight.

'Sorry,' Rose muttered and unwound the strip so that she could start again.

'My dear Mrs Haywood, we hear such dreadful things happening at the training camp,' Mrs Dauntry put in. 'You must be so worried about Rose.'

Edith looked surprised. 'What sort of things?'

'The men are very rough,' said Mrs Dauntry, chins wobbling. 'Lord Kitchener has been so anxious to recruit soldiers that they say the most *unsavoury* types are being accepted.'

'I have heard there have been a few thefts,' Edith admitted.

'It is not just the thefts, Mrs Haywood. They are encouraging immoral behaviour amongst the young women. With almost all the young men in the villages signed up, of course the girls are looking for company – and *more*,' she added with a significant look. 'There have been shocking goings-on.' She glanced at Rose and Sylvia, obviously deciding with reluctance that she couldn't elaborate. 'Some of the things I have heard aren't fit for young ladies' ears.'

'There has been fighting, too,' Sylvia added eagerly.

Rose remembered the brawl her father had broken up outside the Woolpack. 'Some of the local men have been fighting too,' she pointed out. 'It's not just the men from the training camp. We shouldn't be complaining about *them*, surely? They're going out to fight for us like John and Ralph.'

'Oh, Rose, my dear, you are so very young,' Mrs Dauntry said with a patronising smile.

'No one is complaining about their bravery,' said Edith with her usual quiet good sense before Rose could retort. 'It is their behaviour when they are allowed to leave the camp that causes some concern. I believe Charles has spoken to the camp commander about it.'

'Well, I for one will be glad to get away,' said Violet and Mrs Haddington looked dismayed.

'Oh, Lady Miffield, you're not leaving us, are you?'

'I am, I'm afraid. Miffield Hall has been requisitioned as a hospital.' She looked around the dining room with its magnificent fireplace at one end and the portraits of Verney ancestors glaring down from the wall opposite the windows. 'It's rather grim to think of this filled with hospital beds, isn't it? But we must all make sacrifices. Gerald and I will be moving down to the London house for the duration of the war – unless it's already been taken over by Belgian refugees,' she added with her tinkling laugh.

At last all the gauze strips were rolled and they were able to leave. As they had their pony and trap, Mrs Dauntry offered a lift into the village. 'It's on our way,' Sylvia said gaily and although Edith accepted after a momentary hesitation, Rose didn't think she could bear their company a moment longer.

'It's very kind of you,' she said as she pulled on her gloves, 'but I have a headache. I think some fresh air will do me good.'

Feeling sorry for her mother but glad to be alone, she watched the trap bowling down the avenue and then turned to walk back around the house onto the terrace. Rose had heard that in happier days, when Ralph's mother was alive, there had been wonderful parties on the terrace on languid summer evenings and she liked to imagine that she could still hear the chatter and the laughter drifting in the air.

She walked along the gravel paths past the herbaceous borders, all looking badly in need of some attention, and through the gate in the wall to the orchard. As children, she and John had had the run of the hall grounds and the orchard had been a favourite place to play.

One day they had come across Ralph there. Three years older than John, Ralph must have been about sixteen at the time, and Rose, at ten, had been too over-awed by his magnificence to say a word. But she remembered that Ralph had been friendly to John and had even showed him the best way to climb a gnarled apple tree in the centre of the orchard.

Why, oh why, did everything come back to Ralph? Rose kicked a rotting apple away. She *must* pull herself together. It was pointless thinking about him and wasting her life wishing things had been different. They weren't and she just had to accept it.

If only Papa would let her do something useful, she thought with a sigh, she would have something else to occupy her mind.

Until then, it looked as if she would be stuck with rolling bandages and nursing her own bruised heart.

CHAPTER THIRTEEN

Restlessly, Rose wandered around the orchard, seeing if she could remember which tree the boys had climbed. That one, she was almost sure, she decided and reached up to pull off an apple. Her tug set off a cascade of apples bouncing down onto her hat. 'Ow,' she said and instinctively put up a hand to protect her head, only to feel another apple drop onto her and then another.

Puzzled, she looked up and her heart lurched into her throat. A man was hidden in the branches above her and a yelp of fright escaped her. 'What ... what are you doing up there?'

'Ah now, I'm sorry if they hurt you,' he said in the warm lilt of the Irish, apparently unconcerned at being spotted. Now that she looked more closely she could see that he was desperately trying to control a bag of apples, some of which had clearly toppled out of the top and onto her head. 'They slipped out before I could stop them. That's the trouble with apples,' he said. 'They're slippery things.'

Rose drew herself up. 'I said, what are you doing up there?' she repeated. She had been startled at the sight of him, but he didn't appear to be dangerous, in spite of everything Mrs Dauntry had had to say about 'goings-on'.

'I was just helping myself to some apples,' he said with disarming frankness. 'Hold these now, will you?' Without waiting for Rose to agree, he lowered a kitbag stuffed full of apples, and somehow she found herself holding it while he climbed down the branches until he could jump onto the ground.

'Thank you, *a chara*,' he said, taking the bag back from her with a smile that creased his cheeks in a way Rose strongly suspected he knew was charming.

'Have you been *stealing?*' she said in what she hoped was a quelling voice.

'I'm sorry,' he said, 'are they your apples?'

'No, but...'

'Aha, so you're stealing too?'

Rose had forgotten the apple she still held in her hand. 'Yes ... no ... it's quite different!' she said, flustered, and dropped it into the grass. 'I know the Verneys!'

'There you have the advantage of me,' he conceded. 'Do the Verneys send their guests out to amuse themselves in the orchard?'

'I've been rolling bandages.' Rose tried for some dignity. 'I'm just on my way home.'

'Rolling bandages, eh? For the war effort?'

'Yes, of course.'

'You could say I'm supporting the war effort too,' he said. 'The men are all desperate for a decent meal or at least a piece of fruit. And it's not like the Verneys don't have plenty to spare,' he added, glancing around the orchard where there were indeed apples rotting on the trees.

'You should have asked.' Rose hated how priggish she sounded and when he raised his brows, a stupid blush stained her cheeks.

'Ah, sure,' he said, amused. 'Next time I'll stroll up to the front door and ask if I can help myself to some apples, shall I?'

Rose looked away. She knew as well as he did what kind of response he would get.

He hoisted the kit bag onto his shoulder. 'So, Rose, are you going to report me to the constable?'

'No, I–' She broke off to stare at him. 'How do you know my name?'

'I had the pleasure of being lectured by your papa outside the Woolpack once.'

No wonder he had seemed vaguely familiar! 'You were fighting,' she remembered and he held up his hands.

'I didn't start it, I swear.'

'And you *winked* at me.' It was coming back now.

'I am guilty of that, yes. Is winking not allowed in Beckindale?'

127

'You don't wink at people you don't know.'
What was it about him that made her sound so
stuffy?

'Well, that's easily remedied,' he said. 'Corporal
Michael Dingle at your service.' He held out his
hand and Rose couldn't think of a good reason
not to take it. 'Mick to my friends.' She could feel
the warmth of his palm through her glove and
she had to resist the urge to snatch her hand
away.

'I am Miss Haywood,' she said with a haughty
look.

He cocked his head on one side while he
thought about it. 'I prefer Rose,' he said.

Rose was feeling ruffled, and she didn't like it.
She was quite sure that she shouldn't be chatting
to a man who her father would certainly deem
unsuitable, if not just as unsavoury as Mrs Dauntry had warned. He had openly admitted stealing,
but she could hardly march him off to the constable, and besides, hadn't she defended him and
his like earlier?

'I suppose Lord Miffield can spare you an
apple or two,' she said after a moment. 'I won't
say anything to the police or to Lady Miffield,
but I will if I see you here again. Is that clear?'

'As crystal,' he agreed, with another wink.
'Well, I'd better be getting on.' He adjusted the
kit bag on his shoulder. 'I'll be seeing you, Rose.'

'I hope not,' she said to put him in his place,
'and it's Miss Haywood to you, Corporal Dingle.'

She wanted him to feel embarrassed but he just
laughed, vaulted over the orchard wall and was
gone.

Levi whistled as he walked down the track towards Beckindale. This area with its hills and bleak moors was nothing like green and gentle Ballybeg, but he felt more at home here than he did in noisy Bradford, and on this crisp autumn day with the Yorkshire sky a pale blue and the smoke curling up from the chimneys in the village below, he felt his spirits rising.

He had the afternoon off, and for once he was glad to be alone. Nat was writing to Molly again while Mick had disappeared with a wink, no doubt to set up some deal. Levi loved his brother, but he didn't want him around in case he happened to bump into the vicar's daughter.

Rose. Levi hadn't been able to stop thinking about her since that afternoon when he had been sprawled on the cobbles outside the Woolpack and had looked up to see her. Her image had helped him through the daily humiliations of training, helped him grit his teeth and hold out for his next afternoon off.

And now it had come and he was on his way into Beckindale and in a few minutes he might see her again. Levi couldn't imagine that he would have the nerve to speak to her. He just wanted to know if she was as pretty as he remembered.

Mick would know what to say, but Levi didn't want him there. Rose was *his* dream. If they met her, Mick would take over and make her smile and he, Levi, would be left on the sidelines as usual. It wasn't as if Mick would care whether Rose responded or not. For him, flirting was just an automatic reaction to any pretty female. He wouldn't feel about Rose the way Levi did.

Seeing Rose, so pure and so pretty after the dirt and discomfort of the training camp, had changed everything for him. Levi couldn't really explain it to himself, but he held her image inside him like a precious memory.

He had been feeling so homesick until he had seen her. He'd been sick of his brothers fussing and fretting over him, sick of struggling to do the drills they accomplished easily. But mostly sick of the army.

The routine was punishing. Up at half past three in the morning for two hours of drilling and a three-mile march before breakfast. The day was an endless round of drilling, drilling and more drilling on a sticky, muddy parade ground. At least the last couple of weeks there had been some respite from that, Levi thought, though the longer route marches left him with agonising blisters and he had struggled with learning how to use a bayonet.

The sergeant-major had been scathing about Levi's attempt to stick his bayonet into the straw-filled sacks that were hung at intervals across the field. They had to rush towards one, jab the bayonet in the approximate position of a stomach, wrench it free and then rush on to the next.

'What do you think you're doing, Paddy? Giving Fritz a tickle on his tummy?'

The hot summer had given way to a miserably wet autumn and the camp was awash with mud which made it almost impossible to stick to the standards of cleanliness the army set such store by. Levi's nemesis, Sergeant-Major Hobbs, inspected the ranks with an eagle eye. A speck of dust on a boot or a single button less brightly polished than the next might be punished with two hours of extra drilling at the end of the day or an order to clean out the urinal tubs.

Levi might have grown up in a poor village in Ireland, but he had always been coddled by his mother because of his illness and the harsh reality of camp life had been a shock. They slept in wooden huts, the roofs made of little more than brown paper that leaked like a sieve when it was raining, which seemed to be all the time. There was no heating, just the stink and fug of thirty men to a hut. The food was disgusting too, watery stew or bully beef sandwiches made with stale, soggy bread.

Almost all the other men came from Bradford. They were a tough bunch, close knit and so coarsely spoken that Levi had been shocked, but they accepted Mick very quickly. Levi knew that he was lucky and that without him he would have been mercilessly bullied, but it stung that he had to rely on his brothers still.

Levi had been cursing his decision to join up. He couldn't admit how much hated it, not after having taken such a stand over enlisting in the first place. If he hadn't done that, Nat wouldn't have enlisted either, and Levi felt guilty about that too. Nat was a peaceable soul and with Molly expecting their first child, he hadn't wanted to fight.

But now that Levi had seen Rose, it all felt different. If he hadn't enlisted, he would never have seen her.

He was smiling as he crossed the bridge and headed into Beckindale. He wandered up to the church first. Rose's father was a vicar so it stood to reason she would live nearby. The church looked fairly new. Levi thought about going in to have a look, but the memory of his mother and what she would think of him in a Protestant church made him turn away and almost bump into the vicar.

Rose's father.

Levi snatched off his cap and ducked his head. 'Sorry, sir,' he mumbled.

The vicar frowned. 'What are you doing here, boy?'

'I was just ... looking at the church.'

'You're Irish,' barked the vicar. 'Catholic?'

'Yes, sir.'

'Then this isn't the place for you. If you wanted to come in and worship, then of course that would be a different matter, but there has been too much loitering by you men since the training camp was set up. It's causing bad feeling in the village. Get along now, and don't come back unless you've got a good reason to be here.'

'Yes, sir. No, sir.'

Cramming his cap back on his head, Levi walked back down the lane. He didn't dare look back in case the vicar was watching him, so he turned into the main street. A hammering came from the clog maker's shop, the smell of leather drifted out from the saddlery. He passed a butcher, a greengrocer and a sweetshop that reminded him achingly of Ballybeg and being allowed to spend a halfpenny on aniseed balls.

There was a general store, too, which when Levi pressed his nose against the window seemed to sell everything from tea and biscuits to paraffin and candles as well as the bags of cattle feed and coal that were propped up outside.

Most shopping would have been done in the morning and there were few people about. Those that passed Levi gave his uniform a wary look and he began to feel uncomfortably conspicuous until he caught sight of Rose herself and his heart leapt.

There was no mistaking that trim figure and the glimpse of golden hair beneath her hat! She was turning into the post office, a letter in her hand.

Levi's agitation vanished. Crossing the street, he hurried along to the post office and without giving himself time to think, pushed open the door and went in after her. And there she was, standing at the counter, her back to him. The postmistress was all smiles as she weighed the letter.

'Another letter for Mr Verney? Captain Verney, I should say,' she added archly. 'My, he must be glad to get your letters, Miss Haywood.'

'I hope they remind him of home.'

Rose Haywood. Levi stored up the name. She had a musical voice, as pretty as the rest of her. She hadn't seen him behind her but the postmistress was giving him a suspicious stare and he dropped his eyes and tried to look as if he were just standing in the queue.

'You'll be looking forward to him coming home, I expect.'

'Yes, of course. I don't think it will be soon, unfortunately.'

133

'No, the news from the front isn't good, is it?' The postmistress took a coin from Rose and gave her some change. 'There you are.'

'Thank you, Mrs Rigg.' Unaware that he was behind her, Rose turned and Levi stepped quickly out of her way.

'Oh, excuse me,' she said.

'My fault,' gasped Levi, and leapt to open the door for her.

'Thank you,' she said, and she smiled at him as she passed.

She *smiled* at him! A proper smile, unshadowed by any awareness of his uniform. Just a simple, sweet, dazzling smile that left Levi feeling giddy.

In a daze of wonder, he turned back to the counter where Mrs Rigg regarded him with all the suspicion Rose had lacked.

'Turn out your pockets,' she said.

'What?'

'I want to see what's in your pockets,' she said. 'We've had soldiers pilfering in t'shops here ever since that camp opened. I'm not saying you're not doing your duty, son, and good on you for that, but I don't hold with thieving, so if you've got anything in your pockets you shouldn't, you just take it out now.'

'I haven't stolen anything!' Levi emptied his pockets, slamming the few coins onto the counter and showing her the insides. 'There! That's all my money. Satisfied now?'

She nodded, unperturbed by his anger. 'It's as well to check. So, what can I get you?'

Levi didn't want to buy anything from her, but he had better have some reason for being in the post office.

'A stamp to Ireland,' he said sullenly, trying to get back his delight at having been on the receiving end of Rose Haywood's smile.

'No letter?'

He gritted his teeth. 'No. The stamp is for my brother. He's writing to his wife in Ireland at the moment. Is there anything else you need to know or could I just buy a stamp?'

Mrs Rigg raised her brows. 'There's no call for that kind of attitude, young man,' she said.

Levi snatched at the stamp and his change and flung out of the post office, his good mood soured. Rose, of course, had long gone.

Still at least he had seen her. He had heard her voice. She had smiled at him. That was enough, Levi told himself.

There was still half an afternoon to waste. He didn't want to go back to that blasted camp any sooner than he had to and he paused outside the smithy, drawn by the familiar tapping and clanging. Through the open door, he could see the farrier, a big fellow in the traditional leather apron, running his hand down the flank of a sturdy black carthorse. It stood tensely, and when he touched its fetlock, it let fly with a kick that had him swearing through the nails clamped between his teeth.

'Come on, Florrie, mi lass, it's for yer own good,' he muttered.

Levi went in. 'Want a hand?'

The smith looked up with a mixture of surprise and suspicion. 'I didn't see you there. Did you want summat?'

'No, I was just passing.' Levi looked around the cluttered smithy. 'It reminded me of home.'

The smith took in Levi's khaki uniform. 'You at the camp?'

Levi nodded. 'I miss horses,' he said.

'Should have joined the cavalry,' said the smith.

'Should have thought about a lot of things before joining up,' Levi said frankly and the smith nodded.

'Aye, I reckon there's plenty in the same boat. My lad, Billy, he were wild to enlist too. Wouldn't listen to nobody with owt sensible to say.'

He bent back to pick up the horse's hoof, only to jump out of the way as she kicked again. 'Ah, yer bugger!'

'I'll hold her.' Levi went round to her head. 'Now, Florrie, is it? Why don't you keep still while your man finishes, eh?'

Florrie snorted and blew into his ear while he talked nonsense to distract her until the smith straightened.

'That's done,' he said. 'Thanks.' He wiped his hands on a rag. 'Will Hutton,' he introduced himself gruffly.

'Levi Dingle.'

'You know horses, young Levi?'

'A bit.'

'Well, if you want summat to do, why don't you take Florrie out back and bring in Prince? I'd appreciate a hand to finish up.'

CHAPTER FOURTEEN

Maggie rested the pitchfork against the wall and dragged the back of her arm across her forehead. Outside, November had brought plummeting temperatures, but here in the barn the cows created a warm fug. They shuffled and huffed as Maggie cleaned out the straw and laid fresh for them, shoving against their bulk to move them out of the way. She had learnt to like cleaning out the barn, a chore Joe had always moaned about. It was hard, physical work, but Maggie didn't mind that, and it gave her time to think.

She read Ralph's letters until she knew them by heart, and she would mull over what he had told her about life at the front as she forked manure-splattered straw into a wheelbarrow. He was always cheerful, but Maggie could read between the lines and it was clear that the war was not going well. Ralph's promise to be home by Christmas was no longer mentioned by either of them.

It worried Maggie that Ralph's account of shells and shooting, of death and terrible injuries, was beginning to seem normal. It felt as if they had been at war for ever. Things that would have seemed extraordinary earlier that summer were now taken for granted. They were all used to Lord Kitchener's recruitment posters, to the notices urging housewives to practice economy, to rising food prices and the growing lists of casualties that were pinned up on the board outside the post office.

The news from the front was depressing, and Maggie stopped buying a newspaper. It was too much to think about what was happening over in France so she thought about Emmerdale Farm instead. Together she and Frank had managed to finish ploughing the fields and had sowed a winter crop of oats, and soon she would bring the sheep down from the hill to keep them close to the farm in case of snow.

They were managing. Maggie was proud about that. Tom Skilbeck had waited in vain for her to go crawling back and beg him to take over the farm. There were still plenty of folk in Beckindale who pursed their lips disapprovingly at the idea of a woman running a farm, and shook their heads at the unladylike trousers she wore, but Maggie didn't care. She was used to being eyed askance.

Dot brought the news from the village when she came up every morning. So Maggie knew that Ernest Burrows had joined up even though he was only sixteen and his ma had clouted him for a fool when she heard. That Beckindale was a-buzz with stories of terrible war atrocities, of babies butchered and women raped by the Germans. That Ava Bainbridge had bought herself a new hat and was giving out white feathers to anyone she thought should be in khaki and denouncing them as cowards. Clarence Terry had lost three hens and blamed the recruits in the training camp.

The presence of the troops so close to the village was both a source of pride and discontent in Beckindale. In principle, everybody wanted to support the men who had volunteered so promptly to fight for the country. In practice, though, the soldiers with little else to do on their days off roamed around the village and rumours swirled about petty pilfering, drunkenness and brawling, and sometimes worse. Young girls were told to cross the road if they saw a soldier coming.

'Can't you do something about it, Maggie?' Ava Bainbridge had asked in her officious way, tackling Maggie as she left church. As usual there was a cluster of village women around her, bobbing their heads anxiously.

'Me?' Maggie was distracted. Rose had slipped her a letter from Ralph in church and she couldn't wait to get home so that she could read it. 'What can I do about it?'

'The camp is on Emmerdale land.'

Maggie fingered the letter in her pocket. 'It's nothing to do with me, Ava. I wouldn't interfere even if I could.' She hadn't forgotten that it was Ava who had told Joe about her meeting with Ralph, and had made him so angry that he had killed Toby. Maggie would never forgive her for that. 'As far as I'm concerned, these troops are training to go out and fight with our menfolk. We should be cheering them not criticising them.'

'You didn't cheer our menfolk,' said Ava. 'You couldn't even be bothered to come to the parade when they left.'

Maggie stared at her. 'I didn't realise you were keeping track of my movements, Ava.'

'You weren't there, were you? Everybody else was patriotic and turned out, but not you.'

Maggie thought of her cracked ribs, the bruises all over her body. She thought about her desperation to reach Ralph and the bitterness of knowing that she was too late to see more than the man she loved march past her and out of sight. 'I was there,' she said.

'It doesn't matter who was or wasn't at the parade, Ava.' Janet Airey pushed forward. 'We're worried about the young lasses. It's not safe for them to walk the streets now without soldiers making lewd comments.'

'Or even worse,' Betty Porter put in.

'What do you mean, worse?' asked Maggie.

Betty looked flustered by the direct question. 'It's not the kind of thing girls like to talk about, but there have been lots of rumours.'

'Oh, rumours,' said Maggie contemptuously. Beckindale thrived on them as far as she could see.

'I know of two girls – I won't mention them by name,' Janet said. 'They've told their parents they've been, you know, touched up by soldiers. It's upsetting.'

'I'm sure it is,' Maggie said, 'but I don't see what you expect me to do about it. I don't even know the camp commander. He's not going to listen to me. If they've been hurt, the girls should go to the police. Now, if you'll excuse me...'

'Typical!' Ava's voice was shrill and pitched loud enough for Maggie to hear as she walked away. 'Maggie Oldroyd always was too grand to involve herself with village problems.'

'She's probably right about going to the police,'

one of the women said. 'If Joe Sugden was here, it would be different, but the camp commander isn't going to listen to her, is he?'

The support might have come from Janet or possibly Mary Ann Teale, but Maggie didn't turn round to check. She wasn't going to get involved in their petty squabbles. She had a letter from Ralph and right then, nothing else mattered.

Young Bert Clark, the butcher's boy, was Beckindale's first casualty of the war. The news came like a bucket of water in Maggie's face. Until then the war had been something that happened somewhere else, but Bert's death was the slap of reality. Bert was not coming back for Christmas, or ever. There was a gap in the village where he had been that would never now be filled. No more Bert in his striped butcher's apron, weaving along the streets, pedalling too fast on his bike, whistling out of tune. No more Bert with his cheery smile and the tuft of hair that would never stay flat. He had been blown up by a shell in a muddy field in northern France and there was nothing left of him to bury.

The village was sobered by Bert's death for a day or two but then, in the way of things, other news began to take its place: Walter Dinsdale had had another of his horses requisitioned, the price of sugar was going up, Tom Harker's back had gone digging potatoes. And always, the weather, which had turned raw and wet and made for miserable ploughing.

Maggie and Frank had struggled to get a second field of winter oats sown. Maggie led Blossom as she trudged through the mud, dragging

141

the plough behind her, and Frank followed to try and break up the worst of the clods. It was a long, wet day and at one point it rained so hard they had to take shelter in one of the field barns. Poor Blossom had to wait outside, while Frank and Maggie sat on a hay bale by the door.

'We may as well have dinner,' said Maggie, producing the pieces of pie that Dot had wrapped up for them that morning. 'It's a bit soggy, I'm afraid.'

She handed a piece to Frank who took a huge bite. 'Good,' he said through a mouthful of pie.

He spoke rarely, but Maggie was used to him now. If Frank had something to say, he would say it, in as few words as possible.

She was hungrier than she had thought, and she ate her own pie sitting in companionable silence on the bale with Frank. Her trousers and coat were sodden and in spite of her hat, her hair was plastered to her face or straggling, dripping, onto her shoulders. She was cold and wet and uncomfortable, but Frank, who must have felt the same, never uttered a word of complaint, and it was strangely peaceful in the barn, surrounded by the sweet smell of hay, listening to the drumming of the rain on the roof and to Frank chewing contentedly beside her.

'Aren't you hungry?' she asked, noticing that he had left a crust.

'For Blossom,' he said. 'She's a good horse.'

Maggie looked out to where Blossom stood patiently in the rain with her head down. 'Yes, she is,' she agreed. She looked at Frank. 'Like you. You're a good lad, Frank.'

A smile broke out over his face and he beamed at her, delighted by the praise.

'Here.' She gave him the crust from her own pie. 'Give Blossom this too.'

Frank got to his feet and careless of the rain went out to feed the crusts to the horse. 'Good horse,' he repeated as he came in. 'Good lad,' he added pointing at himself and his face screwed up with the effort of maintaining a line of thought. He pointed at Maggie. 'Good farmer,' he said, clearly pleased with himself for making the connection.

Maggie looked up at him, conscious of a warm glow around her heart. Did this big, gentle boy know what that meant to her, she wondered. Good farmer. She was absurdly moved by the compliment.

'Thank you, Frank.'

Maggie was thinking of the exchange as she finished clearing out the barn and went to wash under the pump. What would happen to Frank when she left? She hoped Joe would keep him on.

Grimacing at the cold, she soaped her hands and arms. She had sent Joe brief reports on the farm, telling him what she was doing, and she made sure that he knew what a help Frank had been. In return, she had curt scrawls about his training and the chances of leave. He still had three months of training to go before they would be awarded embarkation leave. Maggie was hoping that Ralph would have come home before then, and that she would be gone.

But she did worry about Frank.

When she went into the kitchen, Dot was at the

143

range, tipping a pan of sizzling fat from side to side. As Maggie watched, she poured in batter for a Yorkshire pudding and slipped the pan back into the oven where Maggie glimpsed an apple pie browning.

'Smells good,' she said. 'I'll lay the table.'

She went to the dresser to find the plates, and it was not until she turned round that she realised that Dot was nervously twisting her apron in her hands.

'I've got summat to tell yer,' she said abruptly.

'What is it?'

'I'm going to work in Bradford.'

'Oh, Dot!' said Maggie in involuntary dismay, putting the plates down with a clatter. 'Oh, no!'

'I'm right sorry,' said Dot doggedly, 'but there's that many posters telling us females to take on jobs so men can go and fight, and I dunno, since Bert died, I feel like I need to do summat. My friend Ellen, she reckons they're looking for women in t'munitions factories so's men can go and fight. Pay's not bad, neither,' she added as if honour bound.

Maggie drew a steadying breath. She hadn't realised how much she had come to rely on Dot to keep the house running until she had to face the prospect of her going. It was a blow she hadn't expected.

She forced a smile. 'Of course you must go. The war's affecting all of us now, and we each have to do what we can. It's just ... I'll miss you,' she confessed.

Dot hunched a shoulder, embarrassed. 'You'll miss my cooking, mebbe.'

144

'Yes, there's that – and Frank certainly will,' she said. 'You know what a terrible cook I am! But I'll miss you as well.'

It was true. She had found Dot difficult at first, but since Joe's departure they had been rubbing along, and Maggie had come to value Dot's no-nonsense practicality.

Dot scowled as if to disguise her pleasure. 'I know we haven't always seen eye to eye,' she said awkwardly. 'I never thought you'd be able to take on running of t'farm, but I reckon you're tougher than you look.'

Coming from Dot, that was nearly as good a compliment as being a good farmer.

'I won't stop you going,' Maggie said. 'It's the right thing to do ... but, oh, Dot, how will I manage without you?'

'I'll ask around in t'village, see if there's anyone fancying being a farm lass.'

But no one wanted to go to Emmerdale Farm. 'I've told them you're all right,' Dot reported, 'but all the lasses are looking for jobs now, and the younger girls, well, their mams don't want them so near the training camp.'

Or near Maggie Sugden, Maggie guessed. She wore trousers, had been involved in a scandalous affair with Ralph Verney, had been beaten up by her husband... She understood why the mothers wanted their daughters to go to a more respectable household.

Hearing the news about Dot's departure and sensing weakness, Tom Skilbeck renewed his offer to take over the farm. 'Would you take on Frank?' Maggie had asked, but he'd shaken his head.

'I don't have time for sentimentality. The boy's not all there, and that's a fact. My men can manage Emmerdale.'

So Maggie had turned him down again and probably made herself another enemy.

Now she summoned a smile for Dot. 'Thanks for asking around, Dot.'

'Mebbe I should stay,' Dot said, looking around the kitchen. She had been ironing that morning and the kitchen smelt wonderfully of freshly pressed linen. A beef pie was browning in the oven, potatoes bubbling in a saucepan. 'There's no way you can do all that you've been doing and feed Frank. I don't want him to starve!'

A faint smile lit Maggie's tired eyes. 'I'll make sure he has something to eat, I promise. I'm not saying it won't be hard, but our troops are dealing with a lot worse. If they can keep going, so can I. What you're going to do is more important, Dot,' she told her. 'Our boys need munitions if they're going to win the war. Go and make shells to beat the Germans, and put Bert Clark's name on them. Don't worry about Frank and me. We'll manage.'

But how? Maggie dropped her head into her hands that night. There was so much to be done. Winter was coming, that was something. Once she got sheep the down from the hill, it should be case of feeding and checking the animals during the cold, and Frank could help with that, but when spring came, there would be lambing and dipping and clipping and crops to be harvested. Feeling her breath coming in short puffs, Maggie made herself slow down. One thing at a time.

Ralph would be home soon. Not by Christmas – she wasn't foolish enough to think that anymore – but sometime soon. He had promised. She just had to keep going until she could be with him again. Maggie imagined his arms closing around her, imagined resting her head on his shoulder. Nothing would seem so difficult then. They would work it out together.

In meantime, she would do what she had told Dot she would do. She would manage.

CHAPTER FIFTEEN

'Look, Papa!' Rose tapped the newspaper as she pushed it under her father's nose. 'The government are calling on women to take up vital war work. That means women like me.'

He passed the newspaper back to her. 'It does *not* mean women like you, Rose. You are barely eighteen.'

'Dot Colton is only eighteen. She's left Emmerdale farm and is going to work in a munitions factory.'

'Dot Colton is not a young lady,' he pointed out. 'Her case is quite different. She will do very well in a factory, but it wouldn't be at all suitable for you. Indeed, Dot's parents are also concerned. The "munitionettes", as I believe they call them, are already getting a bad reputation.'

'For what?'

'For lax morals and indecency,' her father pronounced. 'Earning generous wages and living away from home is encouraging all sorts of bad behaviour. It's out of the question for you to join them.'

What would that be like? Rose wondered. To live away from home, to earn her own money and do what she liked with it? The idea fizzed along her veins. Imagine sitting down to lunch when she wanted to eat, not when her father wanted to dine! Imagine eating whatever she wanted, when she wanted! Imagine choosing to do what *she* wanted to do, instead of what she was allowed to do!

Recently, her rebellious thoughts had almost scared Rose. She had always adored her father – she still did – but since the war her life had felt so constricted. It had never occurred to her before that she might not move seamlessly from a pampered existence in the vicarage to a pampered existence in her husband's house. Naturally, she had imagined herself at Miffield Hall with Ralph, but might she then have been doing what Ralph wanted to do? Eating what he wanted to eat, when he wanted to eat it?

Rose glanced at Edith, who was sitting at the end of the table, pushing the remnants of a lemon pudding around her plate. She noticed the tightness of her mother's jaw sometimes, and her expression when she was watching her husband and thought no one was looking. She never disagreed openly with Charles but Rose found herself wondering more and more often what her mother really thought.

'Papa, I must be able to do *something*,' she tried

again. 'What if I trained as a nurse?'

Her father sighed. 'Emptying bedpans and doing who knows what filthy jobs? My darling, I hardly think so.'

'But Papa–'

He held up a hand. 'I don't wish to hear any more about it, Rose. You are a very young lady, in the fortunate position of being able to stay safely at home with your parents. Your desire to help the war effort is admirable but it will be quite enough to help your mother. You are already rolling bandages and putting together comfort parcels for the troops.'

'And knitting socks. Don't forget knitting.'

'And knitting,' he agreed, rolling smoothly over her bitter comment. 'The most important thing you can do is to write cheerful letters to John and to Ralph, of course. What do you think Ralph would think about the future Lady Miffield working in a munitions factory?'

'Papa!' Rose's cheeks burned. 'I keep telling you, Ralph and I are just friends.'

'I can assure you he would *not* want to think of you doing any such thing,' her father said as if she hadn't spoken. 'The war is an upsetting time, Rose. For all of us. John and Ralph and all the others we love are showing great bravery at the front. We must be equally courageous in making sure that their world is here for them to come back to when the war is over.

'That's why I am anxious about the training camp,' he went on. 'I confess, I hadn't realised what problems it would cause. Which reminds me, Rose my dear, I don't want you wandering around on your own. There are some *very* un-savoury types at the camp. I even came across one loitering around the church.'

'Perhaps he wanted to see the church,' Edith suggested. 'Would you like some more pudding, dear?'

'Not he!' Charles gave his bowl to Rose to pass on. 'Thank you,' he said as an afterthought. 'He was an Irishman, and if he'd ever seen inside anything other than a Catholic church, I'd eat my hat. I sent him off with a flea in his ear.'

Rose thought about Corporal Dingle, stealing apples from the orchard. She remembered his merry eyes and cocky grin. He had been Irish, although she couldn't see him at church.

'Papa, I will be perfectly safe,' she said, passing his bowl down to her mother who served him with a couple of spoonfuls from the dish in front of her. 'I have been walking around Beckindale on my own all my life!'

'Things are different now.'

'Didn't you just say that we mustn't let the war change everything? You know how much I like to walk. I can't wait for you or Mother to want to go with me. It's absurd! I might as well be a pris-oner!'

'Now, Rose, don't exaggerate.'

Her lips tightened. She passed the bowl of lemon pudding back to her father. 'I am not exag-gerating! Mother, tell Papa,' she pleaded.

'Rose will be perfectly safe on her own,' Edith said in her quiet way. 'I agree with you about the unsuitability of her working in a factory, Charles, but we must allow her some freedom. She is sensible enough not to come to any harm in Beckindale.'

Her father subsided, grumbling, as he picked up his spoon and dug into his second helpings. 'Oh, very well, you may go out on your own, but you are to be careful, Rose,' he warned. 'Don't talk to any soldiers or encourage them.'

Encourage them to what? Rose jerked on her gloves as she set off for a walk – on her own! The cold brought colour to her cheeks and her eyes sparkled with resentment as she replayed the conversation over lunch in her head. Oh, she knew that her papa loved her but he was smothering her! She was eighteen now, but he treated her as a child still and she was tired of it. Her privileged existence had never bothered Rose before but now ... surely, *surely,* there was more to life than this?

She walked all the way round the grounds of Miffield Hall and back along the lane to the bridge where she stopped, suddenly irresolute. She wasn't ready to go home but where else could she go?

Feeling stifled, Rose leant morosely on the parapet and looked down at the beck. It was a still, cold day and the surface of the water was glassy, but as she watched a stone skimmed across the river, bouncing once, twice, three times before it plopped into the depths. Peering over, she was able to see the soldier on the little beach below bridge. He had a pebble in his hand and as she watched he bent, and with a clever flick of the wrist sent it bouncing five times across the water, before he looked up and grinned.

151

It was Corporal Dingle.

'Oh, it's you,' she said.

'And good afternoon to you too, Rose.'

'Miss Haywood,' she snapped.

'You look very cross *a chara*. Come down and throw stones in the water. It always works for me when I'm in a temper.'

'I am not in a temper!'

'It's very easy, you know. I could teach you.'

'I know perfectly well how to skim stones,' said Rose.

'Now that I don't believe,' said Mick. 'Skimming stones is not the kind of thing that young ladies know how to do.'

Exasperated, Rose marched to the end of the bridge and jumped down onto the beach without giving him a chance to help her. She took the pebble he offered her, inspected it to see that it was suitably smooth, and without a word sent it bouncing over the water the way Ralph had taught her to do one summer.

'Three bounces. Not bad,' Mick acknowledged. 'You'd do even better if you weren't in a mood.'

Rose scowled at him. 'What are you doing here?'

'Just passing the time. I came in with my brother, Levi, but I had the distinct feeling that he didn't want me around,' Mick smiled. 'I suspect he may have found a girl, and good luck to him if so. He's being very secretive, though.'

'I'm surprised you're not filling the time with a little stealing,' said Rose crossly and he grinned and showed her his empty hands.

'I wouldn't dare after you tore such a strip off

me in the orchard.'

'Hah.' She held out her hand. 'Give me another pebble.'

Obediently, Mick bent and found her a smooth, flat stone. 'Try that one.'

This time, Rose made herself relax. She remembered what Ralph had told her about bending low and flicking her wrist. The pebble skipped beautifully over the water.

'Six!' Rose jumped and clapped her hands in triumph when it disappeared at last. 'Six bounces!'

'I withdraw any suggestion that ladies don't know how to skim stones,' he conceded. 'Who taught you to do that?'

A shadow crossed her face as she remembered Ralph. 'Just someone I used to know.'

'A sweetheart?'

Rose sighed without meaning to. 'No, just a friend.'

His eyes were a warm blue and full of understanding, and she was glad when he didn't pursue it. He tossed a stone in his hand. 'So I was right about stone skimming being good for your temper, wasn't I?'

She gave in with a laugh. 'I suppose you were.'

'Sit down, *a chara,* and tell me what put you in such a tearing rage,' Mick invited her and somehow Rose found herself perching on old boulder.

'I wasn't in a *rage* exactly,' she said, smoothing down her skirt.

'Were you not?' Mick leant back against the edge of the bridge and regarded her with amusement. 'Those brown eyes of yours were fairly snapping when you leant over and saw me!'

153

'I was just feeling ... frustrated.'

'Oh, I know *that* feeling,' he said, one corner of his mouth twitching.

Rose hesitated. Here she was doing what her beloved papa had expressly forbidden her to do. She was talking to a soldier from the camp, and an Irish soldier at that. She had no doubt that her father would call Mick Dingle unsavoury. He was lean and dark with dancing blue eyes and a reckless air to him that tugged at her. She was sick of doing what she was told!

'There's a war on!' she burst out. 'I should be allowed to something to help, but no! All I'm allowed to do is knit!'

Mick laughed. 'That sounds terrible!'

'It is!'

'You roll bandages, too,' he reminded her.

'Oh, yes ... but other girls are going to work in factories or be postmen or drive trains. I'm not allowed to do anything like that.'

'There's not much call for train drivers around here,' said Mick. 'Not many factories either.'

'I know of girls from Beckindale who are going to work in munitions factories in Bradford, but *I'm* not allowed to go. It's not suitable for me, apparently. Nothing is suitable for me because I am useless!'

'I daresay your papa is afraid of what might happen to you in the city. You are not very old, or very experienced yet, are you?'

'How am I to become experienced if I am never allowed to leave Beckindale?' Rose demanded. She tugged off her gloves and held her hands out in front of her, turning them palm up. 'Papa

154

thinks I wouldn't cope with any dirty work but I could try.'

'It would be a shame to spoil those pretty hands, though.'

'And *now* Papa says that I mustn't walk out on my own in case I come across soldiers from the training camp.'

'Which you have done,' Mick pointed out.

'Yes.' Rose sighed. 'He would be horrified if he knew that I was here with you.'

'Because I'm a soldier? Or because I'm Irish?'

'And a thief,' she reminded him with a pert look. 'Although Papa doesn't know about the apples.'

'I can see why he would disapprove,' said Mick, amused. 'And yet here you are.'

Rose's eyes flashed to his face and then slid away. 'Yes, here I am.' She bit her lip. 'I'm tired of doing what I'm told,' she confessed. 'I want to be ... free.'

'Good for you.' Mick applauded. 'So, if I happened to be skimming stones here next Tuesday, do you think you might defy your papa and walk this way again?'

Rose looked at him. 'I don't want a sweetheart,' she said abruptly, but Mick was unfazed.

'Why not? Everybody wants a sweetheart, Rose – sorry, *Miss Haywood*,' he corrected himself at her glare.

'I don't.'

'Are you in love with another man?'

'I thought I was,' she said honestly. 'Now ... now, I don't know. But I know he doesn't love me, and I know I don't want to feel like that again.'

155

Mick clicked his tongue. 'Sure, you don't want to fall in love, but that doesn't mean you can't have fun, *a chara*.'

'You said that before,' said Rose. 'Akara ... what does it mean?'

'Friend,' said Mick. 'It means friend.'

CHAPTER SIXTEEN

Maggie pulled off her trousers and dropped them into the dirty linen basket. She really *had* to find time to do some laundry soon.

She missed Dot. Not just because Dot had kept the house clean, the clothes washed and ironed, and food on the table, but as someone to talk to, a presence in the kitchen when she came in from the farmyard. Dot might have been prickly, but at least she had been there. Frank came in for meals, of course, but no matter how fond of him she had grown, he was never going to be a great conversationalist.

Quickly Maggie pulled on a high-necked blouse and fastened her best Sunday skirt at the waist before pulling on some wool stockings. It had been bitterly cold out when she had been feeding the sheep earlier and she would be glad of the extra warmth under her boots as she walked down to church.

Grabbing her hat and her warmest coat, Maggie ran downstairs. There was just time to shove a joint of beef into the range before she had to go.

A letter for Ralph waited on the table. She had written to him the night before in the unsteady light of a candle. She hadn't had any time to go and get more paraffin for the lamp; that was another job on her list of chores that never got done.

Not long until Christmas, she had written. *Remember how we thought the war would be over by then? There is no sign of it ending yet, I know, so I won't hold you to your promise to be back this Christmas, Ralph my darling, as long as you keep your promise to come home as soon as you can. I hope and pray that by* next *Christmas we will be together and all this anxious waiting will be over. I wonder where we will be? New Zealand? America? I won't mind as long as we're together.*

Where were her hat pins? Maggie scrabbled for them on the dresser. Ah, there! She pounced on them and stood in front of the mirror to pin her hat to her hastily put-up hair.

Writing to Ralph eased her loneliness on the long winter evenings. It was almost like talking to him. Maggie imagined him sitting across from her, how he would laugh when she told him of being knocked over by a cantankerous ram or her disastrous attempt to make a cake. She had always loved watching Ralph laugh and she could picture him so clearly, his cheeks creasing as he threw back his head to reveal the long, strong column of his neck. She could still hear his laughter, still feel the warmth of it as it blew through her like a breeze rippling sunlight over a field of wheat.

She would do anything to hear Ralph laugh now, for real. To be able to reach across the table and touch him, to feel his fingers close around hers. Missing him had been an ache for so long, Maggie was almost used to it, but sometimes it would sharpen into a pain and twist so savagely inside her that she had to suck in a breath to stop herself from crying out.

She longed to see him again, but until then she just had to imagine him frowning at her news of Joe's brusque messages from his training camp near Hull, and the ominous mentions of embarkation leave. *I do not think that can be before May,* Maggie had written. *It is my dearest hope that you will be able to come before then. Even if the war is not over, surely you will get some leave? I do not want to be here when Joe comes back, Ralph. I cannot bear him to touch me again.*

But she tried not to think about Joe too much. Instead she imagined sitting at the table with Ralph after supper and telling him about her days, about the weight of the hay on her back as she struggled out to the sheep through the wind and the rain, about the warm fug in the cow byre and Fly's expression as her legs went in four different directions on an icy patch of the farmyard.

She told him how Edith Haywood had remarked on how tired she was looking and had suggested that Maggie employ a conscientious objector to help on the farm. *I said I wouldn't think of it, of course,* Maggie wrote to Ralph. *How could I take on a coward who refuses to fight while you are out there defending us all?*

158

She told him about the tensions between the village and the training camp, and how Miffield Hall was being stripped of the paintings and furniture he had grown up with as it was converted to a hospital. His father had written to tell him the news as well and in his previous letter Ralph had professed not to mind. His had been a lonely childhood and he had few fond memories of the Hall. *I liked being at High Moor better,* he had said, and Maggie had sighed when she read it. Her home seemed so distant now, her memories of an idyllic childhood and youth drenched in gold and blurred with remembered happiness.

It made her too sad to think about High Moor now. She could think only about getting from day to day until Ralph came home.

At least today the sun was out and there was the hope that Rose would be able to pass her a letter from Ralph. Maggie's spirits rose as she fixed the last pin in her hat, put her own letter into her pocket and pulled on her gloves. Outside she found Frank, stamping his feet against the cold, his hands tucked into his armpits.

Ever alert, Fly jumped up as soon as the kitchen door opened, but Maggie took one look at Frank and told the dog to wait. She went back inside and came out a few minutes later with Joe's woollen gloves.

'Put these on, Frank,' she said. 'They'll keep your hands warm.'

He took them wonderingly. 'For me?'

'Yes, for you.'

He gaped at her as if she had handed him the crown jewels. 'A *present?*'

159

Maggie could just imagine what Joe would say if he knew she had given Frank his gloves. But it was too hard to explain the concept of borrowing to Frank and besides, Joe wasn't there. She would have to find another pair of gloves if Joe came back in winter.

If she was here, she reminded herself. The thought that she might not be gave Maggie a shiver of excitement.

'Yes, a present,' she said firmly.

A huge smile brightened Frank's usually stolid expression as he put on the gloves and turned his hands this way and that as if he could hardly believe his luck. Maggie wondered if it was the first time he had ever had gloves to wear.

The two of them walked down to the village every Sunday now. The Pickles were Chapel so Maggie sent Frank home to his mother with his wages for the week and went on to St Mary's where she could be sure of seeing Rose Haywood.

She had tried to tell Rose what it meant to her to be able to correspond with Ralph, but Rose had waved her gratitude aside. Maggie had used to think of the vicar's daughter as spoilt and frankly a little silly, but she had changed her mind. Rose wasn't silly at all. She might be pretty, but there was strength in the set of her chin, spark in her brown eyes. Maggie tried to imagine how she would feel if she loved Ralph and had to accept that he loved someone else, and she knew how hard she would find it. Rose not only dealt with that, she was helping Ralph and Maggie be together.

The more Maggie saw of Rose, the more she

admired her, but she felt sorry for her too. Compared to the freedom her own father had given her, Rose seemed to live a cramped life in the vicarage, and the war had only made things worse as far as Maggie could see.

Having checked that Frank had washed under the pump that morning, they set off together down the track with Fly trotting ahead. The dale was spread out below them, glittering in the sharp light. Rimed with frost, the tops of the dry-stone wall glinted like diamonds. Beneath Maggie's sturdy boots, the mud had hardened into icy ridges and on either side, teasels emerged rigid and sparkling from the tussocks of white-rimmed grass.

Frank kept lifting his hands to admire his gloves and Maggie smiled at his simple delight. The cold pinched at her cheeks and made her teeth ache, but she kept hands stuffed deep in her pockets where could feel her letter to Ralph. Slender as the connection to him was, it set a warmth glowing deep inside her. On a day like this, it was impossible to believe in the war being fought in France, impossible to think that she might not see him soon.

She parted ways with Frank as the road up from the bridge bent round towards the main street. 'You'll come back for milking?' she said as she always did. Frank nodded but she could tell that he was too wrapped up in the pleasure of having gloves of his own to listen to her. She smiled as she watched him go, his hands held up by his sides so that everyone could see his gloves. Frank might forget but Nancy Pickles would send him

161

back in good time.

Maggie was still smiling as she walked up the road past the village hall. A crowd was gathered outside the church as she rounded the bend, and something about the atmosphere made her pause, her smile fading. There was a sombre air to the scene, jarring in the brightness of the light and her steps slowed as a nameless dread pooled in her stomach. People were huddled together in small groups, talking in low voices, but silence fell as Maggie stepped into the churchyard.

At the church door, Rose Haywood was weeping in her mother's arms. Maggie stopped at the sight, her heart banging painfully. Over Rose's bent head, she could see Edith's devastated expression.

Oh, no, not John, thought Maggie. Please, God, let it not be John.

Edith had seen her. She murmured something to Rose, who straightened and shook her head before squaring her shoulders. Her pretty face was ravaged with grief as she met Maggie's eyes.

Thud, thud, thud. Maggie's pulse was booming in her ears and her stomach churned. Rose was walking towards her, the congregation parting silently to let her through. Maggie was seized by the urge to turn and run away, but her boots seemed fixed to the stone path and she could only stand, trapped, unable to move while Rose kept coming.

'Maggie.' Rose stopped a few feet away. Her voice was barely more than a thread, her face white.

'Is it John?' Maggie asked hoarsely and Rose

162

shook her head.

'No, it's not John.' She swallowed and her soft mouth trembled so much that it took her several attempts before she could get the next words out. 'It's Ralph.'

'Ralph?' Maggie heard herself say, as if from a great distance.

'Ralph is dead.'

Maggie stared at her. She heard the words, but they made no sense. 'No,' she said definitely. 'No, he isn't.'

'I'm sorry, Maggie. I know ... I know how much he loved you, how much you loved him.'

'Ralph isn't dead.' Maggie's fingers closed over the letter in her pocket. She would know if Ralph were dead. This was some cruel trick. 'He's not,' she said fiercely.

'I'm so sorry...' Rose's voice cracked.

Maggie backed away, shaking her head. 'No,' she said and put out both hands as if to ward off a blow.

Rose swallowed hard to steady her voice. 'The telegram came last night, and Lord Miffield called for Papa. I didn't know how to get word to you.'

Putting her hand back in her pocket, Maggie pulled out the letter. 'But I've got a letter for him,' she said, as if that proved the news had to be wrong.

Rose just shook her head. 'I'm sorry,' she said again.

Maggie's breath was coming in short gasps. Deep inside an anguish was slowly uncoiling. 'What ... how?' she managed.

163

Rose moistened her lips. 'He was fighting at a place called Ypres. I think ... Papa said he was killed by a shell. Lord and Lady Miffield are much distressed,' she whispered. 'They were going to London tomorrow but now ... I don't know.'

Maggie stared at her blindly. Ralph, *dead?* Ralph, with the dancing smile in his eyes, Ralph with his warm hands and warm mouth. Ralph, who had promised to come back. Rage gusted through her. He had *promised!*

There was a hand around her throat, throttling her of air, horror twisting in her belly. Maggie squeezed her eyes shut. She wanted to rewind time, to the cheerful way she had walked down the lane enjoying the sparkling air. She would walk past the village hall once more but this time, there would be only a few stragglers outside the church. Everyone else would be inside, preparing to pray for the troops, thanking God that the casualties had been few so far.

But when she opened them again, Rose was still there, her face distressed,

There would be no going back, no unsaying the words.

Ralph was dead.

Ralph was dead.

Ralph was *dead.*

1915

CHAPTER SEVENTEEN

'Mother of God, my feet!' Nat pulled off his boots and socks and collapsed back onto the cot.

'What feet?' Beside him, Mick was lowering his bare toes into a bowl of cold water with a grimace. 'I can't even feel mine anymore. Twenty miles with full kit! Whose idea was it to join the army?'

'Yours,' said Nat with the closest he ever came to a sour look.

'I didn't think they'd make us march up and down every one of the bloody Yorkshire Dales. In the rain.'

'That's your trouble, Mick. You *don't* think.'

Levi could hear them sniping at each other but their voices seemed to be coming from a long way away. Around them, men were groaning and grumbling, and the stench of feet and wet wool socks in the hut was almost overpowering. Levi lay splayed on his cot. His whole body pulsed with exhaustion. His feet were raw and throbbing with pain, but almost worse than that was the humiliation of having to be carried home by his brothers.

He had had the first blister before the end of first mile. After ten miles he had collapsed and begged Nat and Mick to leave him to die where he lay.

'We can't do that,' Mick had said, hauling him

167

back to his feet. 'We promised Mammy we wouldn't let any harm come to you. What do you think she'd say if she knew we had left you by the side of the road?'

He and Nat had shared out the weight of his rifle and pack between them which had helped Levi to limp on for a while, but they had had to carry him for most of the last five miles.

He was never going to make a soldier.

'Ah, it's not been all bad, has it?' Mick was saying as he inspected his feet gingerly. 'Look what a dab hand you turned out to be with a rifle.'

To his and everybody's surprise, Nat had shown unexpected ability for shooting. Mick was noted for his running speed and agility – learnt from years of getting out of scrapes, Nat said – and there was talk of him doing specialist training as a scout, although he was more interested in learning to drive.

Levi wasn't good at anything. He was clumsy and fumbled with a gun. He couldn't keep up on the route marches. He gagged at the smell of the latrines. He had even fainted when one of the cooks had cut off the end of his finger when serving Christmas lunch in the canteen.

'What are we going to do with you?' Nat had said humorously as he shoved Levi's head between his knees.

Levi knew his brothers worried about how he would cope when it came to real fighting. He was worried too. He should never have enlisted, he knew that now. He wasn't cut out to be a soldier, that was obvious, but there was no way he was going to desert, and besides he had reached the point where even the prospect of fighting seemed better than staying in the camp for another two months.

Training had been one long humiliation. Whenever he could, Levi slipped away to help Will Hutton at the smithy. At least there he knew what he was doing. He preferred Will's dour acceptance to his brothers' fussing, and there was always the chance of catching a glimpse of Rose Haywood.

After Will's son, Billy, had been killed at the front, Rose had come to the smithy with her mother to ask if there was anything they could do. Will, turning in on himself in his grief, had answered in monosyllables. Levi had stood almost near enough to touch Rose, close enough to see the sadness and distress in her brown eyes, and he felt guilty at the thrill he felt when she had turned to him as they left and said that she was glad that he was there to keep Will company.

'I'm training,' he had heard himself say. 'I can only come on my days off, but I'll do what I can.'

'Thank you.' She had pressed his hand. *Pressed his hand!* 'I'm sure that'll be a comfort to Mr Hutton, even if he doesn't show it.'

Taciturn at the best of times, Will had become even more withdrawn since Billy's death, and Levi was ashamed that the farrier's grief had been the cause of making him so happy.

He never got so close to Rose again, but Levi didn't mind. Just a glimpse of her walking along the road or disappearing into a shop was enough to make him happy. He didn't always see her, though he often dawdled past the vicarage on his way back to camp from the smithy, keeping a wary eye out for the vicar.

Concerned for Will Hutton and consumed by thoughts of Rose Haywood, Levi was spending all his free time in Beckindale and had seen little of his brothers. So when Mick clapped him on the shoulder a few days after the route march, just as he was about to set off for the village, he felt instantly guilty.

'We never see you now, Levi,' Mick said. 'Where do you hide yourself on your afternoons off?'

'I help the farrier. His son died at the front.'

'Oh. There was me thinking you must have a girl down in the village.'

Levi flushed. He didn't want to tell Mick about Rose. 'No, nothing like that.'

'Well, could the smithy spare you for a family outing, do you think? Nat and I thought we'd go up the hill,' said Mick with a wink. 'See if we can catch us a rabbit or two as a change from bully beef. What do you say? Are your blisters up to a walk yet?'

Levi grimaced inwardly at the thought of a climb in his boots, but Mick was right, he'd hardly seen his brothers recently. 'Sure, I'll come,' he said.

'Good man.'

It was quiet on the hill. Pockets of swirling mist clung damply to their faces as they climbed up to the moor above the training camp. Mick kept up a stream of jokes and self-deprecating stories but Nat, evidently delegated to shoot rabbits with his rifle, was looking unhappy. He was probably homesick for Ballybeg and for Molly.

Still, it was nice to be out with his brothers again. This was what he had dreamed of when he had stowed away from Ireland, the three of them together, a team.

He was glad when Mick declared rest. They collapsed onto the heather to catch their breath before Mick glanced at Nat and then sprang up to admire the view.

'Mick, can you not sit still for a minute?' Levi complained, rolling his eyes at Nat, who smiled weakly in return.

'It's a grand view from here. You can see all the way to Beckindale. Come over here, Levi.' Mick beckoned and from force of habit, Levi did as he was told. 'Is that the smithy down there, next to the pub?'

Levi peered in the direction of his pointed finger. 'No, smithy's further ov–'

He broke off at the sharp crack of a rifle behind him. For one frozen moment, he was simply puzzled, and then pain blossomed in his leg. Screaming, he fell onto the tussocky heather. 'Jesus! My leg! My leg!' He clutched it as Mick and Nat bent anxiously over him. 'What ...what...'

'By Jesus, that was fine shooting, Nat,' Mick said admiringly. 'Now hold on, Levi, we're going to get you fixed up.'

'Aaargh! My leg, it's broken!'

'It might be, yes. Is it very painful? Sorry about that, but we didn't know what else to do.'

'What?' Bewildered by the pain, Levi blinked up at his brothers. 'What are you saying? You shot me *deliberately?*'

'We had to. We promised Mammy. You're not

171

going to war, Levi.'

'*What?* You bastards!' Tears of humiliation, rage and pain filled Levi's eyes. 'You could have killed me!'

'No fear of that,' said Mick. 'Nat's an ace with a rifle now. We're sorry, but we needed to put you out of action and we had to do it here where we could help you. We wouldn't be able to do much if you were hit by a shell out in the trenches, now would we?'

Being Mick, he made it sound completely reasonable. 'We talked about it and this was all we could think of to do. Neither of us liked it, but it's for your own good.'

His own good! Levi would have laughed if his leg hadn't felt as if it was on fire. The best he could manage was to tip his head back with a groan.

'Here.' Mick produced a hipflask. 'We came prepared. Have a drink of this. It'll help.'

'What is it? Poison?' Levi ground out between teeth gritted against the pain consuming him.

Mick had the nerve to grin. 'It's whiskey. Irish, of course.'

'I don't want it.'

'Come on now, you've had a shock.' He held it to Levi's mouth and in spite of his protests Levi ended up swallowing some. The fiery liquid burned down his throat and he choked and spluttered, but it did help him with the agony of their attempts to tie a bandage around his injured leg.

'That's the best we can do,' Nat decided, looking nearly as grey as Levi. 'We'd better get you down to the hospital straight away.'

Mick squatted down next to Levi, who was panting against the pain. 'This was an accident, all right Levi? You don't want Nat to go to prison, do you?'

'I want you both to go to hell!'

'That's my boy,' said Mick with a twisted smile. 'Come on then, Nat. We'll have to carry him. Up you come, Levi.'

Levi's scream of protest at the burst of agony that followed was cut short when mercifully he blacked out.

He came round in the camp hospital, where he spent three weeks before being discharged. He would have a permanent limp, the doctors confirmed, and was no use to them as a soldier.

'Will you go back to Ireland now?' Nat asked hopefully.

'The hell I will.' Levi had no intention of doing what his bloody brothers wanted. Go back to Ballybeg and have to admit that his grand stand had all been for nothing? Back to smothering by his sisters? Back to being the baby, the weakling? He'd rather be shot in his other leg! 'I'm staying right here,' he said.

He might not have been enjoying life in the army, but Mick and Nat had no business taking the decision out of his hands, Levi thought bitterly.

'We did it for you,' Mick tried telling him, but Levi only turned his face away and refused to listen.

It felt strange to hand back his uniform and put on civilian clothes again. Hoisting his bag over his shoulder he took his crutch and set off down the track for the last time, burning with resentment still. He had hated the training camp, but he hadn't wanted to leave like this.

Will Hutton raised his brows but showed no other sign of surprise when Levi struggled into the smithy. 'What happened to you?'

Levi's leg was sore and he collapsed, panting with effort, onto an upturned barrel. He poured out the story of his brothers' treachery to Will, who listened without comment.

'They've made me look a fool!' he raged.

Will wiped his hands on a rag. 'Mebbe,' he said. 'And mebbe they've saved your life,' he said. 'Mebbe I wish I'd shot Billy in t'leg before he joined up.'

Deflated, Levi rubbed his leg. He had hoped for more understanding from the farrier. 'They want me to go back to Ireland but I won't do that. Can I stay here and work for you?'

'I can't afford to pay you anything,' Will warned. 'But Billy's not coming back. You can have his room and board if you want to help me wi' horses.'

It was the best he was going to get, Levi realised.

'There you go,' said Mick when he and Nat came to see how Levi was getting on. 'Working with horses was what you always wanted to do.'

That was true, but Levi had no intention of letting either of his brothers think they had done him a favour.

'What I *wanted* to do was make my own decisions,' he retorted. 'Everyone in the village thinks I hurt myself deliberately to get out of fighting.

They call me a shirker to my face.' His voice was bitter.

'Better than calling you dead,' said Mick flatly. 'It's done now, Levi. Hate us if you want, but you've got a chance to make something of yourself now. This farrier seems a decent man. He doesn't think you're a shirker, does he?'

'No,' Levi had to admit.

'And has no one else been friendly to you at all?'

Levi hesitated. 'No, not really.'

Although that was not quite true.

Levi's only consolation for what had happened had been the fact that he would be able to stay near Rose. And incredibly, she had somehow found out what had happened to him, and far from accusing him of being a shirker, she had actually come to the smithy to see how he was. She knew his *name!* She had asked after his leg and sympathised with how painful the shooting must have been. She had said that she was glad that he would be able to help Will.

It had almost been worth being shot.

Levi hadn't asked himself how Rose knew so much about what had happened.

But when he hobbled into the Woolpack that night, he had soon learnt that the rest of Beckindale was far less inclined to be understanding. He was met by silence and a wall of blank faces.

'A pint of your best,' he said to the landlord as confidently as he could and put some coins on the bar, but Percy Bainbridge shook his head.

'We don't serve shirkers here. Take your money elsewhere.'

Levi's face burned. 'I was injured while training.'

'That's not what we heard.' There was a murmur of agreement from the men at the bar, and Percy jerked his head in the direction of the door. 'Go on with you.'

Shaking with humiliation, Levi had gathered up the coins and limped out, letting the door slam closed after him.

Worse was to come two days later. Levi was minding his own business, hoping to see Rose as he hopped on his crutch down the main street when he was accosted by the landlady at the Woolpack. According to Will Hutton, Ava Bainbridge was the chief busybody in the village.

'I've got something for you,' she said.

Levi stopped in surprise. 'For me?'

From her basket Ava produced a white feather and made such a show of handing it to him that everyone passing stopped and stared.

Levi went red and then white. 'I don't want your damned feather!' Snatching it from her hand, he threw it onto the ground. 'I am not a shirker!'

'What else would you call somebody who'd shoot his own leg rather than go and front with our other brave soldiers? Coward!' Ava's voice rose shrilly. 'You should be ashamed of yourself.'

'Now, Ava.' An older woman with a plump face sent Levi a half apologetic look. 'The boy's been injured, you can see that.'

'I've no sympathy for him, Mary Ann, none at all! If he had been injured by a German bullet, that would be different.' Ava looked at him with contempt. 'We don't want your type in Beckindale,' she said, and she stalked off, leaving Levi in the middle of the street, burning with rage and humiliation, the white feather at his feet.

CHAPTER EIGHTEEN

Spring was coy that year, flirting with the occasional mild day before dancing back to allow a raw wind to scour the dale once more. Maggie cursed the sleety rain that stung her face as she inspected her flock, but it fit her mood. There might have been sunny days and mild days over the winter, but for Maggie nothing could relieve the coldness inside her. She hadn't felt warm once since she had walked away from the church that day.

Rose had tried to stop her, but Maggie backed away, her rigid control starting to crumble terrifyingly. The vicar had come over then. He had urged Maggie to come into the church and pray. He said it would be a comfort. But Maggie didn't want to pray, for Ralph or for herself. How could a god who blew Ralph into a haze of pieces offer her comfort?

'No, I have to go,' she had said. 'I have to go.'

'Where are you going?' Rose called anxiously after her.

Maggie didn't answer. She didn't know. She just knew that she had to get away.

She had walked blindly that day, Fly anxious by her side. Over the bridge, up the track, past

Emmerdale Farm ... walking faster and faster until she was flinging herself up the hillside. Refusing to allow herself time to stop, or to think, or to feel, Maggie scrabbled over frosted tussocks, her shoes skidding sometimes on icy patches, panting in her desperation to get higher, to leave the galloping pain behind her.

At length, exhausted, she collapsed onto a limestone outcrop. The sun was still shining, the air still crystalline. A peregrine falcon circled overhead, pitilessly marking its prey, and as Maggie watched, it folded its wings and dived.

Another death, but life would go on. The sun would keep rising, the earth would keep turning, the hills were going nowhere, but there would always be an absence now, a gap in space where Ralph had been.

She would never see him again, never touch him again. He was gone, and this time he was never coming back. The hope that had kept her going the past few months was brutally snuffed out, and the future she had longed for now yawned, dark with desolation and despair.

Maggie wanted to scream, to cry, to rain down curses on God and the Germans and the generals who were waging this cursed war, but she couldn't. Her grief was lodged in her throat, an agonisingly tangled clump of sadness and hurt and fear and rage that could not be swallowed down or choked up.

Sensing her distress, Fly whined and put her paw on Maggie's knee. Maggie rested her hand on Fly's head in return and drew a shuddering breath. Far below, the frosty roofs of Emmerdale

Farm sparkled in the winter sunlight. Her heart might be broken, her last hope gone, but the cows still needed to be milked, the sheep still needed to be moved off the hills before the snow came. The oats she and Frank had sown would come up, and they would have to be harvested.

And she would go back because what else could she do?

Maggie felt as if her heart had shut down. Perhaps it had no alternative, when feeling was too painful to contemplate. She moved stiffly, awkwardly now, as if she had found herself in a body that didn't belong to her.

Winter that year was a bleak and bitter one, and not just for Maggie.

The war went on. Hartlepool, Scarborough and Whitby were shelled by German ships and over a hundred people died, shocking news that brought the war uncomfortably close to home. The list of casualties grew ever longer. Alfred Porter was shot in the lung and died in hospital. Jack Airey lost a leg and was in hospital in France.

One morning not long before Christmas, Maggie came out of the stable to see Rose, neat as a pin, picking her way across the farmyard in her clean boots. She held out two letters.

'These came,' she said baldly.

Maggie wiped her hands on her trousers and took the letters very carefully, turning them over to see her name in Ralph's familiar writing. Her throat closed painfully. Funny, she had thought she had stopped feeling, but it seemed that grief could still rake at her with savage claws.

'I didn't want to distress you,' said Rose, her

voice thin and wobbly with her own tears, 'but I thought you'd want to have them.'

Maggie nodded, rigid-jawed. 'Thank you,' she managed.

'Lord and Lady Miffield have spoken to Papa about a memorial service for Ralph. There can't be a funeral because ... because...'

'Because there's no body,' Maggie finished for her in a hard voice. 'Because he was blown into a thousand tiny pieces and there's nothing left to bury.'

Rose covered her face with her hands. 'I can't bear it,' she said brokenly.

'You can,' said Maggie. 'You will. You don't have a choice.'

'Will you come to the service?' Rose lowered her hands on a sigh. 'Everyone will be there.' She hesitated. 'Papa has spoken to Lady Miffield. She has said she would make no difficulties about you going. I think she truly mourns him, as we all do.'

Maggie looked past Rose to the fells on the other side of the valley. From where she stood, she could see High Moor, where she and Ralph had fallen in love. 'I don't need a service to re-member him,' she said.

The service would remember Ralph the aristo-crat; Ralph the heir to the Miffield estate; charm-ing, handsome Ralph. It wouldn't remember the boy he had been, running wild with her in the hills above High Moor, or the man who had laid her back in the heather and loved her.

'No, I won't go,' she said.

'It might be a comfort,' Rose suggested but Maggie shook her head, her expression bleak.

'Nothing is a comfort now,' she said.

'I'm sorry, Maggie.' Rose's eyes shimmered with tears. 'I'm so sorry.'

Maggie held the letters tightly in her hands. 'Thank you for everything you did, Rose,' she said with difficulty. 'I know you loved him too.'

Unable to speak, Rose nodded and turned away, leaving Maggie to read Ralph's last letters to her alone.

I'm due some leave after Christmas. I'll come home then, my darling. Wait for me. Yours forever and always.

The words wavered so badly that Maggie could hardly read them. Tears crowded her throat and threatened to suffocate her, but still she couldn't cry. Pressing the heels of her hands hard against her eyes, she waited until she could push the grief back down inside her once more. Then she put Ralph's letters away with the others, scrubbed her face and got back to work.

It was a bleak Christmas. Maggie sent Frank home for two days and milked the cows herself. She took Elijah a plum pudding that Dot had made before she left, but otherwise she spoke to no one. In previous years she had been to church on Christmas Eve and sung carols with the rest of the congregation, but she hadn't set foot in church since Ralph's death.

Unable to forgive God for killing him, she spent Christmas alone at Emmerdale Farm, loneliness snapped around her heart like a vice. Grief was snipping and slicing at her until she was pared down to essentials. There was no softness to Maggie now, no warmth. She was hard work and

181

pride, and nothing else, trudging across a barren landscape into a barren future because there was nothing else to do.

She had trudged as far as March and now the sheep were about to lamb. Following Elijah's instructions, Maggie brought the sheep down to the field behind the farmhouse, a process that had been easier than she had expected. All she had had to do was to dangle some hay in front of the sheep and they followed her obligingly down the hillside in single file, with Fly bringing up the rear and nipping at any stragglers.

Once in the field, Maggie closed the gate and looked at the sheep huddling together against the sleety rain. They looked back at her.

'Let nature tek its course,' said Elijah. Maggie had nothing to do but wait.

The first lamb was born on a day when the rain fell like curtain rods. Maggie nearly missed it. The ewe had found a private place among the bumps and hollows of the land behind tufts of rushes to give birth, and by the time Maggie saw it, the lamb was already on its feet and suckling, careless of the weather.

It gave her a jolt to see it, battling so tenaciously against the elements.

Her first lamb.

Day by day, the flock grew, and Maggie found herself pacing the field hour after hour, whatever the weather, chasing away the crows and foxes that were quick to take advantage of a newborn lamb. She hadn't been expecting the spurt of pride and pleasure she felt every time she counted a new addition to the flock. The pregnant ewes clearly knew more about the business than she did, and Maggie discovered a new respect for their stoical endurance.

Most of the lambs were born without fuss. The first time Maggie came across a ewe struggling to give birth, she was taken aback by the rush of concern. There was no time to run to Elijah's cottage for advice and besides, she couldn't go to him every time she had a problem with the sheep. She would have to deal with this herself. Maggie made herself stop and remember everything he had told her.

Squatting down, she examined the ewe carefully. The lamb seemed to be stuck and Maggie was afraid that if she didn't help it out, it would die and its mother with it. Reaching into the bag she carried with her according to Elijah's instructions, she pulled out a jar of butter and slathered it over her right hand and arm.

'Sorry about this,' she muttered to the ewe as she bunched her fingers and thumb into a cone shape and cautiously pushed inside it. She could feel the lamb's nose but no hooves.

What was it Elijah had said? Biting her lip, praying that she was doing the right thing, Maggie gently manoeuvred the lamb's head back into the uterus until she could locate the legs and help them into position.

'Now, up you get, lass,' she said, hauling the ewe up, and watched in triumph as the lamb slithered out.

She had other successes – saving a lamb in breech position, helping a ewe give birth to twins – but when that first lamb wobbled to its feet and

183

began to suckle, the ice around Maggie's heart began to crack at last.

There were failures too: lambs that died, born in the middle of the night when she wasn't there to help, three dead ewes. It was frustrating, but what could she do? She couldn't be in the field all day and all night, though she often got up in the small hours and carried her lamp up to the field, just to check on the sheep.

By the time the last ewe had lambed, Maggie was exhausted. Leaning on the dry-stone wall, she surveyed her flock with pride. She never tired of watching the lambs suckling, their tails wagging contentedly.

As if to atone for its earlier disappointments, spring had burst back with a glorious burst of colour. A pale blue sky arched over the hills, already hazed green with new grass. The field banks were bright with yellow celandine while paler primroses clustered along the walls. The black-thorns bloomed a dense, dazzling white, as if someone had thrown a tablecloth over them, while new leaves on the trees unfurled an intense, vivid green and the hedgerows were busy with birds cheeping and twittering.

Ralph was still dead. Missing him was still a dull ache inside her but as Maggie turned her face up to the sun and thought about her sheep grazing contently, she let herself believe that the long, bleak winter was over at last.

CHAPTER NINETEEN

'Where are you off to, Rose?'

Rose bit her lip. She had hoped to slip out of the back door without being seen but her father had come out of his study just as she was tiptoeing across the hall to fetch an umbrella. 'Just for a walk.'

'It's pouring!'

'It's just a shower.' Rose pulled the umbrella out of the stand. 'And I'll have this.' April had been characteristically fickle, frequent cloudbursts interspersed with breezy sunshine. 'It'll pass.'

Charles Haywood frowned. 'I don't like the way you wander around on your own so much, Rose. It's not safe, particularly not this afternoon. The troops are leaving for the front tomorrow. This is the end of their embarkation leave and they'll be in a wild mood.'

Rose knew the company at the training camp would be marching out the next day. She was on her way to say goodbye to Mick Dingle, and there was a hollow feeling in the pit of her stomach at the thought.

'I'll be fine, Papa,' she said as patiently as she could, but he wasn't reassured.

'These men are not gentlemen, Rose. You have never come across men of this type before and I'm afraid that if you found yourself in a difficult situation, you couldn't rely on them to behave as

185

a gentleman would. It's not their fault,' he went on as she opened her mouth to object. 'Different classes have different values. The war has upset the conventions, and we must face the fact that while these troops are bravely going to do their duty, many are what in other times we would undoubtedly call riff-raff.'

Rose thought of Mick Dingle. He would be riff-raff as far as her father was concerned.

It was hard to remember now just how it had happened, but that unplanned encounter with Mick under the bridge had turned into a regular meeting whenever he could get away from the camp.

At first, the secrecy of the meetings had been a distraction from her grief. Rose had mourned Ralph all the more for knowing had he never been hers. She had found herself telling Mick about Ralph and Maggie and she thought that he had understood. He hadn't offered sympathy, and he hadn't told her to consider herself lucky compared to others. Instead he had teased her and challenged her and made her smile again, after Rose had been sure that she never would.

She hadn't told her parents about Mick. She knew they would be horrified. Her father especially seemed determined to keep her away from what he called 'undesirable elements' from the camp roaming the village. Rose had no doubt that he would think Mick undesirable. He would not admire Mick's resourcefulness or his lovely lilting voice. He would be unamused by the humour glinting in the navy-blue eyes, unimpressed by Mick's frankness in describing himself as 'fresh from the bog'.

Rose herself was clear-eyed about him. Mick was no knight on a white charger, no Ralph, and she had been careful to keep their friendship light. She could hardly imagine anyone her parents would consider less suitable as a friend for her. She guessed stealing apples was the least of Mick's dubious activities, but he made her laugh and he made her feel alive. When she was with him, her senses sharpened, and the most familiar of sensations felt new and fresh: the smell of woodsmoke on the air, the rush and bubble of the beck, the swing of her skirts as she walked.

Mick gave her a glimpse into the world beyond the vicarage, a new and exciting world of music halls and moving pictures and motor cars. Rose liked the way he told stories against himself. She liked the reckless glint in his eyes, the way he seemed to live every day as if it might be his last.

As it soon might be. Tomorrow his company would be on parade in Beckindale. He would be marching off to war, to France, where he would fight and where he might die as Ralph had died.

She wasn't in love with him, Rose insisted to herself. She was too sensible for that. When Mick flirted with her, she always fixed him with a stern eye.

'Are you trying to make me fall in love with you by any chance, Corporal Dingle?'

And Mick would always grin. 'Is it working, Miss Haywood?' he would reply hopefully.

'Certainly not,' Rose always said.

But she would miss him.

Now she buttoned up her coat and fastened the

belt. 'I will be perfectly safe, Papa.'

'Let me go with you–'

'No,' she interrupted him. 'I ... I need to be on my own.'

Rose felt guilty when his face changed. She knew that he thought that she was still mourning Ralph, and she did miss him – oh, she *did* – but she had to say goodbye to Mick and there was no way her father would let her go if he knew who she was meeting.

The rain drummed on her umbrella as she walked briskly down to the bridge and across to slip into the grounds of Miffield Hall. She and Mick had fallen into the way of meeting in the woods at an old summer house built by Ralph's grandfather, but long abandoned and now forgotten. A few mildewed wicker chairs rotted slowly in the summer house but there was a wooden bench under the windows where she and Mick could shelter from the weather if necessary while they talked.

In spite of Mick's flirtation, talking was all they had ever done. Lately, though, Rose had found herself looking at Mick's mouth sometimes and feeling an unsettling warmth uncoil in the pit of her stomach as she wondered what doing more than talking would feel like.

Mick was waiting for her, tossing his cap restlessly in the air. He threw it aside as Rose hurried up the steps. 'Good afternoon to you, *acushla*.'

'*Acushla?* That's a new one.' Rose shook the rain from her umbrella and propped it by the door. Mick was always teasing her with Irish endearments. He called her his treasure, his heart, his sweetheart, although Rose had no way of knowing whether he was translating accurately for her or not. She didn't take them seriously, anyway.

'Ah, *acushla* is special. It's a word we use for the one who makes our heart beat faster,' Mick told her. 'My darling, you might say.'

'I wouldn't say anything of the kind,' said Rose primly.

'Not even now that we're saying goodbye?'

Her face changed. 'I hate this war,' she said as she sat on the wooden bench. Mick had tried to sit on one of the wicker chairs once and it had promptly collapsed. 'I can't believe that tomorrow you will be going off to fight. There are so many terrible things happening, not just at the front, but here too. I have to lie to my parents. You had to shoot your brother.'

Mick sat down next to her and stretched out long legs in front of him. 'How's Levi doing?'

'I feel sorry for him.' Mick had told her what he and his brother had done and had asked her to look out for Levi. 'He's lonely,' she said, thinking of the time she had gone to see Levi at the smithy. 'No one will believe that he didn't shoot himself deliberately so he's having a hard time.'

'Not as hard a time as he would have at the front,' said Mick. 'He's a dreamer, is Levi, but he's a good boy at heart. He's not for forgiving us yet, but he didn't snitch on Nat, and I'm proud of him for that.'

'I'll do my best to be a friend to him while you're away,' she promised.

'Thank you, Rose,' he said seriously, and to lighten the atmosphere, she corrected him as she

189

had done the first time they met. It had become a private joke.

'Miss Haywood, please,' she said crisply and was glad to see Mick grin.

'I'm going to miss you, *acushla*.'

'I'll miss you, too,' Rose admitted. She tipped her head back against the window. 'It's strange. I do hate the war, but part of me is glad about it too. I would never have met you otherwise.'

'And that would have been a tragedy.' Mick reached out and took her hand. 'The war's mixed everyone up. Everything we took for granted before, now we're not so sure about. That's not a bad thing.'

Rose looked down at their entwined fingers, and the feel of her palm pressed against his set her heart slamming against her ribs. 'Are you frightened, Mick?'

'Not yet,' he said. 'I will be when we get to the front, I'm sure of that, but I'm not going to think about that yet. I'm going to think about how nice it is to sit here with you, to hold your hand, and to enjoy the fact that it's stopped raining.'

'I am,' Rose confessed abruptly. 'I'm frightened, not just for you and John and everyone else who's fighting. I'm frightened that I'll never go anywhere, do anything. I'll just stay in Beckindale and life will pass me by while my father stops me doing anything he thinks is unsuitable.'

'You've been meeting me,' Mick pointed out. 'I'm sure he'd think that was unsuitable, wouldn't he?'

'Oh, yes,' she said on a half laugh.

'Well then, I don't think you need to worry,' he

told her. 'I think you're more of a rebel than you think you are.'

Rose liked that idea.

'Are you rebel enough to write to me?' Mick asked. 'I wasn't going to ask,' he said when she looked at him in surprise, and his fingers tightened around hers. 'I know your family would never approve of me, *acushla*. I know we don't have a future together. I told myself this would be goodbye for ever, but now that you're here, I don't want to do that. I'm not much for writing, I have to admit, Rose. I don't have much schooling, but it would mean a lot to get a letter from you every now and then.'

'Of course I'll write,' she said.

Mick brightened. 'How will we manage it? I won't be able to write to you at the vicarage.'

'No, Papa would have a fit!' Rose thought about the way she had forwarded letters for Ralph and Maggie. 'Do you think Levi would help us? If I go to the post office to send a letter to you, the whole of Beckindale will know I'm writing to you. Hannah Rigg is nearly as bad a busybody as Ava Bainbridge. She knows everybody's business, and word would get back to my father straight away.'

Rose couldn't bear the thought of her father finding out. He would be bitterly disappointed in her and worse, he would be angry. He was an indulgent father, and she loved him dearly, but he wouldn't rest until he had put a stop to her relationship with Mick, of that she was sure.

Mick was pleased with the idea. 'I'll ask Levi. He'll do it for me,' he said confidently.

Disentangling her hand from his, Rose got up.

191

'If I write to you, would you do something for me in return?' she said nervously.

'Anything,' said Mick without hesitation.

'Would you kiss me?' she heard herself say. Unable to look at him, her eyes skittered around the summer house but she could feel his astonished shock. 'I know it's very forward of me,' she hurried on before she could change her mind, 'but I've never been kissed, and the way the war is going, I never will be. I'd just like to know what it feels like.'

'That doesn't seem to be asking too much,' said Mick slowly.

She turned to face him. 'So will you?'

'It would be my pleasure, Miss Haywood.' Smiling, Mick got to his feet and Rose suddenly felt foolish.

'I don't know what to do.'

'Well, first we'll take off your hat,' said Mick, expertly removing the pins and laying the hat on the bench. 'That's better.'

Rose was having trouble with her breathing. 'Now what, Corporal Dingle?'

'Why don't you put your arms around me, Miss Haywood?'

Hesitantly, she slid her arms around his waist, thrilling at the hard, solid feel of his body. 'Like this?'

'Exactly like that.' There was a hoarse edge to Mick's voice as he took her face between his hands and gently traced his thumb over the curve of her mouth.

'And now?' she whispered, tangled up in longing and a deep thrum of anticipation.

'Now we wonder just how good this is going to feel,' he said, his voice reverberating through her hands. 'Now we admit to ourselves that we've wanted to do this for months, since the day we met in that orchard. *Now*, I kiss you.'

With dreamlike slowness, he lowered his head, angling it to touch his mouth to hers, gently at first but then more insistently, his lips warm and persuasive. The floor of the summerhouse seemed to drop away beneath Rose's feet and she clung to him with a hum of pleasure, her bones melting in a giddy rush of delight. She hadn't dreamt it would feel like this, that it would make her blood surge with hunger, that it would feel so right.

Mick's lips trailed from her mouth to her ear. 'I think you're getting the idea, Miss Haywood,' he murmured and Rose laughed shakily.

'I don't know about that, Corporal Dingle,' she said. 'I might need to try again, just to make sure I've got the hang of it.'

Mick smiled and dropped his hands from her face to pull her closer. 'I'd be happy to oblige, Miss Haywood,' he said.

CHAPTER TWENTY

Sick with shock, Levi stared at the summerhouse. He had followed Rose on an impulse, after seeing her walking so purposefully away from the village. He'd been curious about where she was going, especially when she turned off the lane and into a

193

little used path through the grounds of Miffield Hall.

The thought that she was on her way to meet a man had wormed its way into his head and wouldn't be shaken. Levi was used to thinking of Rose as perfect, shining out of reach of mere mortals. The idea that she would stoop to secret meetings was unsettling. He nearly turned back but forced himself to limp on and see for himself.

He had watched her go into the summerhouse. He'd seen her shake out her umbrella and say something to someone inside. She was definitely meeting someone there, he thought, disappointed in her. Someone not welcome at the vicarage.

From his position half hidden in the bushes, Levi couldn't see clearly through the mildewed windows. It wasn't until Rose moved before the open door that he could see her clearly and for a nasty moment he was afraid that she was looking straight at him, but the next moment she had turned and a man stepped into view beside her.

Mick.

Mick.

Churning with bitterness and envy, Levi watched as Rose put her arms around his brother, watched as Mick bent his head to kiss her before turning to slam his hand into a tree in disgust.

Rose ... and Mick!

It wasn't fair! Levi's eyes filled with tears. Mick, Mick, Mick!

Mick had ruined his life, he realised, always interfering, always treating Levi like a child, always one step ahead so that it was impossible for Levi ever to catch up. Mick was older, Mick was braver, Mick was funnier, Mick was more charming. Always more, more, more than Levi.

And now, when he had finally fallen in love, Mick had the woman he adored too.

Levi's palm stung where he had hit the tree. Resting his forehead against the rough bark, he made himself take deep breaths. It wasn't Rose's fault. Anyone could see that she was sweet and pure. Mick had taken advantage of her innocence, just as he had always taken advantage of Levi's youth and inexperience to force Levi to do whatever Mick thought best.

Well, that was going to change, Levi vowed. He had been drifting and dreaming for too long. From now on he would be selfish and tough like Mick. He would make his own way and damn the consequences.

As for Rose, she might have toppled from the pedestal on which he had placed her, but that was a good thing, wasn't it? It meant he could try his damnedest to win her from Mick.

For the first time, Levi was glad that his brothers had disabled him. Perhaps he was a cripple, but at least he wouldn't be at the front. Anything might happen to Mick there, while Levi would be safely in Beckindale with Rose. He would make himself indispensable to her, Levi decided. It was Levi she would turn to when she was worried or sad, Levi who would comfort and console her, who would win her round with his undemanding friendship.

Resolved, he straightened from the tree. All was not lost. He cast one last look over his shoulder at Mick and Rose, still entwined in the summerhouse, and turned away with a bitter smile. He would leave them for now, but his time would come.

Feeling conspicuous in his civilian clothes, Levi skirted the crowd lining the main street for the parade to farewell the troops from the training camp. He had considered staying at the smithy, but Will Hutton had told him that he should go. 'Your brothers are going to war,' he'd said brusquely. 'Go and say goodbye in case you never see them again. You don't want them busybodies saying you're not as patriotic as you should be, neither,' he'd added.

So Levi had come. He could manage without his crutch now which made it easier to make his way through the press of soldiers and villagers. He found Nat and Mick, and Nat's eyes had filled with tears when he saw Levi. 'Forgive me, Levi?' he'd said, clasping him in his arms.

Levi thought of all the times his eldest brother had looked out for him and he closed his eyes and hugged Nat back. 'Of course I do. You be safe now, Nat. Molly will be wanting you home unharmed.'

When it was Mick's turn to say goodbye, he gave Levi a brotherly buffet on the shoulder. 'You make us proud now, Levi.'

Strange how you could love someone and hate them at same time, Levi mused. All he had ever wanted was to be like Mick, but since seeing him with Rose, everything had twisted up inside him. At one level he knew that Mick had no idea of how he felt about Rose and that he hadn't taken her from Levi deliberately, but that wasn't how it felt. Loving Rose was the only thing Levi had ever had for himself, and now Mick had spoilt that too.

And then Mick had the nerve to ask Levi to act as a go-between. He was to post on Rose's letters to Mick, and pass Mick's to her, as if all he was good for was a postman. It was on the tip of Levi's tongue to refuse before he remembered that it would be the perfect excuse to see Rose regularly. It wasn't as if Mick could write properly anyway. Rose would soon get tired of his illiterate scrawls and he, Levi, would be here to take Mick's place.

'Sure,' he had said. 'I'll do that for you, Mick.'

Now the troops were starting to line up outside the Woolpack, Mick was clearly not the only soldier who had found a sweetheart in Beckindale during training. There were some tearful farewells taking place, not without some disapproving looks. Levi overheard a cluster of villagers discussing the news that someone called Doreen Bates had got herself into trouble and there hadn't been time to arrange a wedding. A dour-looking Yorkshireman was prowling among the troops with a ferocious scowl, clearly looking for someone. Mr Bates? Levi could see one of the Bradford men who had been in the same hut as the Dingle brothers skulking behind his fellows and wondered if he was avoiding Doreen's enraged father.

In spite of the tensions that had existed, Beckindale had turned out in force to show its support. Bunting fluttered in the stiff breeze and a brass band was playing.

Not everyone was impressed. 'I won't be sorry to see the back of them,' grunted a youngish man in a farmer's cap. Levi had seen him at the smithy. His name was Robert Warcup and he managed the home farm at Miffield Hall. Farming was a reserved occupation so Robert hadn't enlisted. Did Ava Bainbridge hand him white feathers, Levi wondered.

'I dunno why we have to come and wave them off. Them lads have been nowt but trouble,' Robert was grumbling.

'Oh, Robert, they're going to fight the Germans,' his pretty wife said. 'We have to support them. When I heard what the Germans did to those poor babies in Belgium...' Her voice broke and Robert put his arm round her shoulders.

'Now, Polly, don't take on so,' he said uncomfortably. 'Remember what the doctor said? There's no reason we shouldn't try again for a baby.'

Levi moved on when he spotted Rose standing with the vicar and his wife further down the street. He made his way as close as he dared without the vicar seeing him. Rose was looking pretty in a dusky pink dress and a becoming hat. She kept standing on tiptoe to scan the crowd. Looking for Mick, Levi was bitterly sure.

Mrs Haywood moved away from her husband to talk to a striking young woman standing next to Levi.

'Have you anything from Joe?' Rose's mother asked.

'Not recently.' The younger woman sounded reserved. She carried herself very erect and Levi thought she looked very proud in spite of her dowdy hat and the coat worn thin in patches.

'He must be finishing his training soon, too?'

'I think so.' She hesitated. 'I don't know if he will come home before he goes to the front or not. He did mention embarkation leave a few months ago, but I haven't heard anything since.'

'So it's just you and Frank Pickles?' Mrs Haywood looked concerned when the other woman nodded. 'You must be so tired, Maggie, my dear. I wish you would think again about employing some more help.'

'No one will come and work at Emmerdale farm,' the woman called Maggie said. 'Ava Bainbridge has seen to that.'

'You mustn't pay too much attention to Ava.'

'I don't,' she said briefly, 'but other people do.'

'Why don't you think again about the possibility I mentioned to you before?'

Maggie stiffened with hostility. 'The conchie?'

'Hugo is a Quaker,' Mrs Haywood corrected gently. 'His conscience won't permit him to fight but he is very willing to help the war effort in other ways. He is an acquaintance of friends of mine in York. I don't know his story but I gather that he would like to get away from the city. He would be a strong man, Maggie. You could put him to good use.'

'Thank you, Mrs Haywood, but Frank and I are managing all right for now.'

Levi felt sorry for the unknown Hugo. A strong man who wouldn't fight? He wouldn't receive a welcome in Beckindale, that was for sure.

Edging round the crowd, he passed Ava Bainbridge, the landlady of the Woolpack, who had given him the white feather. She was wearing a ridiculous hat, a monstrosity of which she was clearly very proud, and Levi was delighted to see her register that one of her neighbours was coming towards her sporting exactly the same model. They stared at each other in outrage, like a couple of cats, arching their backs and hissing and spitting.

'Where did you get that hat, Mary Ann?' Ava asked with awful dignity.

'In Ilkley, same as you did, I don't doubt. You're not the only one allowed to buy yourself a new hat, Ava.'

Glad that someone was standing up to the poisonous Ava, Levi sidled onwards. Beckindale had shut him firmly out, but eavesdropping on all these conversations was teaching him a lot about the community that was to be his home, whatever they thought.

A weeping woman was being comforted by a friend. 'You shouldn't have come, Betty. It's too soon after losing your Alfred.'

Betty dabbed at her eyes with a crumpled handkerchief. 'I just wanted to show my support. I complained about the training camp, I know, but look at them. They're just boys, and they're going out to fight them blasted Germans, just like Alfred did.'

Children ran excitably through the crowd, weaving between legs and skirts. 'Iris Bainbridge, come here at once!' Levi heard Ava shriek as a little girl darted giggling across the street in pursuit of a boy. 'Iris!' she called again, but the child ignored her. Pursing her lips, Ava turned to a sulky looking girl beside her. 'Sarah, go and get her.'

'Get her yourself,' said Sarah.

The women beside Levi, who were also listening to the exchange, sucked in their breath audibly. 'Ava's got no control over those children, Janet,' one of them said.

'Stepchildren,' Janet corrected. 'It's not the same.'

'I see why Percy married again – he can't look after t'pub and three children – but he'd have been better off with Lizzy Clark, don't you reckon? Ava doesn't know owt about being a mother.'

Janet sniffed. 'Too busy being queen bee of Beckindale.'

'Oh, Ava's all right,' her friend said comfortably. 'She just likes to know what's going on.'

'What's with her and Maggie Sugden anyroads, Joan? I know Maggie's a bit hoity-toity like, but Ava *hates* her.'

'I can't believe you don't know that!' The other woman leant closer. 'Ava had her eye on Maggie's brother at one point.'

'Andrew Oldroyd? Died of diphtheria?'

'Pneumonia, I think it was. Anyway, Ava asked Maggie if she would put a good word in for her, like. Fancied herself up at High Moor. And Maggie said no, Andrew would rather dig out his liver with a spoon than get involved with a sly spiteful madam like Ava. Or words to that effect.'

'Ava wouldn't have liked *that*.'

'She didn't.'

Levi was beginning to feel quite kindly towards Maggie, who was presumably the same Maggie who refused to have a conscientious objector working on her farm.

The crowd stirred at the stamp of boots as the troops fell in. Levi heard the vicar's booming voice – 'They're off!' – and slipped back to stand behind Rose who was waving her flag while people started cheering and whistling.

She was tense, Levi could tell. Doubtless still looking for Mick. Craning his neck to look past her, he saw his brothers at last. There was Nat, and there, next to him was Mick, cock of the walk as always.

Rose had seen him too. He knew because her shoulders relaxed and she started waving her flag with extra fervour.

Mick had spotted her too. His face lit up and he grinned back and blew her a kiss.

The vicar bristled. 'Damned cheek! Sorry, my dear,' he added as his wife raised her brows at his swearing. 'But how dare he!'

'I don't think he was blowing you a kiss, dear.' Levi was sure he picked up a sardonic note in Mrs Haywood's voice and he looked at her with interest. She seemed so meek and mild-mannered, but perhaps there was more to her than appeared.

'I'm aware of that, Edith.' The vicar was plainly in a very bad mood. 'He was blowing *Rose* a kiss, and I was objecting to that. The insolence of it! Treating my daughter as if she were one of his...' Feeling his wife's eye on him, Charles Haywood broke off with a harrumph. 'These fellows are getting above themselves. Blowing kisses at young ladies! I'd like to see him horsewhipped.'

'Oh, Papa,' said Rose. 'It didn't mean anything.'

But when she turned her head to watch the troops march out of sight, Levi knew with a vicious twist of envy that she was lying. Of course Mick's casually blown kiss had meant something to her. It had meant everything, as the vicar would have understood if he'd been able to see his daughter's expression as Levi could see it.

One day, he swore, Rose would look at *him* like that.

CHAPTER TWENTY-ONE

No sooner had the battalion marched out than another moved into the training camp and the cycle started again. The war had become almost commonplace, Maggie began to think. She was getting used to long columns of men in khaki tramping along the lane or climbing over her walls, to the sound of bugles and rifle shots and barked commands from the camp.

The notices in the newsagent's window were full of events in strange sounding places far, far from Beckindale, not just in France and Flanders but further east: Constantinople, the Dardanelles, Gallipoli. Next to the notices was pinned a list of the most recent casualties, some of them appallingly long. When Ralph had marched out, the war had seemed a matter of honour and of glory. Now Maggie wondered if anyone remembered what they were fighting for.

Then came news of the Zeppelin raids on London and the war seemed commonplace no longer. Maggie had never been to London or seen an airship, but she could imagine how terrifying it must be. She looked up at the blue spring sky and pictured an unearthly machine floating overhead, like something from another world. She thought about what it would be like if it rained fire on the farmyard, exploding the stable and the byre, reducing the farmhouse to rubble, killing the cows and the hens and Fly. Killing *her*.

Every time Maggie thought she was getting used to the war, there was a new horror. Walking down to the village to buy soap one day in May, she saw a cluster of people around the notice board. That was never a good sign.

'What is it?' she asked Mary Ann Teale, who let her through.

'Read it for yourself.'

'Them blasted Germans!' Janet Airey was saying, her voice shaking in outrage. 'They're savages, they are. A thousand killed! A *thousand!* Women and children!'

Polly Warcup had a hand over her mouth and her eyes were full of tears. 'Oh, those poor children. Babies too. I can't bear to think of it!'

Maggie's mouth tightened as she read the notice for herself. The *Lusitania,* sailing from New York to Liverpool, had been sunk by a German U-boat off the coast of Ireland and more than half of the two thousand people on board had perished, including many women and children. She walked back up the track thinking of how terrified they must have been as they thrashed in terror and the cold, dark Atlantic closed over their heads.

So many young people had left Beckindale already to help fight the enemy one way or the other: Dot, George, even Joe. Should she join them? There was no reason for her to stay at Emmerdale Farm now. Ralph was dead.

She had no one to wait for, no one to miss her if she left.

But still the animals had to be fed and the land tended. She couldn't abandon them. Wasn't she doing as much for the war effort running the farm as she would working in a factory? Maggie put down her basket to struggle with the gate that Joe had never fixed. Her fight against the Germans would be here, helping to feed the country.

It was a struggle with just Frank to help her, though. There were times when Maggie was so tired at the end of the day that she thought about going back to Edith Haywood and asking again about the Quaker. But Ralph had given his life to the war. How could she contemplate working with someone who refused to fight as Ralph had done?

There had been no word from Joe for weeks. Maggie had sent the occasional brief letter to tell him what she and Frank had been doing but it was so long since she had a reply that she stopped writing and began to hope that he had abandoned interest in the farm altogether. He had said that he hated being a farmer. Maggie would be happy if he stayed a soldier, if that was what he wanted. After what Joe had done to Toby, she would be glad never to see him again. Let him go away and start a new life after the war. That would be fine by her. They wouldn't need to go to the trouble of a divorce. It was not as if she would ever want to marry anyone else. Her capacity for love had died with Ralph.

It was a warm evening in May when Maggie wished Frank goodnight and watched him walk across to his room over the stable while she pumped five big buckets of water from the well. It had been a long day and she was tired, but she had promised herself a bath.

Together she and Frank had shovelled all the muck from the privy and the farmyard manure onto a sledge before harnessing it to Blossom. The horse had dragged it up to the fields where the cows had been enjoying the young grass and they had spread the muck out as a fertiliser. It wasn't the nicest of jobs, but it had to be done and it would be worth it when the grass grew long and sweet for hay to see the stock through the winter.

They both stank afterwards. Frank had stripped down to his trousers and washed under the pump before milking the cows while Maggie cleaned the muck from her face and hands and exchanged her filthy work trousers for a cool skirt. Tying on an apron, she had put together a supper of cold beef and bread with a slice of plum pie.

She couldn't wait to sink into that bath and scrub away the stench.

The evening light slanted over the fells and touched the dry-stone walls with gold as she filled the buckets. While she pumped, she watched the swallows swooping in and out of their nests under the eaves. It felt good to know that the animals were all fed and safe. Even Fly had curled up in her bed in the barn, while Frank, she guessed, would be asleep already. She had the farmhouse to herself and the prospect of a bath to ease her aching muscles.

After labouring backwards and forwards with the water for the tin tub, she heated a kettle on the stove and poured that into the tub. It would be worth the effort, she told herself. And it was. She lowered herself into the tub with a long exhale of pleasure as she slipped into the warm, clean water.

Soaping herself all over, Maggie luxuriated in the feeling of self-indulgence. It had been so long since she had made the time to have a bath instead of scrub in the bowl with a jugful of warm water.

She had left the door open to let the evening light flood into the kitchen. It striped the flag-stones and slanted across the tub where she lay. Closing her eyes against the golden dazzle of it, she tipped her head back against the rim. Don't think about anything, she told herself. Don't spoil the moment. Don't remember Ralph now.

But it was no good. He was there in her mind, impossible to dislodge. Ralph smiling at her. Ralph holding out his hand to help her jump down from a rock. Ralph pulling her towards him, sliding his hands through her hair, bending to kiss her.

Ralph blown to bits.

Ralph dead.

Ralph gone.

Grief twisted cruelly inside her. During the day

she could forget him but as soon as she was alone like this, the longing for him rolled over her. Maggie pressed her fingers against her eyelids, but still the tears leaked out.

There was no point in crying. It wouldn't change anything. Fly was barking, at a fox perhaps, and the water was cooling. She should get out, but she couldn't summon the energy to move.

'Hullo, Maggie.'

Maggie's eyes flew open and she sat up with a gasp of fright, making a grab for the towel she had laid ready on the chair nearby.

A dark figure was silhouetted against the light in the kitchen door but she recognised the voice.

'Joe!' Maggie's heart was hammering in her throat. The towel had slipped from her fingers onto the floor and she groped for it desperately while covering her breasts with one arm. 'What are you doing here?'

'It's my farm, in't it?'

Joe stepped into the kitchen. He was leaner than she remembered, now that she could see him properly and the khaki uniform made him look bigger. Meaner.

'I thought you were training in Hull,' she said. Where was that towel? She was horribly exposed like this and her fingers felt thick and clumsy as she felt for the towel.

'Got embarkation leave, haven't I? Thought I'd come back and say goodbye to my wife.'

'I wish you'd let me know you were coming.'

His face darkened. 'I don't have to ask permission to come to my own home.'

'No, but I could have got a meal ready for you.'

Maggie spoke as evenly as she could but she was scared. He was looking at her in a way that made her skin crawl, and something unpleasant was shifting behind his eyes.

'Give me a minute and I'll get dressed,' she said as casually as she could.

Joe moved forward without taking his eyes off her. 'No hurry,' he smirked. 'Don't be shy. I'm your husband, remember?'

'It's been six months. We're more like strangers now.' Maggie set her teeth and lifted her chin. 'I'd be obliged if you would look away.'

'You'd be obliged!' he mocked her. 'You haven't changed. Still Lady Muck, looking down your nose at me. I've been away training to fight for t'country, and the least I deserve is a decent welcome home by my wife,' he said, kicking the towel out of her reach.

'You forfeited any welcome when you killed Toby,' said Maggie.

There was nothing for it but to get up, naked as she was. She couldn't sit in the tub all night. Forcing herself not to flinch as he leered at her body, she reached calmly for the towel but he flicked it away once more.

'Don't bother to get dressed. It's a long time since I've had a woman.'

Maggie's eyes snapped, anger vying with fear. 'You're not having one tonight,' she told him and looked around for something – anything – to cover herself.

'You don't get to say no.'

'I do,' she said, forcing her voice to stay steady. 'I say no.'

'You're my wife,' he reminded her. 'You promised to obey me and I'm telling you to come here.'

He was like a bull with a lowered head, practically pawing the ground, his eyes hot and dangerous. Maggie's pulse was pounding in her head, her heart jerking with horror. She had let herself forget about Joe. What a fool she had been!

Could she reason with him? 'Let ... let me get you something to eat first,' she managed but Joe shook his head. He had stripped off his jacket and was fumbling at his shirt, at his fly.

'I want you down on your knees,' he said, his voice thick. 'It's the least you owe me.' He ran a tongue over his lips and Maggie shuddered in disgust.

She stood, naked, her eyes flickering frantically around the room as she considered her options. She could scream, and Frank might hear, but what if he tried to help her? Joe was capable of killing the boy when he was in a rage. And what if Frank let Fly out? Fly would come to protect her, Maggie knew. She couldn't bear to lose another dog to Joe. At least in the barn, Fly was safe.

She could run for it instead, but where could she go with no clothes? The last few months had made her strong and fast, but Joe had been in training too. He would be stronger, faster. He would catch her.

What if she could hide? The parlour? Perhaps she could pull something in front of the door or find something to defend herself with. Her eyes flickered to the kitchen knives but sensing what she was planning, Joe shifted around the table. He was stalking her the way he would try and catch a pig.

Making a split decision, Maggie feinted left and then ran for the kitchen door, but Joe was even quicker than she had thought. She was barely at the door before he had grabbed her by the wrist and jerked her round, bringing her naked body against the rough khaki of his trousers where he was hard against his fly.

'Let me go!' she spat and beat at him with her free hand but Joe's blood was up, and he fetched her a backhanded blow that sent her sprawling on the flagstones.

'By God, I should have done this a long time ago,' he muttered, pinning her down with his knees while he unfastened his fly.

'No! No!' Maggie bucked desperately against the weight of him. She beat and clawed at him, but he batted her hands away. He was panting and his eyes were glazed. Struggling was only making him more excited but she couldn't stop herself.

'Get off me!' she cried and raked her fingers down his cheek. 'Get off, get off, get off! I hate you!'

Face stinging from the scratches on his cheek, Joe cursed and clamped a sweaty hand over her mouth as he levered her legs apart with his knee.

'Keep still, damn you!' he grunted.

Half suffocated by his palm, Maggie was tiring, but she wouldn't give up. She bit at his hand, she scratched and she hit, but she couldn't shift him and when he thrust into her, everything went dark with pain and disgust.

Later, she couldn't have said how long it went on. She lay, defeated, gagging under the stench and sweat of his hand, while Joe bucked and plunged and grunted and felt shame swamp her. She who had prided herself on her independence had not been able to save herself from this. She was nothing now, just a lump of flesh Joe could do what he liked with, and so she squeezed her eyes shut and blanked out her mind and endured until he emptied himself inside with an inarticulate cry.

He flopped on top of Maggie, almost crushing her, before rolling off her at last. 'Next time just do as you're bloody told,' he said.

Beaten, bloody, Maggie levered herself agonisingly off the floor. Without a word, she crawled to the door and retched into the dust. The sun was still slanting its gentle light into the farmyard. The swallows were still darting after insects. Fly had fallen silent. Frank, it seemed, was still asleep. Somewhere high on the hill a lamb was bleating for its mother.

Maggie's head was ringing. She was torn and bleeding and pain hammered at her but worse, far worse, was the sense of degradation and disgust. She had felt cleaner spreading muck on the fields.

Somehow she made it to the trough. Greedily she drank water straight from the pump, letting it splash over her face, only to vomit it all up a minute later. The rag Frank had used to wash earlier had been wrung out and draped over the pump to dry. Maggie used it to wash herself all over, scrubbing furiously at herself as if she could rub away the memory of how Joe had pinned her down and made her powerless.

She wouldn't go back to the house. She couldn't. She staggered to the barn instead and heaving open the heavy bar, she practically fell inside into the familiar smell of straw and cows. In her kennel, Fly whined.

Maggie opened the door and let the dog lick her in wordless comfort. They curled up in the straw together.

And in the morning, Joe had gone.

CHAPTER TWENTY-TWO

'What's that?' Rose lifted her head, startled by the strange rumbling sound. It had started as a low hum but was getting louder and louder. In quiet Beckindale, where the clanging from the smithy, the peal of church bells and the bellowing of calves being castrated vied for the honour of loudest noise, the sound was disconcertingly out of place.

She had slipped out to meet Levi Dingle in the ruins of the old watermill by the bridge. When they had first arranged a meeting, he had suggested the summerhouse in the grounds of Miffield Hall. Rose was surprised that he knew of it.

'It would be private,' he said. 'I don't think anyone ever goes there.'

She and Mick had. It had been their special place, and she didn't want to spoil those memories with anyone else.

'It's too far,' she said. 'The mill ruins are more convenient.'

Something ugly flashed across Levi's face, something that gave Rose a jolt, but the next moment he was smiling, and she decided that she must have imagined it.

'Whatever you want, Rose,' he had said.

She didn't like Levi calling her Rose. Oh, she and Mick had made a joke of him calling him Miss Haywood rather than Rose, but she hadn't meant it, and Mick had known that. Her name in Levi's mouth felt uncomfortably intimate but Rose didn't feel able to insist that he should address her as Miss Haywood.

She found Mick's brother unsettling. They had been meeting for three months now, whenever Rose had a letter to send to Mick, or Levi had one to pass to her. He always brought her a present although all Rose wanted was the letter from Mick. Today it was a posy of flowers.

'Thank you, Levi. They're charming,' she had said, forcing a smile. She couldn't wait to be alone so that she could read Mick's letter, but it seemed rude to rush away, especially when she knew how lonely Levi must be.

The farrier was the only other person who would talk to him now that Ava had suggested that he had shot himself in order to avoid going to the front. Naturally, the rumour had spread like wildfire, and Levi was firmly branded a cowardly shirker. Rose had tried to counteract the gossip by suggesting that he was the victim of an accident and should be pitied, but Ava had merely looked contemptuous.

'Oh, my dear Miss Haywood, you are such an innocent. Of course every shirker has a hard luck story. You really mustn't let a man like that, an Irishman too, take advantage of your trusting nature.'

Rose had clenched her fists but how could she insist that she knew the truth without giving away her relationship with Mick?

So when Levi invited her to sit down, she never made an excuse to leave, although Mick's brother made her uncomfortable at times. He was an intense young man with an unnerving habit of staring at her. Mick had told her that Levi was a dreamer, but he didn't seem dreamy to Rose. She sensed a core of bitterness and anger in him that left her feeling uneasy. He seemed to be dabbling in some questionable activities, too. Rose didn't like to enquire too closely about where he had acquired a bicycle, or how he had been able to afford the box of chocolates that he had presented her with the first time they met.

'There's plenty more where that came from,' he had said. 'Just let me know.'

Now Rose got to her feet and listened to the sound growing ever louder. Was this what it had been like for the poor people who had heard a strange noise and looked up to see a Zeppelin airship looming above them before it dropped bombs on them?

Don't be ridiculous, Rose told herself. The Germans were hardly going to target Beckindale, were they?

Still, the sound was ominous.

'What is it?' she asked Levi.

'Sounds like motor cars to me,' he said, and they clambered up onto the tumbledown wall to have a better look.

'You're right. There!' Rose pointed as the first truck came round the bend and drove carefully over the bridge. It had canvas sides painted with a great red cross.

'It's an ambulance,' said Levi. 'Lots of ambulances,' he added as the first was followed by another and another and another until they formed a great snake winding along the narrow country lane and disappearing out of sight at either end.

'They must be going to Miffield Hall,' Rose said.

Rose watched the ambulances trundling past, appalled to realise just how many injured men were being transferred to the new hospital. Behind those red crosses were men who had been at front, who had been shot or had a limb blown off or breathed in vile poison gas. They would not even be the worst injured, but patients well enough to be recuperate. 'There are so many of them,' she said, shaken.

'They'll be wanting cigarettes,' Levi thought out loud. 'I'll get hold of some in Bradford and sell them on. It's not like most of them will be able to get down to the village shop, is it? I reckon I could make a tidy profit.'

Rose looked at him in dismay. 'You can't make a profit out of the fact that they're injured!'

'How else am I going to live?' he asked bitterly. 'I'm no use with this leg now, even if anyone in Beckindale would give me a job.'

'I thought you were helping Will Hutton.'

'For bed and board, but I've no money of my own unless I earn it using my wits,' he told her. 'Luckily I've got a few irons in the fire. I've got contacts in Bradford who can get me cheap cigarettes, chocolate and beer,' he boasted. 'I've got a nice little sideline going with one of the sergeants at the camp. He gets a cut, the new recruits get a few luxuries and I make a profit. Everyone's happy.'

'But isn't the black market illegal?' Rose asked.

Levi shrugged. 'You don't get anywhere sticking to the straight and narrow,' he said. 'Mick taught me that.'

Rose wanted to protest that Mick would never do anything criminal, but she remembered how she had first met him, stuffing his kit bag with Lord Miffield's apples. Perhaps he was a rogue, she admitted to herself, but Mick wouldn't do anything *bad*.

Should she say something to Mick? He had asked her to be a friend to Levi, but she didn't want to worry him while he was at the front.

'Be careful,' she said to Levi. 'I wouldn't want anything to happen to you.'

'I will be,' he promised her with one of his disquieting stares.

'And these flowers are lovely but you mustn't spend any money bringing me presents,' Rose went on.

'I like giving you presents.'

'That's sweet of you,' she said uneasily, 'but it's really not necessary. You're doing enough for me already, keeping me in touch with Mick.' She pulled a letter from her pocket and handed it to Levi. 'Will you send this one back to him?'

'Of course,' he said. 'I'd do anything for you, Rose. You know that. Anything at all.'

The last ambulance drove slowly over the bridge and disappeared up the lane that led to Miffield Hall. Rose followed it with her eyes. What if Mick were in the back? Or John? Oh, she was so tired of doing nothing! Every time she wrote to Mick she cringed inwardly a how little she had to tell him. You're more of a rebel than you think you are, he had said, but she wasn't rebelling. She was still waiting for her father to give her permission to do more than roll bandages and knit.

But that could change.

Abruptly making up her mind, Rose jumped down from the wall. 'I need to go.'

'I'll walk with you,' said Levi instantly.

'No, you mustn't, Levi. You don't know what my father's like,' she tried to explain as she did every time they met. 'If he got wind of the fact that I was meeting you, he would be furious. I'd be all right, but I don't want to think what he would do to you. I'm sure he could get you sent away from Beckindale. He's got a lot of influence. Mick and I were always careful never to be seen by anyone.'

There it was again, that flash of dislike in his expression, so quickly veiled that she couldn't be entirely sure that she'd seen it.

'Anyway,' she said, 'I'm not going back to the village.'

'Where are you going?'

'To Miffield Hall.'

The ambulances were pulled up on the gravel sweep in front of the hall where Rose used to jump down from the pony and trap, eager to see Ralph. They were all empty now, their drivers leaning against the bonnets and smoking cigarettes. The front door was open. Rose walked in and stood in the hall feeling disorientated. Where once Grieves, the butler, had crossed the tiled floor with a stately lack of speed, now orderlies and nurses in crisp aprons and starched caps rushed to and fro. A patient, his head swathed in bandages, was slumped in a wheelchair under the magnificent grandfather clock that must have been too old or too awkward to move. It ticked remorselessly over the bustle.

Nobody paid any attention to Rose. She had to catch a nurse by the sleeve to ask if she could see whoever was in charge.

'Can't you see we're busy?'

'I know,' said Rose. 'I'm sorry. I don't mind waiting.'

The nurse sighed. 'Wait in there,' she said, nodding her head at what had been Lord Miffield's study.

'What name shall I say?'

'I'm Rose Haywood. Miss Haywood.'

'I'll tell Matron you're there, but you might have a long wait.'

She bustled off, and Rose pushed open the door to the study. She had never been in there before, but she suspected she wouldn't have recognised the room anyway. It had been roughly partitioned, and there were patches on the walls where pictures and bookcases had been removed.

Rose sat on a hard chair and smoothed Mick's letter out onto her lap. His spelling was terrible and his writing little better than a scrawl, but the recklessness and humour that had drawn her to him was there and she smiled as she read about being billeted on farms and kicking a pig out of its sty for a dry bed. *That old pig was not hapy,* Mick wrote.

She had read and reread the letter many times before the door opened and the matron came in. She was a formidable-looking woman with iron-grey hair. 'Miss Haywood?' she said brusquely. 'I am sorry to keep you waiting but as you will have seen, we have had an influx of new patients today. What can I do for you?'

Rose had risen to her feet, Mick's letter in her hand. 'I want to help.'

'Are you a trained nurse?'

'No. No, I'm not.'

The matron sighed. 'The men here are very badly injured, Miss Haywood. They need specialist care. I am sure you are anxious to do what you can, but my patients are my priority and I am afraid that without training you would just get in the way. Forgive me for being blunt.'

Rose was intimidated but she thought of Mick and held her ground.

'I don't want to get in anyone's way,' she said, 'but there must be something I can do. What do the men do when they are recuperating? Couldn't I read to them, perhaps, or write a letter for someone who can't manage it?'

'That may be possible,' said the matron after a moment. 'Many of the patients are blinded or have lost an arm, so someone to help with writing might be useful.' She studied Rose critically. 'You are a gently bred girl, I suspect, Miss Haywood. I must warn you that you would see some shocking sights on the wards. Do you have a strong enough stomach?'

'I don't know,' said Rose honestly, 'but if I'm going to be sick, I promise to wait until I'm on my way home.'

A smile flickered over the matron's face. 'Very well. Do you have some time now? I know of one man who is very anxious to send a letter home and none of my nurses has had time to sit down with him.'

Rose stuffed Mick's letter into the pocket of her jacket. 'I've got plenty of time,' she said.

'Rose, where on earth have you been? Your mother has been beside herself with worry.'

Her father was furious when Rose went home at last. Dazed with the enormity of what she had seen, she dropped into a chair and looked around as if finding herself in another world.

'I've been at the hospital,' she said.

At the vicarage, afternoon tea was being served in the drawing room. Outside the open windows, fat bumble bees drowsed over the lavender and Arthur, home for the summer holidays, was moodily cracking a croquet ball through the hoops on the lawn. Her mother poured tea from a silver pot into bone china cups and saucers while her father loomed in front of the fireplace, glowering at Rose.

'Oh, Papa, if you had seen those poor men!' The

matron's warning had not prepared Rose. She had gagged at the smell of carbolic soap which only partly masked the stench of blood and pus and vomit. A row of beds now stood in Lady Miffield's drawing room where once they had taken tea. The carpets had been rolled up, the fireplace boarded over and the pictures and furniture put into storage. Now it was just an echoingly large room, the sound of groans and muffled cries of pain overlaid by the squeak of the nurses' shoes on the new linoleum floor.

She saw men with bloody bandages covering the stumps of amputated limbs, men missing a foot or an arm or in one case both legs blown off below the knee. Others were wrapped like mummies, with only their nose and mouth uncovered. Rose couldn't imagine the terrible damage that must have been done to their faces.

'I sat with a sergeant today. He's completely blind and in so much pain, but he wanted to write to his little girl, so he dictated to me and I wrote the letter for him. He loves her so much, Papa, and he wrote so bravely and cheerfully to her ... it broke my heart!' Remembering Sergeant Donald's stoical endurance and the tenderness of his words to his beloved daughter, Rose had to choke back a sob.

Her father frowned. 'This is exactly why I didn't want you to go to the hospital, Rose. It's too upsetting for you.'

'I *should* be upset, Papa! These men have been injured fighting to protect us!'

'I am well aware of what we owe them, Rose, but my concern at the moment is for you. I don't like the idea of you being exposed to such scenes. I don't want you to go back there.'

'Of course I am going back,' said Rose, taking a cucumber sandwich. 'The soldier in the bed next to Sergeant Donald said I had a lovely voice and I promised I would go and read to him. Do you think he'd like some Dickens?'

'Rose,' her father said awfully, 'I cannot permit it. Especially not after today.'

'Why, what has happened?'

'Mildred has just resigned!'

'She's going to be a plumber's mate in Keighley,' her mother added.

'Really?' Rose was astounded. 'How marvellous of her!'

'It is *not* marvellous,' her father said, handing his cup and saucer to her mother for more tea. 'Who do you think is going to cook and clean now? Now that all the girls have gone off to get jobs, we won't be able to replace Mildred, so your mother will need you to help her run the house.'

Rose glanced at her mother. 'We're going to have to learn how to cook?'

'I'm afraid so,' said Edith composedly.

'Gosh.'

'So you see, you won't have time to go back to the hospital,' Charles said, accepting his teacup back with a nod of thanks.

'I don't agree.' To his consternation, her mother looked him straight in the eye. 'What if it were John lying in a hospital unable to see to read or to write to us? Rose has promised to go back and she should. I will manage the housework,' she said quietly. 'I'm sure she will help me when she can.'

CHAPTER TWENTY-THREE

In July, Frank enlisted.

'But Frank, you're only fifteen!' Maggie said in dismay when he told her.

Frank wouldn't meet her eyes. 'I'm a big lad,' he mumbled, clearly parroting what he had been told at the recruiting office. Maggie knew that after nearly a year of a war that didn't seem to be going anywhere it was getting harder and harder for the Army to recruit volunteers, but surely they weren't reduced to boys?

'You're still too young, Frank. Why did you go along? Aren't you happy here with Blossom and the cows?'

His face worked. 'I'm not a coward,' he said.

'Who said you were?'

'Mrs Bainbridge.'

Ava Bainbridge. Was there no end to the trouble that woman could cause? Maggie kept a tight rein on her temper as she coaxed the story out of Frank. Ava, it seemed, had presented Frank with a white feather and told him that it was his duty to sign up.

As carefully as she could, Maggie tried to explain to Frank that Ava was wrong and that his duty was still to stay where he could do most good, at Emmerdale Farm. She would go with him to the recruiting office, she said, and explain that a mistake had been made.

But once an idea had taken hold of Frank, he was unshakeable. He didn't want to be a coward or be called a shirker. He dug in his heels and insisted that he was old enough to do his duty.

He came to say goodbye, bashful in his new uniform. He took a prolonged farewell of each of the cows and of Blossom and then bent to pat Fly. Maggie's throat ached with unshed tears as she kissed him. 'I'm proud of you, Frank,' she told him, straightening his collar. 'You're a good lad, and you'll be a good soldier. You do what the officer tells you, and when the war is over, there'll always be a job for you at Emmerdale Farm.'

When he left, she had to cover her mouth with her hand to stop her face crumpling. How many more goodbyes would there be before this cursed war was over?

And now she had something else to worry about. This was the fourth morning she'd been sick and the first she'd made it to the privy on time.

Leaning against the wooden wall of the privy until the sickness faded, Maggie had been unable to ignore the truth any longer. This sickness in the mornings and the strange tingling sensation in her breasts. She hadn't had the curse since before Joe came back. Maggie's mind skittered around the memory of what he had done to her then: the smell of his sweaty palm over her face, the brutal thrusting, that horrifying sense of powerlessness.

And now she was pregnant.

Swamped by a great wave of lassitude, Maggie had to force herself outside and away from the stench and the flies. The privy was no place to

225

linger, especially not in high summer.

Fly was waiting for her, her bright eyes fixed anxiously on Maggie's face. 'Oh, Fly,' Maggie had sighed, bending down to stroke her. '*Now* what am I going to do?'

When Frank had told her about enlisting, Maggie had come so close to giving up. Why struggle on? she had asked herself. Why not let Tom Skilbeck take over? She could go and work in a factory. She could leave Beckindale and all its memories behind.

But now everything had changed. Now there was a child to think of.

Maggie laid a hand on her stomach. There was nothing to feel yet, just the rough cotton of her work trousers but it was there, she was sure.

A baby.

Her baby – and Joe's.

She could get rid of it. The thought hung in the air. There were all sorts of folk-remedies to encourage a miscarriage. Nobody would blame her if she tried one. Nobody would know.

Nobody would care.

But Maggie knew that she couldn't do it. Already she felt fiercely protective of the new life growing inside her. It might be Joe's child, but it would be hers too.

Since Ralph died, she had been existing. She had kept going because there had been no alternative. Now she had a child to work for. Emmerdale Farm would do its bit to feed the country during the war, but it had a future now too. It was an inheritance, to be built up and passed on to this child and to future generations.

So when Tom Skilbeck came sniffing around as soon as he heard about Frank, Maggie told him that she wasn't interested in letting him have any more. 'Come on, now, Maggie,' he said. 'I'm trying to help you out here. You've done well, I'll give you that, but even Frank's gone now. Even you can't think a lass can run a farm like this all by yourself.'

'I'm getting some help,' she said.

'Who? There aren't many young men left at all, and the older ones won't work for a woman. No one will work for you, Maggie, and you know it.'

But Maggie only put up her chin. 'We'll see,' she said.

As soon as Tom had stomped off, she put on her hat and walked down to the vicarage. Edith Haywood showed no surprise at seeing her. She made Maggie tea and they sat in the kitchen. All their lives had changed, Maggie thought. A year ago, Mrs Haywood would not have known how to make her own tea.

'When is the baby due?' Edith asked and Maggie put her cup unsteadily back in its saucer.

'How did you know?'

'I have had three children, my dear,' said Edith with a faint smile. 'Have you seen a doctor?'

Maggie shook her head. 'I can't afford a doctor. Besides, I helped enough lambs into the world earlier this year to know what's going to happen. It's a natural process. If the sheep can manage without a doctor, so can I.'

Edith lifted her hands in a gesture of acceptance. 'Still, you must look after yourself. You'll be exhausted if you try to do everything yourself.'

227

'I know. I've changed my mind,' Maggie said. 'Do you think your friend from York would still like to come and work on the farm?'

'I can get in touch with Hugo and ask him to come straight away,' said Edith. She paused. 'I think you're making the right decision but are you prepared for the fact that it won't make you popular in the village?'

Maggie gave a short laugh. 'No change there, then.'

She wrote to Joe that night. She told him about the baby and that she expected it would be born sometime in January. She told him about Frank and that she had had no choice but to employ a conscientious objector to help with the heavy work. Then she took it down to Hannah Rigg in the post office and sent it off. Joe's unit had been sent to Egypt and she didn't expect to hear back for some time. Until then, she would do whatever she had to.

On a sticky August evening when the heat of the day shimmered still on the track, Maggie came out of the byre to see a quiet-looking man wrestling with the gate at Emmerdale Farm.

She put down the can of milk and watched as he stopped and studied the gate for a moment before working out the trick of it and opening it so that he could step through. Putting down his suitcase once more, he fastened the gate behind him and turned to see Maggie.

After only a moment's hesitation, he walked across the farmyard, looking ridiculously citified in his tweed suit and polished shoes. When he got closer, he stopped and lifted his hat.

'Mrs Sugden?'

'That's me.'

'I'm Hugo Dawson. I believe you're expecting me?'

'I had a letter, yes. You're the conchie.' Maggie made no attempt to hide her hostility. She might have no choice but to employ a conscientious objector, but she didn't have to like it – or him.

Braced for a cowardly type, raving about the iniquities of war, she had been prepared to give him short shrift, but the man who had opened the gate so competently didn't look as if raving was his style. She guessed that he was in his early thirties or so. He was clean-shaven with quiet features and steady eyes. Put him in a uniform and he would make a perfect officer.

And that's what he should be, Maggie thought fiercely. Hugo Dawson should be out in France doing his bit with everyone else and looking out for the likes of Frank, not standing safely here at Beckindale Farm in his tweed suit.

'I am a Quaker,' he said evenly. 'My conscience does not permit me to fight but I am happy to do what I can to help as long as I am not called upon to kill my fellow men.'

'Conscience won't help the boys at the front,' she pointed out with a tart look.

Hugo acknowledged that with a nod. 'No, but I hope I will be able to help *you,*' he said. 'I understand you are running this farm all by yourself?'

'That's right.' Maggie caught herself up. Approve of him or not, she needed this man if she were to keep the farm going. Think of the baby,

229

she reminded herself.

'You'd better come in,' she said ungraciously as she bent to pick up the milk can. 'I'll just put this in the dairy.'

'That looks heavy. Let me take it for you.'

Maggie was about to refuse when she remembered how tired she was. 'You may as well start making yourself useful,' she allowed and watched critically as he picked up the can with ease. He was stronger than he looked, that was something.

Hugo looked around the dairy with interest. He was full of questions: was it true the elderflower bush at the door kept off flies? What happened to the milk once it was in the churns? Did she make butter, or cheese? How long did that take?

'Nosy, aren't you?' she said at last.

'Sorry,' said Hugo with an unexpectedly engaging smile. 'It's an occupational hazard, I'm afraid. I'm a science teacher,' he explained when she looked at him 'I'm interested in how and why things work. Do questions annoy you?'

'I don't know. I've never thought about it.' Joe grunted orders. Frank did as he was told. Dot had known more than Maggie did anyway, or had thought she did. 'I'm just not used it, I suppose.'

'Let me know if it does. I have it on good authority I can be a pest at times.' Hugo smiled, but there was a sadness in it that made Maggie wonder who he was thinking of.

She pointed to the stable. 'There's a room in the loft. You'll see the stair when you go in the stable. It's not much, but it's private. You can sleep there, but take your meals in the kitchen with me.'

'I'd appreciate that.'

His politeness made her uneasy. 'You might not when you find out what a bad cook I am. Have you eaten today?'

'Not since breakfast.'

'You'd better come in then.'

Maggie couldn't remember the last time a stranger had been in the kitchen and she found herself looking at the room through the stranger's eyes, noting the dinginess of the décor.

At one end of the room the range filled the fire-place, flanked by a rocking chair and the chair where Joe had used to sit, leaning back with his legs spread, his hands gripping the arms while he glared balefully into the fire. A tired rag-rug was laid on the floor in front of the range. There was an old sideboard and a table covered in an oiled cloth and there, near the door, was where Joe had raped her.

Maggie stepped round the spot as she always did. 'Sit down,' she said as she brushed crumbs from the table into her hand. She hadn't taken the time to clear up properly after her dinner, and now she wished she had.

She set out cold beef, some stale bread and home-made butter. 'It's not much,' she found herself apologising. 'We eat a hot meal at dinner time.'

In the larder, she found the remains of a pie she had made with the last of the apples stored in the barn loft and some early blackberries she had found. The pastry was stodgy but it would have to do. Not for the first time Maggie wished Dot still held sway in the kitchen. She would put up with a lot of grumbling for Dot's light hand with the pastry or one of the delicious cakes she used to make.

Pulling out a chair, she sat down opposite Hugo and pushed the plate of beef towards him. 'If we're going to get along, we should set out some ground rules,' she said brusquely.

'That sounds sensible.'

'I believe in being frank.' Maggie took a breath. 'I know you've got your own beliefs, but I don't like what you stand for. There are men I care for at the front right now, and others who will never come back.'

Hugo's eyes were an unusual colour, somewhere between green and brown, and flecked with gold. 'I understand,' he said.

Maggie doubted that he did but he was here now and it looked as if he was the best he was going to get.

'Have you ever worked on a farm before?' she asked.

'No.'

'Ever milked a cow?'

'I'm afraid not.'

'Used a scythe?'

'No.'

'Harnessed a horse?'

He shook his head regretfully.

'Well!' She blew out an exasperated breath. 'What *can* you do?'

'I'm a quick learner,' said Hugo with a faint smile.

'You'd better be,' said Maggie, unimpressed. 'You'll need to be up at five in the morning for milking.'

The dew lay thick on the grass the next morning when Maggie showed him how to bring the cows in from the meadow. When Buttercup was in place, she hooked the milking stool closer with her foot and she sat on it to demonstrate how to squeeze the teats so that milk squirted satisfyingly into the bucket. Buttercup was missing Frank and played up, kicking half a bucket of milk into the straw, but Hugo seemed to get the knack of it eventually, and although it would be a long time before he was as quick as Frank, Maggie grudgingly acknowledged that he had coped better than she had thought. There was a calmness about him, too, that seemed to reassure the cows.

After a breakfast of bread and cheese, milk warm from the cow and the remnants of the blackberry and apple pie, Maggie told Hugo that she wanted him to start harvesting the oats that were already cracking and past their best.

'I want you to cut the field in rows,' she said, handing him the scythe.

Hugo examined the scythe carefully, weighing it in his hands for a few minutes before taking an experimental swing and neatly slicing the top off a stand of oats. 'Like that?'

Maggie stared at him suspiciously. 'I thought you hadn't used a scythe before?'

'I haven't,' he said. 'But I obviously need to work out the most effective angle to hold the scythe and how to use the weight of my body. I've seen men scything in the fields, of course, but I never realised quite what hard work it was.'

'Hmm.' Maggie watched him complete the first

233

row. It was far from perfect but she had to admit that it was much better than she could have done. 'I'll bring you out some dinner and something to drink later,' she said as she left him to it.

By the time she went back, Hugo had cut half the field and was bright red in the face and sweating profusely.

'Have a rest,' said Maggie irritably. 'You're no use to me if you pass out.'

Hugo collapsed gratefully into the long grass and accepted the bottle of home-brewed beer she gave him, tipping back his head and drinking thirstily.

Unwrapping the bread and cheese she had brought out to the field, Maggie was annoyed to see that Fly was greeting him effusively, her tail wagging as she nudged her nose under Hugo's arm. She had been used to Frank, but was otherwise usually wary of men. Joe's kicks had taught her to give them a wide berth. But here she was making a ridiculous fuss over the conscientious objector.

'She's a lovely dog,' said Hugo, patting Fly.

'She doesn't usually like men,' Maggie said.

'Dogs have good instincts,' Hugo glanced up at Maggie in her old trousers and a white shirt open at the throat, her arms folded warily. 'She knows she can trust me not to hurt her.'

CHAPTER TWENTY-FOUR

Cursing the damp that set the ache grinding in his bad leg, Levi limped down to the ruined watermill. It was a misty October day and he skidded on the wet leaves in his haste. He was late, and terribly afraid that Rose wouldn't have waited.

He hardly saw her nowadays. She was always rushing off to that blasted hospital instead of staying to talk to him. Sometimes she could barely wait to snatch Mick's letter from his hands and give him hers in return before she claimed that Sergeant This or Private That was waiting for her and that she had to go.

Levi had taken to hanging around the vicarage in the hope of seeing her and exchanging a word. If Rose was on her own, he would catch up with her but she still tried to brush him off. It annoyed him.

'Please, Levi,' she said, walking very fast even though she knew it was hard for him to keep up with his bad leg. 'We can't be seen together.'

Did she think he was stupid? He only ever approached her if the road was empty. He spread his arms and looked around. 'Who's to see? There's no one here.'

'This is a village. There's *always* someone to see,' said Rose. 'I just don't want my father to get suspicious. If he got it into his head that I was

235

keeping unsuitable company, he'd be able to make your life extremely difficult. And if you weren't here, how would I contact Mick?'

It was still all about Mick, Levi thought resentfully. He had thought she would have tired of Mick's stupid letters by now.

Levi nearly slipped on the wet stones, but at least Rose was still there. She was pacing up and down in a long coat and a hat, banging her gloved hands together for warmth.

'I'm sorry I'm late,' he said breathlessly. 'I was just leaving when Will asked if I could give him a hand with some boxes.'

'It doesn't matter.'

'You seem a bit tense,' Levi said anxiously. 'Is anything wrong?'

'The man I love is fighting in a war that shows no sign of ending. What on earth could be wrong?' she snapped and he recoiled.

'I'm sorry, I didn't mean to annoy you.'

Rose took a deep breath. 'No, *I'm* sorry,' she said. 'Don't mind me, Levi. I'm just cold and I'm upset because Sergeant Donald died yesterday. He was my favourite patient.'

Levi couldn't understand why she was so obsessed with the wounded soldiers. 'I bought you some chocolates,' he said in an attempt to cheer her up, but that didn't work either.

'Oh, Levi, I wish you wouldn't.' She sounded impatient. 'You know I can't take presents home without questions being asked.'

'I thought you would like them as a treat,' he said, wounded. It was so frustrating not being able to impress her with gifts.

Rose sighed. 'I'll take them to the nurses, shall I? They never get any treats,' she said, which wasn't what Levi wanted at all. He didn't want faceless nurses at the hospital to have a treat. He wanted Rose to look at him properly and smile with gratitude. One of these days he was going to earn enough to buy her some jewellery. A necklace, perhaps, or a ring.

'If you want,' he said, sulkily rubbing at the ache in his leg.

Rose was digging into the bag she carried. 'I've got three letters for Mick here,' she said. 'Have you got any from him?'

'A couple,' he admitted grudgingly.

'Could I give you these then?' She handed him her letters. 'I must go.'

His face fell. 'Already? But I've only just got here!'

'I promised to read another chapter of *Jane Eyre* to Stanley Owen. He doesn't know the story at all,' she said as if it was surprising.

Levi didn't know the story either, but she wasn't reading to him.

'And I'd like to spend some time with Wilfred Brown, too,' Rose said. Her face was sad. 'He is so badly injured, poor boy, that I don't think he can live long. Yesterday I just sat and held his hand. It is terrible to think that there is nothing else I can do for him.'

'I'm sure it helps, Rose,' he said. 'It would help me if you held my hand.' Too late he saw that his attempt at joviality had missed the mark again.

Rose's expression changed and she gave him a

237

cool smile that effectively set him at a distance. 'I really do need to go, Levi. Could I have Mick's letters?'

Levi pretended to pat his jacket. 'Now where did I put them?' he said, trying to lighten the atmosphere with a joke as Mick would have done, but Rose was unamused.

'Please, Levi,' she said tight-lipped.

Burningly conscious of having got it wrong again, Levi dug in his pocket. Mick always sealed his letters to Rose in a separate envelope and included it in the package he sent to Levi at the smithy, scrawling her name on the front of the envelope so that Levi had no excuse to open it. Levi got a scribbled note with Mick's news too, but it was a poor thing compared to the letters he had to hand over to Rose.

'Here,' he said, pulling them from his pocket and handing them to Rose.

'Thank you.' She turned the envelopes over. 'You said there were two letters.'

'There were.'

'There's only one here.' She showed him.

Levi frowned and felt around in his pockets for real. 'There was another one...'

Rose looked so downcast that he cursed himself for disappointing her. 'There were definitely two letters. I must have dropped it in the smithy. I'll find it and get it to you as soon as possible.'

'I hope nobody else finds it first,' she said, biting her lip. She looked down at the envelope with *Rose* written on it in Mick's untidy handwriting and grimaced. 'If Papa hears of a letter with my name on it floating around the village, he'll be so angry!'

'I'll find it,' he promised.

Rose sighed and looked up as the mist thickened to a drizzle. 'I really must go, Levi,' she said. 'Let me know if you find the missing letter.'

Levi scowled as he watched her leave. After everything he did for Rose, she could never wait to get away! She only cared about Mick, only wanted to talk about Mick. Mick, Mick, Mick: Levi was sick of hearing how much she loved his brother. He had hoped that once Mick was in France she would learn to like him for himself. Look at how well he treated her! He was always giving her presents and looking out for her. Rose barely had to step outside the vicarage and he was there to escort her and protect her, but did she appreciate it? No!

Hunching his shoulders against the chill, Levi scuffed his feet in the grass and sifted through her letters, all to Mick, of course. His brother had always been one for the ladies, but Levi hadn't expected Mick's interest in Rose to last this long. It was usually a case of out of sight, out of mind with Mick. The trouble was that Rose never gave him a chance to forget her: she was always writing him letters.

But what if those letters started going astray? The idea dropped into Levi's mind and lodged there. Mick would start to lose interest, his letters would get less frequent and then tail off altogether. Rose would be upset at first, but then surely she would turn to him, Levi reasoned. He would need to be careful, though. If the letters stopped too suddenly, they would both suspect something and besides, if Rose decided there was no point in writing to Mick, Levi would have no excuse to meet her so often.

But one or two letters could go missing. These things happened in wartime, didn't they?

On an impulse, Levi ripped open one of the letters. *My own dear darling Corporal Dingle,* Rose had begun and his face twisted as he read how much she missed Mick, how much she thought of him, how much she loved him. She had finished: *Your ever-loving Miss Haywood.*

Levi didn't understand why they addressed each other so formally but there was no mistaking the 'dear darling' and the 'ever-loving'.

With an exclamation of frustration, he tore the letter into little pieces and dropped them into the beck. It was starting to grow dark, but he stood there as the fog closed in and watched the swirling brown water carry Rose's letter away.

'Miss Haywood, yoo-hoo!'

Rose waited reluctantly as Ava Bainbridge dodged between a cartload of straw and a gaggle of geese that Janet Airey's youngest was driving down to the beck.

'What can I do for you, Mrs Bainbridge?'

'It's what I can do for *you,* Miss Haywood.' Ava drew a letter from her basket and Rose sucked in a breath as she recognised Mick's writing. 'I think this might be for you.'

'Where did you find it?' she demanded without thinking.

'In the street. Someone must have dropped it. Betty Porter found it and I said I'd pass it on. It is for you, isn't it?'

'Yes, it is. Thank you.' Rose reached for the envelope but Ava smiled archly and held it teasingly out of reach.

'Have I stumbled on a little romance?'

'No, it's from my brother,' Rose lied without thinking.

'Really? Why wouldn't your brother write to you at the vicarage?'

Rose hated the way she blushed when she was caught out in a lie. Her face always gave her away.

'It doesn't look like very educated writing either,' Ava went on. 'I'm sure your brother writes better than this.'

Why hadn't she said she didn't know who the letter was from? Rose cursed herself. 'Very well,' she said through her teeth. 'It's not from my brother. It's a private letter and I'd be obliged if you would let me have it.'

Rose's attempt to sound quelling didn't seem to have much effect on Ava. 'Well now,' she said, 'I'm very fond of the vicar, as you know. I don't like to think of aiding and abetting you in something your dear papa wouldn't approve of. I think it's probably my duty to bring this letter to his attention.'

'Please don't!' Rose said involuntarily. 'I mean, it's really nothing, but I don't want my father upset or worried.' She forced a smile. She wouldn't put it past Ava Bainbridge to have steamed open the envelope and if Papa saw how Mick was writing to her ... it didn't bear thinking about! 'I would be so grateful if you would just keep this to yourself, Mrs Bainbridge.'

'Well, I don't know...'

'How can I persuade you?'

'Oh, it's not a matter of persuasion, but I have often wondered what it would be like to take tea at the vicarage.'

Rose blinked. She had expected Ava to ask for money, not tea! 'You want to come to tea?' she asked to check that she hadn't misunderstood.

'I think I'm good enough to be invited to tea, don't you?'

'Oh, of course,' said Rose hastily, while wondering what on earth her mother would say. But how could she refuse? 'I'll speak to my mother and perhaps we can arrange a visit soon.'

'That would be very nice, Miss Haywood. I'll bring the letter with me when I come, shall I?'

'I'll look forward to it,' said Rose with an insincere smile.

She marched straight to the smithy, hardly caring who saw her. This was all Levi's fault. He hurried her round to the paddock at the back where they could talk undisturbed.

'What is it, Rose?'

'That letter from Mick that you lost,' she said, clenching and unclenching her hands.

'I couldn't find it anywhere–' he began but she interrupted him.

'I know you couldn't, because that cat Ava Bainbridge has it!'

'*What?*'

'And I'm sure she's read it! I could tell by the way she was looking at me. All sweet smiles but underneath she was rubbing her hands!' Rose was practically in tears. She paced around the paddock, careless of the long grass soaking the hem of her skirt, and told Levi what Ava had said.

'She's a horrible woman! She doesn't want money, she just wants to know that she can make me do whatever she wants. First it'll be tea, and then she'll want to come to dinner, or ... or I don't know what, but it'll be something. I'll never be rid of her!'

'She's a bitch all right, that woman,' said Levi. 'She was the one who gave me the white feather and made sure no one in the village would talk to me. But what can she do?'

'All she has to do is show that letter to Papa and he'll find a way to separate me from Mick, I know he will.' Rose's voice trembled on the edge of hysteria. 'You don't know what my father's like, Levi. I love him dearly, and I know he loves me, but he's so set in his views. He would never accept my friendship with Mick, let alone anything more, I know he wouldn't. And I'm only eighteen. It'll be years before I can make my own decisions. It's been hard enough getting him to accept that I go to the hospital. Imagine what he'd say if I wanted to marry an Irishman who wasn't even an officer!'

'You're going to marry Mick?' Levi looked stunned and Rose covered her face.

'I don't know. We haven't talked about it. I didn't even know how much I loved him until he left,' she said, lowering her hands. 'All I know is that I couldn't bear not to have Mick in my life.

'Then I'll just have to get letter back from her,' said Levi.

'How will you do that?' she asked doubtfully as he puffed out his chest.

'Just leave that to me, Rose,' he said. 'I'll make sure that cow Ava Bainbridge never bothers you again.'

CHAPTER TWENTY-FIVE

It was nearly three months before Maggie had a reply to her letter from Joe in Egypt. He was delighted, it seemed, at the idea of a son, and said that he would ask for leave as soon as possible after the baby was born. But what had she been thinking to employ a conchie? She was to send him away immediately or Joe would want to know why as soon as he came home.

Grim-faced, Maggie tore up the letter. If Joe wanted his child to have a farm to inherit, he would have to let her make the decisions and there was no way they would survive at the moment without Hugo.

'Bad news?' asked Hugo, seeing her rip the letter into little pieces. He had spent the morning dipping sheep and his shirt was still damp.

'No,' said Maggie. 'Nothing that matters.'

She set the stew on the table with a dish of potatoes and turnips. Hugo would need something hot after a morning outside in a raw wind.

Her attitude to Hugo was still guarded. It was hard to get over what she couldn't see as anything but cowardice in his refusal to fight, but she had to admit that he was a good worker. He didn't have Frank's instinctive way with the animals, but nor did she have to explain anything more than once. If Hugo didn't know how to do something, he would work it out. He pestered her with questions, though: why did oats have to be turned a certain way? When had she planted them? Had she ever grown wheat or barley? How many fields were given over to hay? Would she leave the sheep up on the moor all winter or bring them indoors? How long would the cows give milk before they had to have a calf?

'Ask Elijah,' Maggie said, exasperated, in the end. 'I don't know.'

She might not like Hugo's refusal to join up like other men, but she knew that she would not have been able to manage without him. He had taken over all the heavy work, although Maggie still liked to check on her flock. In spite of her increasing bulk, she insisted on walking up to the moor with Fly every day.

Hugo had guessed about her pregnancy early on. 'Sit down,' he had said after dinner one day when Maggie made to push back her chair. 'You need to rest.'

'I haven't time to rest,' she said.

'You must. It won't do the baby any good if you wear yourself out.'

Maggie had started to rise but at that she dropped back into her chair. 'How did you know?'

'It's something about the way you stand,' said Hugo, briskly gathering up dishes. 'I noticed it today. My wife used to stand exactly the same way when she was expecting our child.'

Maggie was taken aback. 'I didn't realise you were married.'

'She died two years ago.'

'And the baby?'

'He died too. His name was Joshua.'

'I'm sorry,' said Maggie awkwardly.

'So am I.'

She wanted to ask what had happened to his wife and son, but Hugo said nothing more. He checked there was enough water in the kettle and put it on the range to boil. Maggie watched in astonishment. 'Don't tell me you're going to wash up too!'

'It's not hard,' he pointed out.

'No, but...'

Never once had Joe offered to so much as carry his plate over to the sink. George and Frank had followed his lead and accepted without question that the women would put the food on the table and take it away. In fact, Maggie couldn't remember her father or brother ever clearing away either, or even registering that it was a job that needed to be done.

Hugo seemed amused by her astonishment. 'Anne was a passionate suffragette,' he explained. 'She believed true equality meant men doing women's jobs just as much as women being able to do men's.'

Maggie thought about that for a long time afterwards. Hugo was unlike any man she had ever met before. He looked so ordinary but he seemed to accept the most extraordinary ideas as natural. She wanted to think of him as weak and cowardly, a man who refused to fight and who took on women's work because his wife said so, but there was a solidity and a steadiness and yes, a strength to him that she found reassuring in spite of herself.

She was determined to keep him at a distance all the same.

To her relief, he made no attempt to convince her of his objections to fighting, and if he wondered why her husband had left her alone when he had no need to, Hugo said nothing. He was an intelligent and thoughtful man who liked to read in the evenings. As the weather grew colder, Maggie suggested that he might like to sit by the fire with a book while she sewed. She wasn't being friendly, she justified the invitation to herself. She just didn't want him reading by candlelight in the stable. The fire risk was too great.

So Hugo had been there when the baby moved for the first time. Maggie was letting out her trousers one night when the strangest and most miraculous of feelings made her suck in her breath and put a hand instinctively on her belly.

Hugo must have seen the look of wonder in her face. 'The baby?'

'Yes,' she said with a shaky laugh. 'Yes, it moved.'

He smiled. 'It is a pity your husband isn't here to share the moment with you. I remember when...' He stopped, and a look of such intense sadness swept his face that Maggie knew he must be thinking of his dead wife and child.

'I'm sorry,' she said. 'It must bring back sad memories for you.' She paused. She had made a point of not asking him personal questions, but why not admit that she was curious?

'How did she die?'

She thought at first that Hugo wasn't going to answer. 'There was a fire,' he said at last. 'Anne and Joshua were alone in the house. I don't know how it started – a candle perhaps? They came to get me at the school but I was too late.' He fell silent, staring down at the book in his hands.

'I'm sorry,' said Maggie again. 'What a tragedy.'

Hugo nodded heavily.

'Is that why you wanted to leave York?'

'One of the reasons, yes.' Hugo leant forward onto his knees, the book still clasped loosely in his hands, and gazed into the fire. 'I missed her,' he said in a low voice. 'Anne was so... I don't have the words to describe her,' he said with a sigh. 'She was everywhere in York, and I missed her with every breath. I thought perhaps if I was somewhere else it would help.' He glanced up at Maggie and mustered a smile. 'Your husband is away at war. You must miss him too.'

Maggie concentrated on rethreading her needle. 'I know what it is like to miss someone, yes,' she said. She lifted her eyes to look directly at Hugo. 'But it's not my husband.'

With Hugo taking on the burden of work, Maggie had more time to spend in the dairy again, and she built up a good stock of butter and cheese. 'It's market day tomorrow,' she said. 'I'll take in some of the cheeses to sell. I've got some shopping to do anyway. We need flour and treacle – oh, and more matches – and I'll see if I can find some different vegetables. I'm sick of turnips.'

Hugo fretted that the cheeses would be too heavy for her to carry but Maggie told him not to fuss. 'I'll take the trap. You get on with harvesting those potatoes.'

Blossom's hooves rang out on the cobbles as Maggie led her out to the gate early the next morning, but when she went to untie the complicated twist of twine that had held the gate upright for as long as she'd been at Emmerdale Farm, she stilled in amazement. The twine had gone and in its place was a proper loop thrown over the post. All she had to do was lift it and she could push the gate open. The broken wooden spar had been fixed and the hinges secured firmly.

Maggie turned back and looked around the farmyard. Hugo had made the changes so unobtrusively that she hadn't realised what he was doing. The muck heap had been moved behind the stable. The mess of wire had disappeared and the broken barrels chopped up for a neat pile of firewood. The nettles and the bindweed had been dug up and the barn and stable doors repaired.

She was thoughtful as she drove the trap into Beckindale.

The food shortages she'd read about hadn't had much impact in a farming area but not everyone had their own dairy so Maggie set out her cheeses on the back of the trap confident of selling them all. She blew on her hands to keep them warm and caught the eye of Polly Warcup who was waddling past. It had been so long since she had seen her that she hadn't realised Polly was also pregnant, so she smiled and held out a sample.

'Would you like a taste of cheese, Polly?'

'No,' said Polly rudely and kept on walking.

'Good for you, Polly,' said plump Betty Porter, chins wobbling in outrage. 'You should be ashamed of yourself,' she said to Maggie. 'My Alfred's *dead*. There's Robert Carr gassed and George Kirby blown up by t'side of road and Jim Airey missing a leg and you've got that coward up at Emmerdale Farm! Nobody's going to buy nothing from you while you've got that bloody conchie there!'

George dead too? The news was a dull shock to Maggie. She wanted to be angry but Betty had only said what she had thought herself about conscientious objectors. When Ava Bainbridge turned up, though, it was harder to keep a lid on her temper.

'You may as well give it up, Maggie,' Ava said with satisfaction 'Betty's right. No one in this village is going to touch anything you're selling, not when you're hiding that shirker.'

'Hugo's not *hiding*.'

'Ooh, *Hugo*, is it?' Ava smirked for the benefit of the inevitable crowd that had gathered at the first sign of a confrontation. 'It must be very cosy up at Emmerdale Farm with just the two of you – but then, we all know how you like to have a man hanging around, and you're not fussy about whether it's your husband or not.' She noted with satisfaction that Maggie had gone white and nodded her head at Maggie's swelling stomach. 'I see you're in the family way. Is that the conchie's kid you're carrying, then?'

'It's Joe's,' she bit out.

'Joe hasn't been in Beckindale for over a year.'

'He had embarkation leave in May.'

'Funny how nobody saw him, isn't it?'

'*I* saw him, Ava,' Janet Airey put in fairly. She was an angular woman with five sons and a no-nonsense manner. 'He weren't back for long, mind.'

'It don't take long to father a bairn,' said Mary Ann with a cackle. 'Least, not when my Tom is at it.'

There was some laughter and lewd comparisons of various husbands' staying power before Ava managed to wrench the conversation back on track.

'Having owt to do with cowardly conchies is unpatriotic,' she told Maggie. 'We're all agreed on that. As long as he's at Emmerdale Farm, you can forget trying to sell any produce in Beckindale. So you may as well pack up those cheeses right now because nobody's going to buy them.'

Maggie was furious. 'It'll be a cold day in hell before I do what you say, Ava Bainbridge,' she said.

'You'll see I'm right,' said Ava and swept off.

Maggie glared after her and turned to appeal to the other women. 'Janet? Mary Ann?'

But Janet shook her head. 'Ava gets uppity about things but she's right about this. We don't care for conchies. You'd have been better off letting Tom Skilbeck take care of t'farm.'

Wearily, Maggie began to pack up her cheeses. She was fastening the back of the trap when Nancy Pickles found her. 'I heard you was here, Mrs Sugden.'

'I'm sorry I had to employ a conchie, Mrs Pickles,' Maggie said, 'but when Frank left, I

251

couldn't–' She stopped, registering the starkness in Nancy Pickles' eyes and, too late, the official looking letter in her hand. 'Oh, no,' she said as her stomach pitched queasily with the premonition of horror.

'This came this morning,' said Nancy. 'I'm not much for reading, Mrs Sugden. Would you ... would you read to me, in case I got it wrong?'

'Oh, Mrs Pickles...'

'Please,' she said, pushing the envelope into Maggie's hand. 'I have to be sure.'

Biting her lip, Maggie pulled out a flimsy piece of paper. She had to swallow hard, twice, before she could trust her voice.

'*Dear Mrs Pickles,*' she read out loud. '*I regret very much...*' Her voice cracked and she had to stop and start again. '*I regret very much to inform you that your son Private F. Pickles of this Company was killed in action on the night of the 17th instant. Death was instantaneous and without any suffering.*

Maggie stopped once more and made herself take another deep breath. Frank, with his guileless blue eyes, his shy smile, the tow-head bent over his supper. Frank who had said farewell to each of the cows and had whispered in Blossom's ear before he left. Dead.

'*Your son was taking part of an advance against the enemy,*' she read on after a moment. '*He and four of his comrades were killed by enemy fire. It was impossible to get his remains away and he lies in a soldier's grave where he fell.*'

Her eyes were so blurred with tears that she could barely read the words. '*I and the Commanding Officer deeply sympathise with you in your loss.*

252

Your son always did his duty and now has given his life for his country. We all honour him, and I trust you will feel some consolation in remembering this. His effects will reach you via the Base in due course. In true sympathy, Captain R. Rowland.'

There was heavy silence. 'I wasn't wrong then,' said Nancy Pickles at last.

'No, you weren't wrong.'

'The letter, it said he didn't suffer. I'm glad of that at least.'

The officer might have lied. He wouldn't tell a mother that her son had suffered horribly. She couldn't bear to think of Frank stumbling through the mud, through a hail of bullets, terrified as screaming shells rained down on him. Had he thought of peaceful days at Emmerdale before he died, of fetching the cows from the meadow, of walking behind the plough with Blossom?

'And he did his duty.'

'I ... I am so sorry, Mrs Pickles.' Maggie's voice wavered horribly. 'Frank was ... a good boy.'

Nancy Pickles nodded. 'A good boy,' she repeated slowly. 'Yes, he were.'

'Can I take you home?'

'No, I think I'll walk.' There was a blankness in Nancy's expression that Maggie recognised. It was shock, frantically building a wall inside her to keep out the pain. 'Thank ee, Mrs Sugden,' she said.

Fury and despair roiled sickeningly inside Maggie as she watched Nancy walk away. She wanted to scream and shake her fists at the sky as she had done when Ralph died, but this time God was not to blame. Ava Bainbridge was.

The buzz of conversation in the Woolpack faltered and then petered out completely when Maggie strode in.

'Where's Ava?'

'I'm here.' Ava lifted the hatch and came out from behind the bar, arms akimbo. 'I'd like you to leave. I thought I'd made it clear that you're not welcome in the Woolpack or in Beckindale.'

'Believe me. I don't want to be here, but I have an account to settle with you.' The white heat of grief and fury drove Maggie across the pub, and her expression was so menacing that Ava took a step back.

'If this is about this morning–'

'It's about Frank Pickles.'

'What about him?'

'He's dead.'

Ava's eyes flickered. 'I'm sorry to hear that.'

'You should be, he's dead because of you.'

'You can't blame me! It's not my fault if he was killed in the war.' Ava protested. 'It's sad of course, but that's what happens in wartime.'

'But I do blame you,' said Maggie. 'If you hadn't pushed him to join the army, Frank would still be alive, and Nancy Pickles would still have a breadwinner in the family. He died in terror and in pain because of *you*, Ava. *You* gave him the white feather. *You* made him feel like a coward. *You* told him he should do his duty. He was only fifteen, too young to do what he should have done and tell you to mind your own bloody business for once.'

'I'd like you to go,' said Ava in a shrill voice.

Maggie stepped up, nose to nose. 'I'm not going until you admit you're responsible for Frank's death.'

'Don't be ridiculous!'

'*Admit it!*' Reaching out Maggie grabbed a shank of Ava's hair and pulled it. Ava screamed and struck back and then they were scratching and slapping at each other, shoving and pushing and clawing and spitting, both sobbing with rage, while the rest of the pub watched with astounded interest.

It took four men to separate them. Maggie's hair was straggling around her scratched face, her eyes bright with fury. Her hat was askew and there was a button missing from her coat, and Ava looked even worse.

'Get that bitch out of my pub!' Ava spat. 'She doesn't belong in Beckindale!'

Percy Bainbridge held her back while the other men carried Maggie bodily to the door. 'You killed him!' Maggie yelled over her shoulder, still struggling. 'Frank's death is on your conscience, Ava! I'll never forgive you for what you've done, never!'

CHAPTER TWENTY-SIX

Winter that year came roaring down from the fells without warning. One day it was autumn, all damp leaves and spiralling woodsmoke, and the next the temperature had plummeted. Maggie woke up one morning to a winter dawn streaked ominously with red. Peering through her bedroom window, she saw Hugo, well wrapped-up in a coat and scarf, skidding over the frosty cobbles as he chivvied the cows to the byre for milking, while the breaths of beasts and man hung in white clouds in the rigid air.

'I'm worried about the sheep up on the moor.' Maggie went to the kitchen door and eyed the sky. After milking, while they had been eating breakfast, the sky had clouded over and now hung grey and leaden over the fells. 'It smells like snow.'

'It's only November,' Hugo objected. 'It's too early for snow, surely.'

'Maybe, but I don't want to risk it. I'll bring the sheep down today. I'd rather have them closer to the farmhouse, just in case.'

He looked worried. 'You shouldn't go up on the hills if you think it's going to snow, not in your condition.'

'I'm pregnant, not ill!' she snapped. She should never have admitted that she had been having trouble sleeping when the baby was kicking and hiccupping. Her back was sore too.

'You can hardly lace up your boots! Let me go instead.'

'You don't know the hills,' Maggie pointed out. 'And you don't know how to work Fly.'

'Then I'll go with you.'

'No, I need you here. It's more important to get that field ploughed now if it is going to snow. I can't do that at the moment, but I can get the sheep. It's the sensible division of labour.'

'I don't like it,' Hugo persisted. 'Maggie, you're nearly seven months pregnant. It's too dangerous.'

'Look, who's boss around here?' Maggie demanded, exasperated. 'I should never have mentioned snow and you'd have been none the wiser. Come on, Fly, let's get going. The sooner we find the sheep, the sooner we can get back.'

A few stray snowflakes were drifting through the air as Maggie and Fly set off, but she told herself that it wasn't going to amount to anything. She had on boots and thick socks, and was bundled up in one of Joe's winter jackets, a shawl over her shoulders and a woolly scarf around her neck. Together with a hat, woollen mittens, and a bundle of hay to tempt the sheep on her back, the outfit kept her warm as she climbed, but it was slow going, especially now the baby was so much bigger, and she was glad of the crook Elijah had given her.

Perhaps this hadn't been a good idea, Maggie thought as the snowflakes began to fall thicker and faster until she had to blink them out of her eyes, but now that she had got this far, it would be silly to turn back. She plodded on, Fly at her heels. They both kept their heads down against the swirling snow and it was a relief when they made it up to the moor. Maggie's hands were so cold by then that she could barely open the gate. The sooner she could get the sheep down off the fell, the better.

By now she could hardly see anything, but the sheep came at her call, and she dangled the hay tantalisingly in front of them before sending Fly to gather up the stragglers. The swirl of white was disorientating. Maggie turned to start the downhill trek but she couldn't see the gate she had just come through.

She stood, blinking the snow out of her eyes. She had forgotten how quickly the landscape could change in the hills. The snow was already lying thickly on the ground, draping a white blanket over the clumps of rough grass and tussocky reeds.

There was no need to panic, Maggie told herself sternly. Surely the gate was just over there. Waving the tempting hay in front of the sheep, she set off, and the flock followed obediently behind in single file, Fly nipping at their heels. When she came to a wall, Maggie stopped. Go left or right? She chose to go right, and followed the wall, but it seemed to go on and on, much further than she had expected, and when she did come to a gate, she wasn't sure that it was the right one.

Doggedly, Maggie carried on but her feet were so cold, she began to stumble. Several times she fell over into the snow and had to struggle up. She had to get down the hill out of the blizzard, she told herself, and when it felt as if the ground was at last falling away, she almost cried with relief. If she could just keep going down, she would surely find a familiar landmark.

She trudged on, telling herself that she was heading downhill although by then she wasn't sure of anything anymore, until the ground dropped away altogether beneath her feet. The next thing she knew, she was tumbling through the air and she just had time to cry out before she landed with a thud and everything went black.

Maggie was floating in the dark, rose petals drifting onto her face. How strange, she thought, but it wasn't an unpleasant sensation. In fact, when the falling petals were replaced by the damp rasp of a tongue, she screwed up her face in protest and tried to bat it away.

The tongue persisted and she came round, mumbling, to realise that Fly was frantically licking her face. 'Good dog,' she whispered, still dazed. It was a few moments before her mind cleared enough to realise that she had fallen over the edge of a steep-sided ghyll and was sprawled right by the freezing water.

The baby! Panic-stricken, Maggie felt her stomach. What if she had hurt it? She struggled up onto her elbows but when she tried to get up, a searing pain in her ankle almost made her pass out again.

She was in big trouble.

Trembling, Maggie wiped the snow from her face. 'Fly, get Hugo!' she ordered, and when Fly only whined in concern, she made her voice firmer. 'Get Hugo!' she said again and pointed to the top of the ghyll.

Fly quivered and then scrambled up and out of sight. Maggie slumped back in despair. Why, why, why had she been so stubborn? Now she had put her baby in danger. If only it would move to let her know it was all right, but it stayed stubbornly still in her womb.

Fear had warmed her momentarily but now the cold was creeping back. Awkwardly, she got herself into a sitting position and remembered the hay on her back. Where were the sheep? What if she had lost them too?

What a fool she had been! She cupped her hands and called the sheep as she did whenever she took food to them, and almost wept with relief when a woolly face appeared over the lip of the ghyll. Where one came, the others would follow. She called again as she shrugged the hay off her back, and with a bleat the sheep made its way cautiously down towards her while the rest of the flock came to investigate. They clustered around Maggie as they found the hay, lending her the warmth of their bodies.

Maggie never knew how long she lay there. Any attempt to stand had her screaming in pain and she didn't want to scare the sheep away. For now, they seemed to be content to huddle around her against the snow that trapped them in a blur of white and grey. It was impossible to tell what time it was, or how long it had been since she had set out so confidently from Emmerdale Farm.

When she heard barking, she thought at first that she might be hallucinating, but the sheep began to shift uneasily too.

'Fly!' she tried to call, but she was so cold that she could hardly move her jaw.

'Maggie? Maggie, where are you?' It was Hugo's voice. Maggie squeezed her eyes shut against the tears of relief.

'Here!' she managed, her voice thready but clear.

The sheep scattered as Fly jumped down to Maggie, followed more carefully by Hugo.

'Maggie!' he said hoarsely. 'Maggie, are you all right?'

'It's my ankle. I can't walk.'

'And the baby?'

'I'm not sure... I can't feel anything.' She clamped down on hysterical tears that would only make things worse. 'How did you find me?'

'I was worried as soon as it started to snow heavily. I'd already set off to look for you when Fly came streaking out of the blizzard. She led me straight here.'

'Good lass. Oh, Fly, you're a good dog.' Maggie buried her face in the scruff of Fly's neck. 'You saved me.'

Hugo had crouched down to examine her ankle but it was impossible to tell what she had done to it without taking off her boot. He straightened, his expression grim. 'We need to get out of here. Let's get you home.'

'I don't think I can walk.'

'I'm going to carry you.'

'Hugo, you can't,' she protested. 'I'm too heavy.'

He ignored that. Bending, he stuffed the last of the hay into his pockets and hauled her up into his arms.

'Luckily, you've worked me so hard over the past few weeks I've developed some muscles,' he said.

It was a gruelling trudge through the blizzard. Uneasy off their heaf, the sheep decided to follow the last scraps of hay, and Fly was an anxious escort, darting back and forth to check on Maggie and then the stragglers. Hugo's breaths were coming in great rasps of exhaustion by the time

261

he set her down gently on one of the kitchen chairs.

'We need to get you warm and dry, and then I'll look at your ankle,' he told her, his hands shaking as he lit one of the spills from the mantelpiece and held it to the fire.

Flames were starting to lick at the wood as he clattered up the wooden stairs to find her some dry clothes. Maggie huddled into the chair, shivering uncontrollably, as much from fear for her baby as from the cold. She didn't protest when Hugo took off her hat and gloves and chafed her icy hands to warm them.

'The sheep?' she asked through chattering teeth.

'In the field. Don't worry about them, they're fine.'

'And Fly?'

'She's here. Look.' He nodded his head towards the kitchen door, where Fly lay, uneasy at being inside and completely alert, her bright eyes fixed on Maggie. 'She won't leave you until she's sure you're safe. I'll give her a heroine's meal and extra straw for her kennel later.'

Maggie felt the tears rise up inside her. 'I'm sorry,' she whispered. 'I'm so sorry, Hugo. I was stupid. I thought I could do it all by myself.'

'Hush now,' he said as he pulled off the shawl and began to unbutton her jacket. 'No talking until you've warmed up. Let's get these wet clothes off you.'

Maggie was too numb to care about the decencies as he took off her jacket and the sodden blouse beneath and wrapped a blanket around her bare shoulders before turning his attention to her boots and socks.

He pulled a face as he examined her bad leg. 'It's going to hurt when I take your boot off, I'm afraid.'

'I know.' Maggie managed a ghost of a smile.

'You can scream if you want.'

She did want to, but she wouldn't let herself, clenching her teeth instead at the excruciating jab of pain.

Hugo laid the boot aside with a smile. 'You're a tough woman, Maggie.'

'I'm a Daleswoman,' she said, and braced herself for the agony of removing the sock. 'We don't do screaming at a little bit of pain,' she added breathlessly.

His fingers were gentle as they probed her ankle. 'I think it's just a bad sprain. I'll strap it up but first we need to get you out of these trousers. Can you lift yourself up so that I can pull them down?'

In spite of her throbbing ankle and the cold that still had her in a rigid grip, Maggie was very aware of Hugo's warm hands so close to her waist, brushing against her bare thighs as he eased the trousers down over her legs. He was careful to touch her no more than absolutely necessary and he wouldn't look at her, but her heart had started a slow, painful thud against her ribs.

Her eyes rested on his bent head. He still wore a cap thick with snow that was beginning to drip in the heat of the fire, and all she could see was the firm line of his nose as he manoeuvred the trousers over her ankle, tossed them aside and began to rub her feet gently between his palms.

He glanced up at her, his grey-green eyes start-lingly clear. 'Are you beginning to feel anything yet?'

Maggie thought of the warmth of his hands, the competence of those deft fingers. She thought about how he had carried her down off the hill. She noticed the line of his mouth, how the fire-light threw the angles of his face into relief, and her own hands trembled. With cold, she told her-self.

'Yes,' she said unevenly. 'I think I am.'

She drew the rough blanket around her, very aware that she was sitting in only her camisole and bloomers, while Hugo found a bandage and strapped up her ankle.

'Better?' he asked when he had finished.

'Much. Thank you.'

'And the baby?'

She pressed her hands over her swollen stom-ach, glad to have been reminded of what really mattered. 'I don't know.' She bit her lip. 'It's not kicking but then it doesn't always...'

'I'm sure it will be fine,' said Hugo but she thought that his smile looked strained.

He helped her up to bed, found an extra blan-ket to tuck around the eiderdown and left her with a stern order to sleep.

Maggie was exhausted but she couldn't sleep. She lay in bed, cradling her stomach, and willed the baby to move so that she knew it was alive. All those nights she had lain here wincing at the discomfort and wishing it would be still, and now she would do anything for one of those kicks!

Please let my baby be all right, she prayed as she had never prayed before, not even for Ralph. *Just one kick, a hiccup, anything to tell me I haven't killed my child.*

This was all her fault for being stubborn, for thinking that she could do everything herself. Maggie lashed herself for taking such a risk with her child. She would do anything to undo that wretched walk up to the moor but the damage was done. She could only lie there under the blankets, thinking of the baby she might never see. Her skin was warm, but inside the cold creep of dread seeped deep into her bones.

CHAPTER TWENTY-SEVEN

Maggie woke sluggishly. There was a blankness to the light, a muffled quality to the silence, that added to a dull sense of foreboding. Disorientated, she struggled to pull herself up onto her pillows only to yelp at the bolt of pain that shot up from her ankle and brought back a jumble of memories from the day before: snow, falling, cold, fear.

Fear for her baby. In a panic, Maggie felt her belly and was rewarded at last with a sharp kick that made her suck in her breath. Eyes stinging with relief, she collapsed back onto the pillows. It was only when she had thought she might lose it that she had realised just how much this baby meant to her. It might have been conceived in

265

horror and disgust, but this child was part of her, and she would do anything to protect it.

She would even be sensible, she told Hugo when he knocked on the bedroom door to see how she was.

'I'm glad to hear it,' he said. 'You can spend the day in bed in that case.'

'The animals–'

'Are all fine,' he interrupted her. 'The sheep are in the field just behind the house. I'm going to check on them in a minute. The cows are safely in the byre and have been milked. Blossom has been fed, and Fly is tucked up in the barn with the hens. There must be nearly a foot of snow out there and it's started to snow again. Nobody is going anywhere today,' he said, 'especially not you. You're exhausted.'

Maggie hadn't been looked after since she was a child. It was strangely comforting to snuggle down under the blankets and watch the snow building up on the windowsill. The throb in her ankle was balanced by the pulse of relief about the baby and she drifted in and out of sleep all day.

In the evening, Hugo brought her tea and some bread and cheese. 'How are you feeling?' he asked as she hoisted herself up on the pillows so that he could put the tray on the eiderdown.

'Much better, thank you.'

'Can I sit down?'

She looked at him curiously. 'Yes, of course.'

He perched on the edge of the bed. 'We need to talk,' he said.

'I'm sorry about yesterday, Hugo, I know how

266

stupid I was and that I owe you my life.'

'It's not about yesterday. Or it is, indirectly.' Hugo hesitated, picking his words carefully. 'When the snow has gone, I think I should go back to York.'

'What?' Maggie stared at him, aghast. 'Why?'

'Because if yesterday proved anything, it proved that you can't manage on your own.'

'But I'm not on my own. You're here.'

'You need other people, Maggie,' he said. 'You're too isolated here, and I'm part of the problem. There was no one I could go to for help yesterday. If I went, everyone in Beckindale would accept you.'

'They wouldn't,' said Maggie with a trace of bitterness. 'It's not just you. I've never fitted in.'

'Why not?'

She plucked restlessly at the blanket. 'I don't know... I suppose my father encouraged Andrew and I to run wild at High Moor. Andrew went away to school, but I was never taught to play nicely with the other girls. I didn't care. I was happy up in the fells,' she said, sighing a little. 'The Oldroyds were always proud, too. We liked to keep ourselves to ourselves and made a point of not needing anyone else.

'Then when Ralph and I fell in love, everyone thought I was somehow trying to better myself.' Maggie lifted her shoulders at the absurdity of it. 'I didn't care about being Lady Miffield! I just wanted to be with Ralph.

'Of course, no one would believe that. Ralph wanted us to go away but Andrew had died and my father was ill. I couldn't leave him.' She

267

sighed. 'And so I married Joe and came here, and that was still not the right thing to do. Joe is ... a hard man, a violent man. He thinks that because he's stronger than me, and can hurt me, he's better than me. In Beckindale, they think that because I've got bruises on my face I should be ashamed, but why should I be ashamed? I don't hit myself! But they don't like that. They don't like that I've managed to keep the farm running by myself. They don't like that I wear trousers. They don't like anything about me,' she told Hugo. 'Why should I pretend to be something I'm not just to make them like me?'

'Because when this child is born, you're going to need neighbours,' he said. 'You need to be part of the community, and I'm afraid my presence is making that more difficult for you. If I went back to York—'

'No!' Maggie recoiled instinctively from the idea. 'I couldn't manage without you now, Hugo,' she said. 'Promise me you won't go!'

He sighed. 'All right, I'll stay. But only if you'll promise me that you'll try to get on better with people.'

Her mouth set in a mutinous line. 'Ava Bainbridge will never accept me – and I'm not going to apologise to her about Frank.'

'Ava is just one woman. I think you'd find that the others would be open to you if you made an effort to make friends.'

'I have friends,' she said sulkily. 'The vicar's wife, Mrs Haywood,' she said when he raised an eyebrow. 'And her daughter, Rose.'

'They're not enough,' said Hugo. 'This war will

end one day, Maggie. Your husband will come back and I'll have to go, but you'll still be here. This is your place. Yours and your child's. You need to find a way to belong.'

It snowed all that day and the next. On the third day, the sun rose on a pristine world. The entire dale was coated in a soft white blanket that glittered in the weak winter sunlight and it was another two days before a thaw had set in enough to contemplate taking the trap into Beckindale.

'We're getting very low on stores,' Maggie told Hugo that evening over a supper of bacon, bread and boiled milk. 'I'll go into the shop tomorrow and see if I can get hold of some sugar and tea. We could do with more candles too.' She caught his eye. 'And yes, I'll be friendly,' she sighed.

'Good girl,' Hugo said, exactly as he would to Fly. He grinned and got to his feet. 'I'll see you in the morning.'

'All right then.' Maggie accompanied him to the door. 'Goodnight Hugo.'

'Goodnight Maggie.'

She smiled at him and without warning the air tightened and her mouth dried. This was ridiculous, Maggie thought as her pulse boomed and thudded in her ears. This was *Hugo,* conscientious objector, grieving widower, the last man she wanted to be attracted to. Look away, she ordered herself sternly, but her eyes were snared with his and as the silence lengthened, her breath shortened, she could feel herself leaning towards him as if drawn by an invisible force.

It was Hugo who broke the tension. 'Goodnight,' he said again in a hoarse voice and jerked open the kitchen door to step outside into the farmyard where the snow lay packed down. Maggie closed the door after him and collapsed back against it. She felt very strange. Her blood was pumping and there was a tingling underneath her skin.

'Maggie!' Hugo's shout made her heart leap. Was he coming back? Had he felt the same irresistible tug of attraction?

But when he banged on the door and she opened it, it was clear that she was the last thing on his mind.

'Fire!' he gasped. 'Come quickly, there's a fire in the village!'

Grabbing her shawl, Maggie limped after him to the gate. It was a still, silent night and in the starlight an eerie orange glow in one of the buildings could be clearly seen.

'It's the pub,' she said. 'The Woolpack is on fire!'

Hugo opened the gate and started to run. 'Where are you going?' Maggie shouted after him.

'They'll need help.' She heard the quick fear in his voice, knew that he was thinking of his wife and child. 'Nobody will be able to get through from outside with all this snow, and there aren't enough able-bodied men in the village now.'

Maggie didn't waste time arguing. She let him start jogging down the track through the snow while she ran to the stable and quickly harnessed sleepy Blossom to the trap. By the time she caught up with him, he was nearly at the lane end. He waited for the trap, panting, hands on his knees, and swung up onto the seat so quickly that she barely needed to slow Blossom at all.

Clicking Blossom into a trot, they rattled over the packed snow into Beckindale, where a crowd had gathered outside the Woolpack. The fire had taken hold and there was screaming from some-where and several women in the crowd were weeping. The noise was fearsome, of crackling flames and crashing beams and the shouts of men frantically passing buckets of water along a chain.

'Is there anyone still inside?' Maggie asked anx-iously as she clambered down from the trap as quickly as she could and tugged the reins over Blossom's head. Hugo was already on the ground.

'Little Iris Bainbridge.' Janet Airey twisted her handkerchief between her hands. 'And Ava. Percy thought she'd got out, but nobody's seen her.'

'There's a child in there?' Hugo demanded, horrified.

'Percy tried to go in again, but they held him back. They said it's too dange...' Janet broke off as he turned and ran towards the pub. 'Where's he going?'

'Oh, dear God! Hugo!' Pushing through the crowd that were watching in shock, Maggie was in time to see him plunge into the burning building. 'Hugo!' she cried and without thinking she ran in after him, evading the hands that reached out to grab her. 'Hugo!'

Inside, the smoke enveloped her, thick and black and foul. 'Get back, Maggie,' Hugo yelled, but as she coughed she saw him run up the stairs where a small bundle had collapsed at the top. The fire was a monster, roaring and belching and gobbling, sending sneaky flames leaping through the air. Hugo's tweed jacket was alight, Maggie saw with horror. She whipped off her shawl and when he staggered back down towards her, holding little Iris Bainbridge in his arms, she used it to slap out the flames.

'Take her out,' Hugo said hoarsely, pushing Iris at her and grabbing the shawl which he wrapped around his nose and mouth. 'I think I saw another body. I need to go back.'

'Hugo, no!' Maggie protested, but she was coughing too hard to make sense and she had to get Iris to safety. The little girl was limp in her arms as she stumbled through the smoke towards the door and out into the air, where she was greeted with a great shout.

'Please, somebody help her,' Maggie wheezed desperately. 'I don't think she's breathing...'

To her relief, hands caught her and took Iris from her, but when she tried to go back inside, a blanket was wrapped around her shoulders and she was held firmly back.

'I need to help Hugo!' Maggie strained to get free while the doctor bent over Iris. Hugo had come for her when she needed him and now it was her turn to save him, but the elderly men on either side holding her by her arms ignored her struggles.

'There's nowt you can do now, lass.'

Rose saw Maggie struggling but a deafening crash inside the pub drowned out her words. The crowd murmured in distress and the human chain faltered as it became clear that the buckets of water were a futile effort against the flames.

Rose and her parents had been playing cards by candlelight at the vicarage when they had heard faint shouts and screams. Charles Haywood threw down his cards and strode outside to see what was going on, only to come back with the news that the Woolpack was on fire. 'I must go and see what I can do,' he said.

Rose and her mother waited only to put on coats and hats before hurrying after him. All was confusion when they arrived. Nobody seemed to know what had happened, and rumours swirled through the crowd. According to Mary Ann Teale, the fire had been started by a candle, but her neighbour disagreed. 'No, I heard it were a cigarette.'

At first it was thought that everyone had got out safely, but then the word went round that Ava was missing, and little Iris Bainbridge who was only six. Rose's hand crept to her mouth as she stared at the flames. They had taken a terrifying hold, in spite of her father's efforts to organise a human chain with buckets of water from the village pump. It was impossible to believe that anyone could survive such a conflagration. Rose hadn't liked Ava Bainbridge, but she couldn't imagine the horror of being trapped in those flames.

All the would-be rescuers had been beaten back by the heat of the fire until Maggie and the conscientious objector had arrived and run inside without hesitation. Like everyone else, Rose had gaped at their courage, and shared in the cheer that went up when Maggie appeared with Iris, but there had been no sign of Ava or Hugo, as her

273

mother said he was called.

'That brave man!' Edith murmured beside her. 'How can anyone call him a coward after this?'

Percy Bainbridge sat on the ground, his face grey. He had his arms around his two older children while the doctor treated Iris who was coughing and choking but who seemed to be coming round.

There was a terrible whoosh as part of the roof collapsed, drawing an involuntary groan from the people watching, but it was followed a moment later by a shout. 'What's happening?' The question ran through the crowd. Craning her head, Rose could just see a figure staggering out of the Woolpack with a body in his arms.

'The conchie's found Ava!' Some of the watchers darted towards her to take her from the stumbling man, while others practically carried him to a safer area away from the spitting flames where he pitched forwards and Rose lost sight of him.

'Is he all right?' she asked her neighbours but they couldn't see properly either. The question was passed to the front of the crowd, and the message came back that he was choking fit to burst and his hands were badly burnt, but that he was alive.

'Thank goodness for that!' Rose said to her mother.

'And Ava?' Edith asked.

At first it was thought that Ava had been rescued in time too, and the news that nobody had been badly hurt was greeted with relief and even calls for a celebration. A few watchers even began to drift away, thinking that the drama was over.

But then a different, grimmer rumour began to circulate. The conscientious objector had risked his life to save Ava, but he had been too late. She was dead.

The crowd fell silent as it absorbed the news. They had become used to hearing of deaths on the front, but here in Beckindale, so suddenly and so terrifyingly, so immediate, to learn of Ava's death was profoundly shocking.

Rose looked around the familiar faces. For all their differences, the people of Beckindale were united in their distress. Everyone looked appalled. It was somehow moving to see how neighbours turned to comfort each other, she thought. She was gripping Edith's hand as they waited for Charles to make his way through to them, his face grim after talking to Percy Bainbridge.

Only one face wore a different expression.

Rose hadn't seen Levi at first but as she looked for her father she saw him at the side of the crowd. He was watching the fire and in the reflected light of the flames, it looked almost as if he was gloating. Rose's heart seemed to stop as she remembered with ghastly clarity what he had said when she told him about the letter Ava had found.

Just leave that to me, Rose. I'll make sure that cow never bothers you again.

Horror rippled through her. Oh, dear God, Levi, she thought. Dear God, what have you done?

CHAPTER TWENTY-EIGHT

It was another week before Maggie made it back to the village. The night of the fire remained a nightmare memory of thick black smoke, of the thunderous spit and crackle of the flames, of Ava lying crumpled on the ground and Hugo pitching forward into the darkness.

Dr Barker had examined him and dressed his burns. 'Keep him in bed,' he told Maggie. 'He's inhaled a lot of smoke and we don't want inflammation of the lungs.'

'I'll be fine,' Hugo wheezed. 'I can't stay in bed. The cows still have to be milked and–'

'You'll do as the doctor says,' said Maggie, whose intense relief that Hugo was alive had given way to fury that he had risked his life that way. 'I'm perfectly capable of milking the cows.'

'In your condition?'

Dr Barker put an end to the argument. 'Neither of you should be milking. You'll have to get someone to help for a few days.'

'No one will come to Emmerdale Farm,' said Maggie, defeated, but the doctor just said 'Nonsense!' and sure enough, when Hugo climbed painfully into the trap, Janet Airey came over with one of her sons, a lean beanpole of a boy of about fourteen.

'I'll send my Fred up first thing tomorrow,' she said to Maggie. 'He's not good for much, but he knows one end of a cow from t'other. He'll milk them and see to whatever else needs seeing to until your man's up and about again.'

So Fred Airey trudged up from Beckindale through the snow to milk the cows and lug feed out to the sheep while Hugo lay in the cupboard bed underneath the stairs and fretted about his uselessness.

'That'll teach you to run into burning buildings,' Maggie said but she watched him anxiously for signs of the infection the doctor had warned about.

'I had to,' said Hugo. 'I kept thinking of Anne and Joshua and how I hadn't been able to save them.'

'I know,' Maggie said more gently. 'Just don't do it again, all right?'

It was as if that moment at the kitchen door had never happened. Maggie thought of it sometimes, of that alarming tingle of awareness, that moment when she had been sure that he wanted to kiss her, but could reassure herself now that she had imagined it.

What had she been thinking anyway? She needed to focus on her baby now. The whole idea of being attracted to him was absurd. Hugo was nothing like Ralph. He was just an ordinary man, obviously still in love with his dead wife and grieving for her and their son. And even if he hadn't been, what interest would he have in a woman nearly eight months pregnant with another man's child?

Of course she was worried about him, but only because she needed his help and she couldn't afford to have him sick on her hands.

Hugo tolerated three days in bed and then insisted on getting up again. Maggie accepted the inevitable and sent Fred Airey back to his mother with thanks for his help and slowly life settled back to a kind of normality. Hugo promised not to overdo things, and after a week of watching him with a hawk eye, Maggie decided that she could safely leave him and took the trap into Beckindale to replenish her depleted store cupboard.

A thaw had set in two days earlier and the snow had vanished as rapidly as it had come. The top of the fells were still white, and a few patches of snow lurked along the dry-stone walls but elsewhere the dale was a patchwork of green and brown once more. The bare trees dripped onto the lane as Maggie drove the trap into the village and tied Blossom up outside the village store.

Drawing a deep breath, she pushed open the door and heard the bell jangle over her head as it always did as she was met by the familiar smell of dried fruit and spices. The shelves were emptier than they had used to be, she thought. Tinned fruit was still stacked in pyramids on the shelf next to the treacle and packets of biscuits, but they were more widely spaced. On the top shelf stood big glass jars of sugar and flour, raisins and sultanas, dried peas and nuts, oatmeal and bicarbonate of soda. Once the Websters had made it a point of pride to keep the jars topped up, but now some were almost empty.

The shop seemed to be full of women who turned as one to look at Maggie, and the conversation paused as it always seemed to when she appeared. Mindful of her promise to Hugo that she would make an effort, she clutched her basket and smiled stiffly.

'Good morning,' she said.

She half expected to be ignored as usual, but Mary Ann Teale stepped forward. 'Good morning, Mrs Sugden.' She hesitated. 'How does Mr Dawson do?'

Maggie was taken aback by the question. Weren't these the women who had refused to buy her cheeses knowing that she employed Hugo at Emmerdale Farm? 'He's much better, thank you,' she said cautiously.

'We heard he was in a bad way.'

'The doctor worried about inflammation of the lungs after he inhaled so much smoke and he did have a very sore throat for a while. He still has nasty burns on his hands,' Maggie said as Mary Ann's interest seemed genuine, 'but he won't accept being an invalid.' She smiled at Janet Airey who had come into the shop behind her. 'He would only let Fred help for three days before he insisted that he could manage without any help.'

'That's men for you,' said Mary Ann and there was a murmur of agreement from the other women in the shop. 'Bone-headed! Still claiming it's nothing when they can hardly stand.'

Janet snorted. 'Or the opposite. If my Dick gets a sniffle, he will have it it's pneumonia.'

'Reg is the same,' confided Gladys Webster from behind the counter. 'Makes a terrible fuss about a scratch. I'd like him to try having a baby!'

The women laughed comfortably.

'And you, Mrs Sugden? How are *you* keeping?' asked Joan Carr with a significant look at the bulge under Maggie's coat.

Maggie's first impulse was to put her chin up and say that she was perfectly well, but she glanced at Polly Warcup, the youngest member of group, who was sitting on one of the chairs by the counter and looking as if she could give birth at any moment. Why pretend that she wasn't like everyone else?

'I get tired,' she admitted. 'And my back aches.'

'Mine too,' said Polly with feeling.

'When is your baby due?'

'The end of December.'

'You're a month ahead of me then.'

'I'll be glad to see my feet again,' Polly confided, and Maggie smiled at her.

'I know what you mean!'

There was a pause when the older women looked at each other, seeming to nominate Mary Ann Teale as their spokeswoman by some mysterious unspoken means. 'Mrs Sugden,' she began, but Maggie interrupted her.

'Please, won't you call me Maggie?'

Mary Ann inclined her head graciously. 'Maggie, then. I think I speak for all of us when I say I'm right sorry about the way we treated you when we heard you had a conscientious objector to work at Emmerdale Farm. Those of us with boys at the front, well, it felt as if Mr Dawson must be a coward not to go with them. But we all saw how he rushed into the fire without a thought for himself and we can see now that whatever else he may be, he's not a coward.'

'No, he's not.'

'You neither,' Janet added. 'I wouldn't have had the nerve to go into those flames, and that's a fact. You're a heroine.' The others nodded.

Maggie shifted her basket uncomfortably. 'How is Iris Bainbridge?'

'She's bounced back. You know what bairns are like. You'd never think she nearly died a week ago!'

'I'm glad. What has happened to the family? There was nothing left of the Woolpack.' Maggie shuddered at the memory.

'Didn't Fred tell you? I've taken the three of them to live with me for now.'

Fred had hardly said a word so it was news to Maggie. 'No, he didn't say.' The Aireys had five sons and their cottage was hardly large. 'Where have you put them all?'

'Oh, they've squeezed in. Jack's off to war now and Jim's still in hospital, so we've got a bit of room.'

'I heard Jim had been injured,' Maggie said. 'I'm so sorry.'

Janet sighed. 'Aye, he lost a leg. He were always such a lively lad, it's going to be hard for him, but there, he's alive. We have to be grateful for that.' She glanced at Betty Foster who had no such comfort. 'I'll be glad to get Jim home, though.'

'What about Mr Bainbridge?'

'Margaret Burrows has given him a room next door.'

Hugo had been right. These women were not all like Ava, Maggie realised. They had their own troubles, but in a crisis, they had rallied around

281

to help their neighbours. She felt ashamed of how easily she had assumed that Ava spoke for them all.

'Will he rebuild the Woolpack?'

Janet pulled a face. 'I don't reckon he's got the heart for it now. His brother's got a pub in Leeds. He's talking of taking the children there next year.'

'Poor mites,' said Maggie. 'It'll be a sad Christmas for them.'

'Ye-es,' said Janet. 'But between you and me I don't think they'll miss Ava overmuch. She wasn't exactly the motherly type, God rest her soul.'

'It'll be a sad Christmas for all of us with this blasted war going on,' said Mary Ann.

'It's been a sad year,' Maggie agreed. She hesitated, remembering what Hugo had said about making an effort to belong. 'I wonder...'

'Yes?' Janet prompted when she trailed off.

'Well, I was just thinking, it's Christmas in a couple of weeks. What if we had a party for all the children? For everyone, even? To cheer us all up. We could all bring something to eat and drink, and perhaps we could play some games.'

The women looked at each other. 'That's an idea,' said Betty. 'None of us has much but we could all provide something.'

'I'm not much of a cook,' Maggie confessed, 'but I could bring some butter and cheese and try my hand at a cake.'

'I'm sure I could spare a jar of jam,' said Polly, brightening.

'I've got a ham I was keeping for Christmas, but we might as well share it.'

There was a buzz of conversation as everyone discussed what they could contribute and when the party should be.

'We could use the village hall,' Betty Porter suggested, and Polly clapped her hands.

'And we could have a Christmas tree!'

'I wonder if Lord Miffield would let us take one from his woods?'

'He's in London.'

'I'm sure Mrs Haywood would write to him for us.' Pleased at the enthusiastic reception to her casual idea, Maggie was growing in confidence. 'I'll ask her. And we could invite any of the wounded soldiers who can get to the village too,' she went on. 'Rose Haywood spends a lot of time at the hospital. She might know what they'd like. We can't make Christmas for our own menfolk,' she said, 'but we could do something for them.'

The women nodded their approval. 'That's a fine idea of yours, Maggie,' said Mary Ann. 'You ask Mrs Haywood to find out about the tree and mebbe Miss Haywood can invite those as can come from the hospital. The rest of us'll spread the word in t'village. Now, was you wanting sum-mat in from Gladys here? You may as well take the weight off your feet while you're at it.' She gestured Maggie towards the free chair by the counter.

'Oh, but you were all here first...'

'You go ahead,' Mary Ann urged her. 'It's the least we can do after you brought little Iris out of the fire.'

So Maggie sat on the chair while Gladys Webster measured out flour and sugar and fetched a tin of treacle from the shelf. She rang up all the items on the till and packed Maggie's basket for her as if she were an invalid. 'There you go, Maggie,' she said when she had finished.

Betty stepped forward to help Maggie up from the chair and Mary Ann carried her basket out to the trap. 'You can't be too careful at this stage,' she said, patting Maggie's bump.

It was strange to feel accepted. Maggie was so used to feeling an outsider that she knew she must be coming across as stiff and self-conscious, but when Betty and Mary Ann waved goodbye and smiled, warmth unspooled inside and she smiled back.

Edith Haywood congratulated her on the idea of holding a party and promised to write to Lord Miffield about a tree that afternoon. 'I can't see why he'd say no. And Rose can speak to someone at the hospital about inviting the men, can't you, Rose? Rose?' she added when Rose didn't reply. She was staring distractedly out of the window but at her mother's prodding, she started and promised to speak to the matron about the party.

'Are you quite well?' Maggie asked when Rose accompanied her out to the trap. 'You don't seem yourself.'

'I'm fine,' Rose said. 'It's just been such a horrible time. I can't believe that Ava Bainbridge is dead. I feel sick every time I think about it.' She hesitated. 'How did the fire start, do you know?'

Maggie shook her head. 'I haven't heard anything. It's a terrible thing. It's common knowledge that Ava and I didn't get on, but I wouldn't have wished her dead, and especially not like that.'

'No,' Rose agreed with a shudder. 'I never wanted her dead.'

CHAPTER TWENTY-NINE

'Are you sure you won't come?' Maggie wound a scarf around her neck and buttoned her coat. Her own coat wouldn't reach over her stomach now, so she was wearing Joe's old one over her warmest woollen skirt and sturdy boots. It was Christmas Eve and it was snowing again. It would be a cold walk down to Beckindale.

Hugo shook his head. 'This is something you need to do by yourself, Maggie,' he said.

He had been pleased when Maggie told him about the party. 'You see? It wasn't that hard to make them like you.'

'I'd rather you hadn't had to nearly die in a fire for it to happen,' Maggie had with some of her old tartness. 'Look at the state of your hands!'

He looked down at his hands, where the skin was shiny and red. 'These will heal eventually,' he had said. 'Loneliness doesn't.'

'I wish you'd come,' she said now. 'Everybody's going except you. They would all make you welcome, Hugo. Nobody thinks you're a coward anymore.'

'I'm thinking about the soldiers you've invited from the hospital,' said Hugo. 'Those men have

285

been terribly injured. The last person they would want to meet is a hale and hearty conscientious objector.'

'Not so hale,' said Maggie, digging in the pockets of her old coat for her gloves. 'I've heard you coughing. I wish you'd go back to sleeping in the cupboard bed,' she fretted. 'It would be so much warmer for you.'

'I'm fine in the stable,' Hugo said firmly. He picked up her basket from the table and handed it to her. 'Now, have you got everything?'

Maggie pulled the cloth back and wrinkled her nose as she inspected the contents. She had promised to take cheese and butter to the party and they were neatly wrapped in waxed paper. But she had been determined to make something special too. Leafing through a tatty recipe book that had belonged to Joe's mother, she had decided to make a Yule cake. It didn't seem too hard. She had followed the directions *exactly*, measuring out teaspoons of cinnamon and yeast, and weighing out the currants and raisins with the butter, flour and sugar. She had the right number of eggs, the precise quantity of milk. So why had her cake turned out flat and hard?

'Perhaps I should leave the cake behind,' she said to Hugo, inspecting it with dissatisfaction. She turned it over to show him the burnt bottom. 'It's a disaster!'

'Take it,' Hugo advised. 'When the women of Beckindale see that you've produced a pie like that, they'll never be able to accuse you of being proud again.'

'That's true,' she said glumly as she covered the

286

basket again with a cloth.

'You can't be good at everything, Maggie,' said Hugo, reading her expression without difficulty. 'Be content with being the extraordinary woman you are. You're the strongest woman I know. The bravest – and the most beautiful,' he added almost as an afterthought. 'You don't need to be a good cook too.'

Astounded, Maggie could just stare at him as he reached out and straightened the collar of her coat quite as if he hadn't called her beautiful. 'I wish you would take Fly with you,' he said.

She swallowed. 'It's too cold to leave her outside the hall.' Her voice didn't sound like her own and she had to clear her throat before she could continue. 'I won't do anything silly this time. It's stopped snowing and I can't get lost on the lane into the village.'

'Be careful anyway. It's not that long since you hurt your ankle.' As if he couldn't resist, Hugo traced the outline of Maggie's cheek with his knuckle, letting it linger by the corner of her mouth. 'Enjoy the party, Maggie,' he said. 'I'll be waiting here for you until you get back.'

Face burning, Maggie fumbled with the door. 'Don't let the fire go out,' she managed, hating how husky her voice sounded.

'I won't.'

After a brief thaw, the snow had come back, carpeting the countryside in white once more. The farmyard was criss-crossed with footprints leading from the stable to the farmhouse and from the farmhouse to the byre where the cows were

287

contentedly waiting out the winter. In the field behind, the sheep huddled together in a stoical mass. Hugo waded through the snow twice a day to feed them now that Maggie had grown too big to carry big bundles of hay around.

Maggie drew on her gloves, remembering with a pang how delighted Frank had been with the gloves she had given him the day they had walked into Beckindale together, the day she had found out that Ralph was dead. Over a year ago, Maggie thought as she slipped through the gate and set off down the track.

A year without Ralph. The first agony of grief had faded now to a dull ache that still jabbed painfully at times. She hadn't forgotten him – never that – but she was used to missing him now and those few weeks when she had believed that he would come home and take her away seemed no more than a bittersweet dream.

So much had changed since then. Maggie put her hands on her stomach as she felt the baby kick. How could she have guessed that at the end of this saddest of years, she would have a child to look forward to? That she would have learned to respect a conscientious objector? *Extraordinary*, Hugo had called her. *Strong. Brave. Beautiful.* Maggie pushed his words to the back of her mind, to take out later and examine carefully to see how they made her feel.

Her feelings towards Beckindale were the biggest change of all. Had she changed, or had the village? Either way, Maggie had surprised herself with how much she was looking forward to the party, so much so that when it had started to snow heavily the day before, she had been dismayed in case she wouldn't be able to get down to the village hall in time for the party.

Excitement had been building in Beckindale as preparations were made all over the village. There had been impromptu meetings in the shop and much popping in and out of kitchens as carefully hoarded ingredients were shared and exchanged. Since they all had to economise, they had decided to pool their resources to create a feast. Some eggs from Emmerdale Farm, some treacle from Betty Porter's larder, spices and flour provided by Edith Haywood who had rifled through the vicarage store cupboard to see what she could find.

Everyone wanted to contribute to the party. Polly Warcup had already passed on a jar of blackberry jam in case she couldn't make it on Christmas Eve. 'She looked about ready to pop when I saw her,' Mary Ann had told Maggie when they met in the village hall to make final preparations. 'She's that big, I can't believe she hasn't had that baby already.'

Janet Airey clapped her hands to call the meeting to order. 'We'll need more than a jar of jam,' she said. 'Miss Haywood says a dozen soldiers from the hospital are coming, so we'd better have summat to give them to eat and drink.'

She went round the room and asked for contributions. That was when Maggie had made her ill-advised promise to make a Yule cake. The offers came thick and fast. The baker promised a dozen loaves, the Websters offered packets of tea and candles for the tree. Mary Ann's husband,

Thomas, said he would bring his fiddle and there were old men in the village who could easily be persuaded to play the accordion and the tin whistle. Even Levi Dingle wanted to make a contribution.

'He says he can get hold of some chocolates for the children,' Rose Haywood passed on his offer. She looked uncomfortable. 'I'm not sure where they'll come from,' she added. 'I have a nasty feeling they might be stolen.'

'Well, don't ask him,' Janet Airey advised briskly. 'It's Christmas. I reckon we can all turn a blind eye for chocolates, don't you?'

The snow squeaked under Maggie's boots as she walked down the track. It already lay thick along the top of the walls and rimmed every twig with white, and as she turned onto the lane into Beckindale, it started snowing again, great fat snowflakes drifting silently onto her hat.

Remembering the blizzard up on the moor, Maggie wondered if she should turn back after all. She was heavily pregnant. Everyone would surely understand if she didn't appear.

But she had promised she would be there.

Keep your promises.

And she wanted to be there, Maggie admitted to herself. She had enjoyed being part of the discussions whenever she went to the village, had liked feeling accepted, had even been interested in the snippets of gossip she had heard.

She had begun to feel as if she might belong in Beckindale after all.

So she plodded on, ignoring the cold that crept through her boots and the snowflakes that tangled on her lashes. It would be dark by the time she came home but there was no way she could get lost. There was the Warcups' cottage just ahead, and beyond it the bridge where she had met Ralph the previous summer, before everything had changed. It felt like remembering another world.

Maggie paused for breath to admire Polly Warcup's garden, now little more than graceful mounds of pure white. It was a lovely garden in spring and summer but there was something moving about its sculptural simplicity in the snow.

'Wait! Mrs Sugden, wait!' She had just moved on when she heard frantic calling behind her and she turned to see Polly's husband, Robert, floundering desperately through the thick snow.

'Thank God!' he panted. 'Polly's having her baby and I can't leave her alone to get the doctor. I think summat's wrong. Please, please can you come in and help us?'

'Robert, I don't know anything about babies,' Maggie began, but he was too worried to listen.

'You're a woman, aren't you?'

It was true. She was a woman and a neighbour and if Polly needed help, she would do what she could until the doctor arrived.

Polly was in the kitchen, kneeling on a cushion, groaning. Her arms and chest were supported on a pillow placed on a chair. 'It hurts!' she wept. 'Make it stop hurting!'

Maggie was terrified, but she put down her basket and went over to Polly and put a hand on her shoulder. 'It's me, Polly. You're going to be fine.'

'The baby's stuck,' Polly sobbed. 'I'm going to die!'

'Nonsense,' said Maggie briskly. 'Of course you're not going to die.'

Robert was wringing his hands. 'What shall we do?' he asked Maggie.

'You must go and get the doctor,' she said. 'Or someone who knows what they're doing. I'll try and keep Polly calm.'

'Right.' He seemed grateful to be told what to do. 'Hold on, love,' he said to Polly. 'I'll be back as soon as I can.'

Polly's only response was a scream of agony and he blenched as he rushed out of the door. Maggie took Polly's hand. 'You're going to be fine, Polly,' she said firmly.

'Maggie?' To Maggie's intense relief, she heard Rose Haywood calling her name a few minutes after Robert had left.

'In here,' she shouted, not wanting to leave Polly.

'I was on my way to see if you needed help getting to the party,' Rose said after she had greeted Polly. 'I was worried about you in the snow. And then I met Robert who said you were in here. He seemed in a terrible panic and wouldn't wait. He said something about going to fetch Dr Barker.'

'I hope he finds him soon,' said Maggie grimly. 'Polly here's having a baby and it's not going to hang around. I'm glad you're here,' she said to Rose.

'I don't know anything about having a baby,' Rose said nervously but she unbuttoned her coat and cast off her hat.

'Nor do I, but we're the best Polly's got.'

'All right.' Rose nodded. 'What can I do to help?'

Maggie took a breath. 'Can you boil some water so I can wash my hands?' she said, and while Rose looked around for a kettle, she crouched as best she could next to Polly, who was panting and groaning.

'I think we should see what's happening with the baby, Polly. Are you all right with that?'

'Anything!' Polly bit off another scream.

'Let's lie you down then and I'll have a look.'

'The baby's stuck, I can feel it!' Polly whimpered as Maggie and Rose helped her onto the rag rug.

'If it's stuck, we'll give it a hand. Don't worry about that.' Maggie spoke with more confidence than she felt. 'Rose, do you want to see if you can find some towels or something to protect the rug?'

'Do you know what you're doing?' Rose asked in an undertone.

'No,' muttered Maggie, remembering how confidently she had told Edith Haywood that birth was a natural process, and that if sheep could manage without a doctor, she could too. 'But I've helped birth lambs, and it must be the same principle, surely?'

Grimacing, she got awkwardly to her feet. If she wasn't careful, she'd be having her own baby. She washed her hands and slathered them with the butter she had been taking to the party in the village hall.

'Right then, Polly,' she said. 'Let's see what's going on down there, shall we?'

While Polly screamed and groaned, Maggie managed to feel a tiny foot. 'Looks like this baby is coming out in its own way,' she told Polly.

'Oh, God, I knew it! There's something wrong!'

'Not at all,' Maggie told her, bolsteringly. 'I saw this all the time with my flock when I was lambing this year,' she said, but she exchanged a worried look with Rose over Folly's head.

Where was the doctor?

Rose wiped Polly's forehead. She was appalled at the pain poor Polly seemed to be enduring. Nobody had told her having a baby would be like this!

She fixed a cheerful smile on her face. 'You're doing well, Polly,' she said, hoping that Polly wouldn't ask how she knew. But she had sat with enough of the wounded soldiers in the hospital to know that they didn't want tears or sympathy, they wanted calm and reassurance. 'Everything's going to be fine.'

It would have to be fine. Nobody else could die, Rose thought frantically. She had been feeling sick with worry ever since the night of the fire. Ever since she had seen Levi's expression and remembered what he had said. *I'll make sure that cow Ava Bainbridge never bothers you again.*

And now Ava was dead.

What if Levi had set the fire deliberately? It would make him a murderer and he would say that he had done it for her!

Rose hadn't dared to ask him outright. If he admitted causing the fire, then how could she keep that to herself? She would have to tell someone, and then she would have to explain how she knew Levi. Her father would find out about

Mick. And Ava had *died*. They would hang Levi, and Mick would know that she had been responsible for handing Levi over to the law. He had asked her to look out for his brother, not see that he was sent to prison.

But perhaps Levi *hadn't* set fire to the Woolpack. Rose's thoughts went round and round in her head. His expression might just have been a trick of the light. She had seen him twice since and he had seemed exactly the same as always, with that strange mixture of arrogance and obsequiousness.

Even if she did ask him outright, how would she know if he were telling the truth?

Rose couldn't decide what to do, and the longer she waited, the harder it became to make a decision. There was nobody she could talk to. If only Mick were here! She didn't dare write to him. Someone might read the letter and besides, what could he do from France other than worry?

No, she would have to deal with this terrible anxiety herself, Rose told herself as her thoughts circled endlessly back to the same place.

Unable to bear thinking about it anymore, she had set off to help Maggie and now here she was in Polly Warcup's kitchen while Polly screamed and writhed and sweated. Rose felt guiltily grateful to have something completely different to worry about.

It seemed to take a very long time. Rose lost count of the times she had wrung out the cloth to wipe Polly's face and she could see Maggie casting anxious glances at the door.

'Robert could have found a doctor in Bradford in the time he's been gone!' she said to Rose in an aside. 'I'm afraid Polly's right and the baby's shoulders are stuck. I don't know how much longer she can go on.'

'I think she's weakening,' said Rose in the same low voice. 'We need to do something. The baby might die.'

'Please...' Polly arched with an agonised scream. 'Please, help me!'

'What would you do if she were a ewe?' Rose asked Maggie.

'All right.' Maggie drew a breath. 'Give me some more of that butter.'

Taking hold of Polly's hand, Rose watched anxiously as Maggie manoeuvred her own considerable bulk onto the floor. 'Maggie knows what she's doing, Polly,' she said, ignoring the look Maggie flashed at her. 'She's done this hundreds of times.'

Maggie's face was screwed up in concentration as she felt for the baby.

'Nearly there,' Rose said brightly as Polly's grip tightened so painfully on her hand that she nearly cried out herself.

'Have a push now,' Maggie said after a few minutes and Polly gathered her breath and with an almighty yell, pushed. 'That's it! Another one.'

'Push, Polly,' Rose said, feeling tears on her cheeks. 'Push!'

As she watched, the baby slithered into Maggie's waiting hands so quickly that Maggie very nearly dropped it.

'That's it! Well done!' she cried, and Rose felt giddy with relief as the baby opened its mouth and wailed in outrage. 'You've got a lovely daughter, Polly,' Maggie said and her smile was brilliant. 'Just listen to the lungs on her!'

Her vision blurred with tears, Rose let go of Polly's hand so that she could hold the baby Maggie placed in her arms.

'I'll get some water,' she said shakily. 'We'll clean you up a bit, Polly, before Robert comes back.'

The hospital had inured Rose to blood. She found a clean cloth while Polly wept with happiness and relief. 'Let's make you more comfortable... Oh!' Rose looked up in wonder. 'Um, Maggie? I don't think we can relax just yet. Polly's having twins!'

CHAPTER THIRTY

By the time Robert came back with the doctor, his exhausted and dazed wife was in bed cradling not one but two baby girls. Rose and Maggie had cleaned up the kitchen and were both in the grip of a strange euphoria that had them weeping and laughing at the same time.

'Twins!' Robert was inarticulate with gratitude as he wrung Rose's hand again and again. 'Thank you, thank you!'

'It was Maggie,' Rose protested. 'I didn't do anything.'

'Yes, you did,' said Polly weakly from the bed. 'I needed someone to hold my hand and you were there.'

'That's right,' Maggie agreed. 'I'm so glad you were here, Rose. I was terrified until you came.'

'Have you ever thought of nursing, Miss Haywood?' Dr Barker said, packing away his bag. 'I think you would make a fine nurse.'

'I would love to,' sighed Rose. If only she could convince Papa! 'My parents don't want me to leave Beckindale while the war is on, though.'

'I could have a word with the matron at Mifield Hall if you like,' he suggested. 'She might be able to find a place for you. It might mean starting as an auxiliary nurse, but you are young and at least you would be learning.' He closed the bag with a snap. 'It's just a thought. Have a word with your father.'

'I will.' Rose glowed with hope. And if only she could believe that Levi wasn't responsible for the fire at the Woolpack, she might begin to feel like herself once more. 'Thank you, Doctor.'

'Now, can I escort you ladies to the village hall?'

Maggie put a hand to her mouth. 'I'd forgotten about the party!'

Rose had forgotten too. The doctor pulled out his pocket watch. 'It's not even three o'clock. Plenty of time to enjoy the party before the carol service.'

Rose bent to say farewell to the twins who were sleeping, tiny fingers waving above the shawls Polly had swaddled them in. She stroked their cheeks and smiled at Polly. 'They're beautiful girls. What are you going to call them?'

'Oh, I don't think there's any doubt about that,' said Polly. 'They're Margaret and Rose.'

Rose felt as if she had lived through a lifetime since she had walked over the bridge to find Maggie. She was exhausted but elated and she tingled with awareness as if hearing for the first time the creak and squeak of the snow underfoot or feeling the featherlight drift of snowflakes on her cheeks. This was the night that would change her life, she promised herself. Whatever her father might say, she would learn how to nurse, and she would be able to write to Mick and say that she was doing something truly useful at last.

And she would speak to Levi, Rose decided. She couldn't put it off any longer. She would ask him outright if he was responsible for the terrible fire at the Woolpack and she would take it from there.

Outside the village hall, a gaggle of small boys were running around, shouting and shoving snowballs at each other, but at the sight of Rose and Maggie with Dr Barker they whooped and cheered.

'That's a nice welcome,' said Maggie, laughing. She ought to smile more often, Rose thought. She was beautiful when she smiled.

'Our mam said as we couldn't start eating until you got here,' confided one boy and darted ahead to burst into the hall. 'They're here! They're here!'

A burst of applause greeted Maggie and Rose as they went into the hall and glasses of hot punch were pressed into their hands. In the mysterious way of village gossip, the women had already heard about what they had been doing, and they found themselves at the centre of a group demanding details about the birth. There were gasps when they heard about the twins.

'I *said* she were big,' Mary Ann Teale exclaimed.

'Rose!' Charles Haywood drew her away from the group. 'I cannot believe what I am hearing!' he said. 'Is it true that you have been assisting at a *birth?*' He sounded revolted at the very idea. 'It's not fit for a young lady like you to be exposed to such things.'

'Oh, Papa, it was *wonderful,*' Rose said and burst into tears.

'Come, come, my dear.' Dismayed, her father found a handkerchief and gave it to Rose. 'There is no need to cry.'

She mopped her face with the handkerchief and drew a shuddering breath. 'Oh, I know, but it was just so amazing. And I'm sorry if you dislike it, Papa, but my mind is made up. I'm going to be a nurse.'

Before he could answer, Janet Airey had climbed up onto a chair. 'Right,' she shouted and clapped her hands for attention. 'Has everyone got a glass? I've got a toast to make.'

There were murmurs and shuffling as everyone made sure they had something to drink. 'This has been a bloody year,' Janet said in her blunt way, 'but we're ending it with some good news. Here's to Beckindale's newest arrivals, Margaret and Rose Warcup!'

The hall erupted with cheers and cries of 'Margaret' and 'Rose'.

'And now,' Janet went on gesturing at the tables of food, 'let's eat up this bloody feast we've got here!'

There were more cheers as Janet was helped down from her chair by her dour husband. Rose didn't think she had ever seen Dick Airey smile, but she noticed the affectionate pat he gave Janet when he thought that no one was looking. The intimacy of the gesture made Rose wistful. Janet pretended to swat her husband's hand away but it was obvious that she didn't really mind.

Would she and Mick ever have the chance to grow that comfortable together? Rose hoped so.

Until then, she would do what she could, so she went to greet the soldiers she knew from the hospital and help them with their plates.

She was licking gingerbread crumbs from her fingers when Levi appeared at her side. 'Good evening, Rose.'

Her heart jerked at the sound of his voice. She had been keeping an eye out for him and had just begun to relax at the thought he might not have come to the party at all.

'Levi!' She patted the base of her throat. 'You startled me! I didn't think you were here.'

'I wouldn't have been if I hadn't offered a whole barrel of beer and a big box of chocolates, no questions asked,' said Levi. He tapped the side of his nose. 'A good deal's all it takes to change people's minds. They were all nice as pie when they knew I had something they wanted.'

Tom Teale and three elderly men with whiskers were tuning up on the dais. There would be dancing soon and then they wouldn't be able to talk.

Rose turned to him abruptly. 'Levi. Can I ask you something?'

'Of course,' he said with one of his obsequious smiles.

'The fire at the Woolpack ... I saw you there that night.'

Did something flicker in his eyes? 'The whole village was there that night,' he said. 'Most exciting thing that's happened in Beckindale for years, I should think.'

'Ava Bainbridge died, Levi. It wasn't exciting, it was horrible.'

'She was a bitch. Don't pretend you liked her now.'

'No ... it's just ... you said that you were going to get the letter back for me and now it's gone. It must have been destroyed in the fire.'

'Lucky that,' said Levi with a grin.

The fiddles were starting up and dancers were taking to the floor. She couldn't ask any more now, but she would, Rose resolved. One way or another she would get Levi to tell her the truth about what happened at the Woolpack that night.

Over Levi's shoulder she could see her father frowning. He didn't like her talking to Levi for so long.

'I haven't got a letter for Mick,' she said, making to leave. 'I'll write after Christmas. Shall we meet then?'

'I thought we could dance,' said Levi.

'Oh, I don't think–'

'If you're worried about your father, the rules don't apply tonight,' he said. 'Everybody's dancing with whoever they like.'

Sure enough, there was her mother dancing with Sergeant Owen, who had been enjoying *Jane*

Eyre as she read to him. He had lost the half of his face covered by a thick bandage and his remaining eye was too blurred to read for himself. He was a rough Welshman and under other circumstances her father would certainly never let her mother dance with him.

Maggie was being whirled around by a one-armed corporal. The hall was crowded with other unlikely couples dancing together: Betty Porter and Joan Carr, Mr Bates with his ten-year-old granddaughter, Hannah Rigg and Peter Swales. Even Arthur had taken to the floor with pretty little Molly Pickles. Rose wondered what her father would say when he saw *that*.

The sudden longing for Mick was so intense that Rose gasped and put a hand to her stomach. If only it were Mick beside her, asking her to dance with his reckless smile and the smile that creased one cheek. If only she could put her hand in his and let him draw her against him so that she could rest her head on his shoulder.

But Mick wasn't there. Levi was, and in that moment, Rose hated him for not being his brother.

Levi's eyes narrowed at her reluctance. 'After everything I've done for you, it would be a shame if another of Mick's letters went missing, wouldn't it?'

'Is that a threat, Levi?' Rose was proud of how steady her voice sounded.

'Of course not. I'm just asking you to dance.'

He held out his hand and Rose had no choice but to take it.

Maggie saw Rose looking downcast as she danced with Levi Dingle and was saddened. Rose had been so happy as they walked down from the Warcups' cottage, chattering about her plans to be a nurse. Maggie hoped the vicar hadn't talked her out of it.

It was a wonderful party. She was astounded at the array of food the women of the Beckindale had been able to assemble. One of the more prosperous farmers had donated a ham, which took pride of place in the middle of the table, surrounded by fruit cakes and mince pies. There were fruit pies and boiled puddings and jam tarts. Cakes and pikelets and scones. Gingerbread and plum pudding. Cheese cakes and parkin and treacle toffee. And less excitingly, bread and creamy farmhouse butter and the cheese Maggie had brought from her dairy.

Even her Yule cake had been there.

'What's this supposed to be?' Janet had demanded, taking it out of basket and holding it up for everyone to see.

Maggie flushed with embarrassment. 'It was meant to be a Yule cake.'

'Oh, aye?' Janet's lips twitched. 'It's not like any Yule cake I've ever seen. What do you reckon, Betty?'

'They're not usually quite so flat,' Betty said taking the cake and examining it with mock seriousness. 'But maybe this is Maggie's own version. It's interesting what you've done with the bottom,' she added solemnly, displaying the charred base to much laughter. 'Is that a speciality of Emmerdale Farm?'

Maggie couldn't help laughing. 'I followed the recipe exactly,' she protested and it felt good to know that they were laughing with her and not at her.

'I've got a light hand with cakes.' Joan Carr patted her arm. 'I can teach you how to make it,' she said.

Maggie smiled. 'I'd like that.'

The hall was crowded, and although some familiar faces were missing, there were others to fill the gaps, soldiers from the hospital, with bandaged heads or wooden legs or sleeves pinned where an arm once had been, but all ready to join in with the spirit of the season.

A Christmas tree stood at the end of the hall. It was decorated with little candles and the chocolates Levi had procured nestled in its branches. Maggie saw little Iris Bainbridge tiptoe up to the tree and take a chocolate, glance around quickly to see if anyone was watching, and pop it in her mouth.

As the dark winter afternoon drew in, the candles were lit with great ceremony and the rest of the chocolates distributed amongst the children. Maggie was glad to see that all of Frank's younger brothers and sisters were there, part of a gang of wildly excited children that ran in and out of the hall and chased each other across the dance floor. All except Molly, who at fourteen had suddenly grown up and wasn't short of partners to dance.

Nancy Pickles sat on one of the chairs ranged around the edge of the hall, rocking a sleeping child on her lap while she talked to Bert Clark's mother. Percy Bainbridge was there, too. He wasn't dancing, but there seemed to be plenty of women fluttering around him, making sure that he had an extra large slice of cake. Even Tom Skilbeck had come, leaning against the wall next to William Hutton, his harsh face carved with new lines of grief for his dead daughter. He nodded at Maggie across the room but didn't say anything.

When there were only crumbs left on the plates and even Maggie's Yule cake had been eaten, a space was cleared for dancing in the middle of the hall. Tom Teale started with his fiddle, and then the accordion and tin whistle joined in and soon everyone was tapping their feet.

Determined to enjoy herself, Maggie danced with everyone brave enough to take a heavily pregnant woman for a turn on the floor – or with arms long enough to reach around her: with the vicar, with Mr Webster from the village shop and with Betty Porter's husband. Henry. She danced with Frank's younger brother, Ned, and with another of Janet Airey's lanky sons. She danced with almost all the soldiers, too. Her chest ached to see how badly hurt they were and how gallantly they made light of their injuries.

She didn't ask about their experiences of the war. For that short time there was a tacit agreement to forget the war, its miseries and privations, the griefs and anxieties they all felt, the tensions and slights of everyday life. None had a place inside the warm, bright hall where the village gathered together in good cheer and community to celebrate Christmas 1915 the best way they could.

At five o'clock, the soldiers headed back to the hospital, the smaller children were taken home to be put to bed and the very elderly decided that they had had enough. Almost everybody else walked up to the church through the snow for the Christmas Eve service.

Maggie hadn't intended to go. She hadn't been to church since Ralph had died, and she had decided to go straight back to the farm. She was very tired after all the dancing, too, but it had been such a good party that she found herself carried along and into the church.

Enveloped in the smell of old, cold stone and musty hassocks and surrounded by her neighbours, Maggie listened to the Reverend Haywood's sonorous voice and remembered the previous Christmas, spent alone and in a despair so deep she had thought it impossible ever to be happy again. She thought about the soldiers still huddled in the trenches at the front or, like Joe, fighting in a country so strange she couldn't even imagine it.

Then she thought about Polly's babies, tiny Margaret and Rose, and about the child inside her, kicking restlessly. What kind of world would they grow up in? What joys and sorrows awaited them?

When the congregation filed out of church, it was to find that the snow had stopped and the clouds had cleared. Maggie shook hands and wished everyone a happy Christmas and walked down to the bridge. The world was dark and rigid with ice, but above her arched an ink-black sky a-glitter with stars so bright she could see the outline of the fells. *Silent night,* she remembered the words of the beautiful carol they had sung together in the church. *Holy night.*

At the bridge, she paused. If she strained her eyes, she could just make out High Moor in the starlight. Her childhood home. Having to leave it had left her lonely and adrift and she had clung to the idea of it as her home when she first married Joe.

But now, now it was different, she realised. The farm was home now. It was hers, not Joe's. She thought about Fly, about Blossom, the cows and the flock of sheep she had worked so hard with that year. She thought about Hugo, keeping the fire going for her. 'I'll be here when you get back,' he had said.

There was no sign of the war ending and the future was uncertain, but she had Hugo to help her. She had friends and a place in Beckindale. She had animals that depended on her and in a few weeks, she would have a child of her own. She had hope, where once there had been none. For now, that was enough.

Pulling the collar of her coat closer against the cold, Maggie smiled and set off up the lane, heading home to Emmerdale Farm.

EMMERDALE 1918:
FACTUAL OVERVIEW FOR THE BOOK

Many of the stories in this book have been inspired by real accounts, diaries and letters of men and women from Yorkshire who lived through the Great War, including stories from Esholt – the real Yorkshire village – on which the Emmerdale set is now based. Whilst Emmerdale is a fictional village, it embodies the community life of villages across the whole of the country; villages that hold the stories of ordinary men and women whose lives were transformed entirely in 1914.

The country had never mobilised in such a way; as sons, husbands and brothers marched out of villages across Yorkshire, women were thrust into jobs typically done by men, and with that work came a new era of female liberation. Maggie Sugden's story is inspired by a real farmer's wife, Annie Marriott. In 1914 Annie's husband George enlisted and left his milk dairy the sole responsibility of his wife. For the next four years Annie successfully kept the dairy running, as well as bringing up her young children. George returned in 1918 with a shrapnel wound to his leg and sadly died in 1920 of septicaemia. For the first time in history, women just like Annie proved they could take on any role a man had done and played an enormous part in winning the war.

The story of Rose King working as a nurse at Miffield Hall is based upon real accounts from Temple Newsam, a country house outside Leeds. The house became a fifty-bed hospital for injured soldiers run by Lady Dorothy Wood, wife of the owner. First used for Belgian officers in 1914, it gave comfort and care to thousands of men who had been wounded, gassed or suffered the devastating psychological effects of shell shock.

But not all soldiers were lucky enough to make it to hospitals in England; just over 700,000 British soldiers would never return. Across Britain mothers, sisters and wives were robbed of their men. In Esholt, the village the Emmerdale set is modelled on, Joshua Booth – the son of the real Woolpack landlord – was killed in 1917 by a stray shell in the trenches of Ypres, leaving behind his young sweetheart Winnie. Winnie would never fully get over the loss of her first love and kept all the precious letters Joshua had sent to her from the trenches until her death in 1992.

The Dingle brothers appearing at a training camp on the edge of the village was inspired by real accounts of Raikeswood Camp in Skipton, which opened in 1915 to house the newly formed Bradford Pals. The opening of the camp resulted in young recruits flooding the area; going on route marches through the local countryside; seeking their own entertainment in the evenings and forming new relationships with local women.

It is easy to imagine the three Dingle brothers amongst the fresh-faced trainee soldiers fraternising with local villagers.

The war transformed the country; for all the loss and pain endured there were also huge advancements in technology, class and gender roles. Suddenly the heir to an estate like Miffield was fighting alongside the penniless Dingle; the old order fell away and with it came the vote for women in 1918 and new opportunities for a modern Britain. There is not a village, house or street in England that was not touched by war, and its legacy is still felt today. We must never forget the great sacrifice made by so many; the gallant acts of bravery and the quiet stories of transformation of these ordinary men and women.